Bodo Lehwald

# *Resonance of the Hidden*

Lena Berg investigates volume 2

Crime novel / Thriller

Bibliographical information of the German National Library: The German National Library lists this publication in the German National Bibliography; detailed bibliographical data can be accessed on the Internet at http://dnb.dnb.de.
The automated analysis of the work in order to obtain information, in particular about patterns, trends and correlations in accordance with Section 44b UrhG ("text and data mining") is prohibited.



Cover design: © Bodo Lehwald

Publisher: BoD · Books on Demand GmbH,

In de Tarpen 42, 22848 Norderstedt, bod@bod.de

Print: Libri Plureos GmbH, Friedensallee 273,

22763 Hamburg

ISBN: 978-3-7693-1849-4

Bodo Lehwald

# Resonance of the Hidden

Lena Berg investigates, Volume 2

## Dedication

I dedicate this book to my son Robin,
whose support, advice, and unwavering confidence in
my abilities have helped me realize this dream. You are
not only a wonderful son but also a true source of inspiration.

I would also like to thank Lea, your amazing wife, who
has supported my journey with understanding and patience, as well as my family, whose strength and encouragement have always been by my side. Without all of
you, this book would not have been possible.

With much love and gratitude,
Bodo

## About the Author

Bodo Lehwald, born in Westbarthausen in 1960, is a passionate crime writer who blends real-life settings with gripping investigations in his novels. Inspired by his love for East Frisia and his enthusiasm for crime fiction, he began writing in 2023. His books are known for their authentic characters, atmospheric descriptions, and thrilling plots.

With *Murder in Emden*, he laid the foundation for his crime series featuring detective Lena Berg. *Echo des Verborgenen* is her second case, but each book can be read as a standalone.

More about the author and his books at:
🌐 **www.bodo-lehwald.de**

## Chapter 1

*2003*

At the Zungenkai, where the grey sea meets the city of Emden, the cranes of the Broder shipyards towered into the sky like steel sentinels. Their massive shapes were reflected in the murky water, roughened by the steady rain. The salty smell of the sea mingled with the sharp, metallic aroma of machine oil and the faint vapours of rust. Over the quay lay a soundscape of rhythmic groans and the dull hammering of heavy machinery—an industrial orchestra that epitomized the heartbeat of the city.

Heinrich Broder stood in his office, looking out. The rain-stained window showed him a familiar scene that had taken on a depressing heaviness in recent weeks. In the past, this view had filled him with pride: the mighty cranes, the ships launched here as a testimony to his vision. But today, the cranes seemed less like triumphant symbols and more like sombre memorials to an era that was about to end.

He ran a shaky hand over his face, his skin taut under the rough touch. The coffee in his cup had long since gone cold, yet he clutched it tightly as if the porcelain could give him stability. The news that reached him that morning had weighed heavily on his shoulders: a major order from Scandinavia—a reliable source of income for years—had gone to a competitor from South Korea. "They've knocked the price down," Karl Niemeyer, his chief engineer, had said when he broke the news. Heinrich had only looked at him silently, unable to find the *words. It wasn't just an order—it was a warning signal, a crack in the façade of his life's work.*

*He turned away from the window and walked to the heavy, dark-wood desk, its surface marked with countless scratches and water stains. On the left-hand side lay a black folder, inconspicuous but menacing in its presence. It had been handed over a week ago by Andreas Falk, an old acquaintance known for his unorthodox methods. The name on the cover was etched into Heinrich's mind: Dmitri Sorokin.*

*A knock on the door made him flinch. He took a deep breath before calling out in a calm voice,*

*"Come in."*

*Karl Niemeyer entered, his face as tense as the wrinkles on his forehead.*

*"Heinrich, we need to talk. The men in the hall... they have questions."*

*Heinrich nodded curtly.*

*"Tell them I'll be right there."*

*But when the door closed behind Niemeyer, Heinrich remained seated. His gaze wandered back to the folder. The name seemed to challenge him. Dmitri Sorokin. A man with the kind of resources Heinrich desperately needed—but also a man known for his ruthless business tactics.      Heinrich's hand trembled as he reached for the folder.*

*The decision before him would not only determine the future of his shipyard, it could irrevocably change the fate of his family and the city.*

*The folder felt heavy in his hands as he slowly opened it. The paper inside was immaculate, the text printed in precise black. But it wasn't the contents that took his breath away—it was the name. Dmitri Sorokin.*

*A soft click made Heinrich jump. The door to his office had opened again, and Andreas Falk entered. The man looked as if he had stepped straight out of an advertising brochure for success: tailored suit,  expensive perfume, a smile that inspired both confidence and caution. "So you haven't thrown the folder away yet," said Falk, closing the door behind him. Heinrich snorted and leaned back in his heavy leather armchair. "A good sign, you say? Looks more like my last stand to me."*

*Falk sat down opposite him, his smile unchanged. "You're in a difficult position, Heinrich. We both know that. But Dmitri Sorokin is not just any investor. He is a solution."*

*"A solution that brings its own problems."*

*Heinrich's voice was calm, but its harshness made Falk pause.*

*"He's... efficient," Falk finally replied, pulling out a gold lighter that flashed in the light. "He offers you exactly what you need: capital, modernization, access to new markets. And all he expects in return is... let's say, a partnership."*

*"Partnership," Heinrich repeated, letting the word melt on his tongue as if it tasted bitter. "A partnership that could cost me my independence. Do you know what this shipyard means to me? To this city?"*

*Falk leaned forward, the smile disappearing.*

*"I know what it means to you, Heinrich. But I also know what will happen if you do nothing. Without this deal, you'll have nothing in a few years—no shipyard, no workers, no city that's proud of you."*

*The words hit Heinrich like a blow. He fell silent, his gaze fixed on the folder. The names and numbers blurred before his eyes. The truth was that Falk was right.*

*Without modernization, the shipyard was doomed. But was he prepared to hand himself over to Sorokin?*

*"He wants more than money," Heinrich finally muttered. "I know these kinds of men. They give you what you need, but in the end, they take everything."*

"Maybe,"

Falk admitted.

"But sometimes all we need is a chance—a small step to preserve something big."

He stood up and smoothed his cuffs.

"Think about it, Heinrich. Sorokin will be in Hamburg tomorrow evening. He's expecting you at the Hotel Atlantic."

Heinrich watched Falk leave the room without waiting for an answer. The rain drummed against the windows, and the monotonous ticking of the grandfather clock filled the silence. He felt like a man balancing on the edge of a precipice—forced to take a step without knowing whether he would fall or fly.

He reached for the folder and closed it. Tomorrow he would be in Hamburg. But not to capitulate. If Dmitri Sorokin wanted to make an offer, then Heinrich would ensure that the conditions were in line with his principles. At least, that's what he told himself.

The next morning began with a cool, rain-soaked silence. Heinrich had hardly slept. The night had been a restless up and down of thoughts, plans, and doubts. As the first rays of sunlight crept through the window, he was already sitting at his desk, staring at a blank notecard. He had *planned to organize his thoughts and structure his arguments for the meeting with Sorokin, but the pen in his hand wouldn't move.*

*The door opened quietly, and Marie Hoffmann, the long-time housekeeper, entered. Her steps were as quiet as always, and she carried a steaming cup of coffee. "Mr. Broder, you've hardly slept," she said, her voice concerned yet reserved.*

*Heinrich did not answer immediately. Instead, he took the cup and looked at it briefly.*

*"Marie, if you had a problem—one that could destroy everything you've worked for—would you solve it on your own? Or would you ask for help from someone you might not fully trust?"*

*Marie paused, her hands tightly clasping the tray. She weighed his words carefully before answering.*

*"It depends, Mr. Broder. Sometimes it's wiser to accept help, but you have to know what the price is."*

*Heinrich nodded slowly. The price—this was exactly what had kept him awake that night. What would be the price of accepting Sorokin's help? And could he pay it without losing himself and everything that was important to him?*

*Later that morning, he sat in his office with the heavy door closed behind him and went through the documents Falk had left him. Sorokin was no ordinary businessman. The little information available painted a picture of a man as charming as he was ruthless—a man who swept through the European industry like a storm, rarely leaving anything untouched.*

*A knock at the door interrupted his thoughts. Karl Niemeyer entered, his brow furrowed.*

*"Heinrich, the men have heard about the lost mission. They're talking... about cutbacks, about redundancies. Some say the shipyard is finished. Heinrich closed the file and stood up.*

*"We're not finished, Karl. As long as I'm here, this ship-yard won't sink."*

*"But how?"*

*Karl asked, his voice quivering with  concern.*

*"How will you manage if we don't modernize? The machines are old, and the competition is faster and cheaper. We need a solution."*

*Heinrich's jaw tightened. He knew Karl was right, but it hurt to say it.*

*"I'm working on it,"*

*he finally said. "That's all I can tell you at the moment."*

*Karl nodded slowly, but his eyes revealed his doubts. As he left the room, Heinrich slumped heavily into his armchair. The ticking of the grandfather clock seemed louder than before, almost like a countdown.*

*In the early evening, Heinrich finally packed his things for the journey to Hamburg. The rain had subsided, but the sky remained grey and oppressive. Before leaving, he took one last look at the shipyard. The cranes reached into the sky like scarred fingers, and the halls looked deserted and bleak in the fading light.*

*As he got into his car, he felt the weight of the moment. This meeting would change everything— perhaps for the better, perhaps for the worse. But one thing was clear: there was no going back.*

*The rain had turned into a fine mist when Heinrich Broder parked in front of the magnificent façade of the Hotel Atlantic. The building radiated the   splendour of times gone by—large golden letters above the entrance, a red carpet leading up the steps—an impersonal luxury that made Heinrich seem strangely out of place.*

*A porter in an immaculate uniform opened the door for him, but Heinrich hesitated for a moment before entering. The interior was opulent: marble floors, crystal chandeliers, and a subtle scent of polish and expensive perfume lingered in the air. People in elegant clothing* moved as if in a ballet, each step perfectly set. Heinrich felt the weight of his simple, dark travelling bag in his hand—a sign of his own reality amidst this spectacle.

He reported to reception, and the attendant led him through long, quietly lit corridors to a secluded   conference room. The heavy wooden doors opened with a muffled sound as Heinrich entered.

The room was silent, except for the soft crackling of a fireplace blazing in one corner. A man stood in front of the fire. Dmitri Sorokin. Tall, slim, wearing a tailor-made suit that emphasized his athletic build. His hair was dark, his eyes grey—cold and penetrating. He turned, a smile showing more control than warmth on his lips.

"Mr. Broder,"

Sorokin said in a quiet but firm voice.

"Welcome. I hope your journey was pleasant."

"Tolerable,"

Heinrich replied curtly as he put his bag down. He stopped, sensing the distance the room created between them despite its limited size.

Sorokin pointed to an armchair at the solid wooden table in the centre of the room.

*"Please, have a seat. We have a lot to talk about."*

*Heinrich accepted the invitation but did not sit down. His posture remained tense, his hands resting flat on the tabletop. Sorokin, on the other hand, appeared relaxed. He took his time to open a carafe of crystal-clear water and pour a glass. "Water?" he asked casually.*

*Heinrich shook his head. "I'm not here to drink."*

*Sorokin's smile widened, though it did not become friendlier.*
*"Of course not. You're here because you have to make a decision. And I'm here to help you with that."*

*"Help?" Heinrich's voice was calm but sharp. "I've heard what your 'help' looks like. You come in, invest, and in the end, you own more than you promised."*

*Sorokin tilted his head slightly, as if examining Heinrich's words like a chess player analyzing his opponent's next move.*

*"You're right, Mr. Broder. I never take less than I deserve. But I also never give less than I promise."*

*He leaned back, his grey eyes fixed firmly on Heinrich. "Your shipyard is a jewel—a symbol of tradition and ex-cellence. But it's also a relic. Your machines, your pro-cesses—they come from a different era. If you want to modernize, you need capital. And capital... costs."*

*Heinrich's heart beat faster. The words struck true. He knew Sorokin was right, yet something inside him resisted the thought of giving this man anything.*

*"And what do you expect in return?" Heinrich finally asked. "What exactly does your capital cost?"*

*Sorokin smiled—a smile that made Heinrich's blood run cold.*

*"Access, Mr. Broder. Access to your infrastructure, your contacts—your loyalty. Nothing more."*

*"That's all?"*

*Heinrich's voice sounded hollow, though he tried to remain calm.*

*"That's all you need to know,"*

*Sorokin replied gently. "The rest is just... business."*

*Heinrich withstood Sorokin's cold gaze, feeling the man's words gnaw at his resistance. It wasn't just the offer; it was the unspoken threat woven into every sentence.*

*Heinrich's hands clenched into fists on the tabletop as Sorokin continued speaking in his calm yet firm voice, as if weaving a web of words that tightened around him.*

"Loyalty, Mr. Broder," Sorokin repeated, leaning back and turning the glass in his hand.

"That's the only price I ask. You keep control, the shipyard stays in your hands, and I'll take care of it—make it shine again: more efficient, more modern, more competitive."

"And what happens if I refuse?" Heinrich asked, forcing himself not to look away.

Sorokin's smile disappeared. His face remained calm, but something cold flashed in his eyes.

"Then everything remains as it is. Your outdated machines, declining orders, the rumours among your workers. And finally... someone else will take over the shipyard. Someone without your values, without your history."

He paused, sipping from his glass.

"That would be a shame, wouldn't it?"

Heinrich felt a mixture of anger and powerlessness rising within him. This man spoke of tradition and history, yet threatened to destroy everything Heinrich had built.

"You're playing a dangerous game, Mr. Sorokin. Do you think I'm someone who can be blackmailed?"

Sorokin placed the glass on the table, and its quiet clink filled the room. "This is not blackmail, Mr. Broder. This is reality. The world has changed, and you have two choices: change with it, or be left behind."

The words echoed in Heinrich's mind. He knew Sorokin was right, but the thought of surrendering himself to this man was unbearable. He searched Sorokin's face for a crack in his façade of control and superiority, but found nothing—only the cool, unwavering presence of a man who knew he was in control.

"I need time," Heinrich finally said, his voice heavy with tension.

Sorokin nodded as if he had expected exactly that. "Of course. Take all the time you need. But remember, Mr. Broder: time is a luxury we sometimes can't afford."

He stood up, his customized suit gliding like a second skin.

"I'll be here until tomorrow evening. When you've made up your mind, let me know."

With these words, he left Heinrich alone in the room.

The silence was oppressive. Heinrich sat motionless, his eyes fixed on the glass of water before him. The man's words had thrown him off course. It wasn't just the *offer—it was the knowledge that Sorokin sought not only capital, but power over everything Heinrich had built.*

*He got up, went to the window, and stared out into the rain-soaked night. The city's lights blurred behind the droplets on the glass. For the first time, Heinrich felt small—like a chess piece on a board dominated by someone else.*

*Yet, something stirred deep inside him—a determination he didn't fully understand. He would not surrender control to Sorokin without a fight. If there were a way to save the shipyard without betraying his principles, he would find it.*

*The streets of Hamburg disappeared into darkness as Heinrich drove back to Emden.*

*The city's lights glided past him, barely noticed, while his thoughts lingered on Dmitri Sorokin's words:*

*"Loyalty... time is a luxury... access."*

*The weight of the decisions ahead seemed unbearable. But it wasn't just the pressure to save the shipyard—it was the question of what would remain of him if he failed, or if he chose the wrong path.*

*When Heinrich arrived at his villa late at night, only silence greeted him. Marie Hoffmann had left the hallway light on, as she always did when she knew he would return late. He hung his coat on the hook and stepped quietly into his study.*

*The room was dark, except for the faint glimmer of the grandfather clock in the corner. Heinrich went to his desk, pulled open the bottom drawer, and took out a small, leather-bound book.*

*His diary—the only thing that brought him clarity in these moments.*

*He sat down, opened the book, and let his eyes wander over the yellowed pages. The entries told the story of his life—the founding of the shipyard, the triumphs, the setbacks, the mistakes. Heinrich ran his fingers over a page he had written years ago:*

*"The shipyard is not just steel and machines. It is family, it is home. Everything we create carries our soul out into the world."*

*But today, the shipyard felt like a burden—a legacy crushing him. Heinrich picked up his pen and began to write. The words flowed as if he had to rid himself of them before they swallowed him whole.*

*"Today I met a man who could change everything. Dmitri Sorokin—a name that hangs like a shadow over my thoughts. He offers salvation, but I see the chains that come with it. If I agree, I will save the shipyard.*

But at what price? And if I refuse... will there even be a shipyard?"

He paused, the pen hovering over the page, then continued more slowly, almost hesitantly.

"I don't know if I have the courage to choose truth when the lie is easier. Perhaps that is the greatest betrayal—not just of my family, but of myself." He closed the diary and put it back in the drawer. Before closing the drawer, he hesitated. A sudden thought made him pause. He reached for a small key lying on the edge of the desk and locked the drawer. For the first time, he felt a sense of relief—as if he had kept something important, something meant only for him. But deep down, Heinrich knew that the diary would not only guard his secrets—it might one day reveal his truth.

# *Chapter 2*

*The dull roar of lorry engines vibrated in Heinrich Broder's chest, reverberating across the shipyard. Between the towering cranes and endless rows of containers, he seemed like a lost figure in a sea of steel and concrete. The wind clawed at his coat—sharp, biting—but the real chill that made him shudder came from something far deeper than the weather.*

*The air was thick with diesel fumes, metal, and damp concrete. Somewhere, a crane groaned, its deep, resonant creak like an agonized breath. Three men in black jackets moved with eerie precision, their hoods pulled low over their faces. They unloaded the containers with a mechanical efficiency—every movement deliberate, almost ritualistic. Not a single word was spoken. It was the kind of silence that made Heinrich uneasy.*

*A noise behind him.*

*He flinched, spinning around too fast.*

*A shipyard worker stood there, his face weathered, his sharp eyes scrutinizing Heinrich with a look that carried more than curiosity. With his hands buried deep in the pockets of his grease-streaked jacket, the man exuded an unspoken challenge.*

*"Mr. Broder?" His voice was rough, marked by years of labor under open skies. Heinrich's stomach tightened. His fingers instinctively gripped the fabric of his coat*

*before he forced himself to relax. "Special assignments," he said, keeping his voice casual. "Not our concern."*

*The worker nodded slowly, but skepticism lingered in his gaze. Heinrich stood his ground, resisting the urge to shift his weight, but the silence between them thickened. When the man finally moved on, Heinrich didn't feel relief—only the gnawing sensation of being watched.*

*His eyes returned to the men at the containers.*

*One of them stood slightly apart, taking a slow drag from a cigarette. His gaze rested on Heinrich—calm, assessing, unshaken. The smoke curled lazily around his face, his expression unreadable. Relaxed. Almost indifferent.*

*But the message was unmistakable.*

**We see everything.**

*Heinrich lowered his gaze and turned away, quickening his pace as the wind drove him forward. But the weight of those eyes clung to the back of his neck like invisible chains.*

*Inside, it was quiet.*

*But not the comforting kind of quiet.*

*The air felt heavier than usual, thick and unmoving. The steady dripping from the roof—normally a small, familiar sound—had stopped. The absence of it unsettled him in a way he couldn't quite explain.*

*He shrugged off his coat, stepped toward his desk—*

*And stopped.*

**An envelope.**

*No return address.*

*It was placed carefully, deliberately. Not simply left behind, but positioned—waiting for him.*

*His fingers trembled as he picked it up. His palms were damp. Without realizing it, he wiped them against his trousers before turning the envelope over in his hands. The paper was thick, unnaturally heavy, as though the words inside carried a weight beyond ink and meaning.*

*He slid the letter out.*

**No exit. No mistakes. We are watching you.**

*His throat turned dry.*

*The letter sagged in his hands, but the words burned into his mind, searing past his defenses. A cold, creeping panic slithered up his spine, gnawing at his self-control. His right eyelid twitched, rapid and involuntary.*

He reached for the phone and dialed Andreas Falk.

It rang. Once. Twice. A third time.

It felt like an eternity before Falk finally answered.

"Heinrich."

No greeting. No pleasantries. Just his name, clipped and unreadable.

Heinrich exhaled sharply.

"He's threatening me, Andreas,"

he said, his voice hoarse. "Sorokin… he's watching me. What if he—my family—?"

"Stay calm." Falk's voice cut through his panic like a blade. "As long as you do what he asks, nothing will happen. But one thing is clear—"

A beat of silence.

"There's no way back."

Then the line went dead.

Heinrich slowly lowered the receiver. The envelope slipped from his fingers, landing crumpled on the floor. The living room was bathed in warm light, but the atmosphere remained cold. Katrin sat curled in an armchair, a book resting on her knees.

When Heinrich entered, she set it aside, her gaze following him—not with concern, but with quiet expectation.

"Dad."

Her voice was pleasant, but distant.

He sank heavily into the armchair across from her. His fingers drummed against the armrest, his jaw tightening.

"Katrin, I… I wanted your advice."

A raised eyebrow.

"You're asking me?" A slight smile, dry and knowing. "That's new."

He hesitated, choosing his words carefully.

"The shipyard is under pressure. I had to make a decision."

Katrin closed her book with slow deliberation.

"You've always treated the shipyard like your personal empire, Dad. Maybe it's time to let go."

A sharp pang shot through his chest.

*"This is no time for reproach,"* he snapped. *"Everything I do, I do for you. For the family."*

*"For the family?"* Katrin leaned back, her eyes piercing through him. *"Or for your pride?"*

*The words landed like a slap.*

*He shot up from his chair, hands clenched into fists.*

*But Katrin didn't flinch. She remained composed, her expression unreadable. A fleeting smile brushed her lips, but there was no warmth in it. "Maybe you should ask yourself what really matters to you, Dad."*

**Hundreds of kilometers away.**

*In a lavish hotel suite, Dmitri Sorokin lowered his phone, his fingers drumming lightly against the polished tabletop.*

*A satisfied smile curled at the corner of his mouth.*

*Outside, lightning slashed across the night sky. The wind howled against the windows.*

*"He's playing exactly as expected,"* Sorokin murmured, *his voice tinged with amusement. He lifted his glass, swirling the dark liquid inside. "Soon, he'll realize he stopped deciding a long time ago." He took a slow sip.* **"A peasant who still believes he's a king."**

# *Chapter 3*

**2024**

The old warehouse of the Emden shipyard was a place frozen in time. Amidst rusted machinery and heaps of discarded metal parts, the steady patter of rain on the corrugated iron roof seemed to echo forgotten secrets. The dim glow of aging overhead lights flickered in the damp, stale air—as if reluctant to let the darkness fully prevail. Since the early hours of the morning, Erik Meyer and Timo Reinders had been clearing away obsolete tools and bulky metal parts from this forsaken space.

"Damn, watch out, Timo!" Erik barked as his colleague nearly knocked over an old metal crate. "This place is dangerous enough."

Timo winced, wiped the sweat from his brow, and gently set the crate aside. "Sorry, man. That wall—there's something off about it."

Erik followed Timo's gaze. In the far end of the hall, where light barely reached, a section of wall appeared out of place. The bricks were roughly grouted, as if hastily patched together.

"This doesn't fit here at all," Erik murmured, running his calloused hand over the uneven stone. "Maybe they bricked something up without caring about the finish." Timo shrugged. "Well, we're supposed to clear everything out anyway. Want to see what's behind it?"

After a brief hesitation, Erik nodded. "Alright, but be careful."

With hearts pounding, they fetched a crowbar and began to loosen the first bricks. Piece by piece, the mortar crumbled until, at last, a heavy wooden door emerged—its surface ravaged by rust and damp.

"Hey, this thing could collapse any second," Timo muttered as he lowered the tool.

"Give me a hand," Erik requested. Together, they pressed against the rotten wood. The door creaked open in a long, reluctant groan, releasing a gust of cool, moldy air that seemed to carry echoes of the past.

As that ancient breath swept out, the incessant drumming of rain began to fade into a foreboding silence. The eerie whisper of the past was replaced by the distant sound of approaching sirens—a reminder that reality was reclaiming this forgotten place.

Inside, the room was shrouded in total darkness. Only the faint beam of a torch revealed dusty tools huddled together, and the air felt unmoved for decades.

"Wow..." Timo exhaled in awe, allowing the narrow cone of light to wander across the room. "It's like no one's been here for ages." Then, the beam settled on an object— a chair placed in the far corner. Slowly, as Erik stepped closer, the shadow on the chair resolved into a ghastly figure: a mummified corpse with its hands bound behind its back, its leathery skin and sunken features frozen in a silent, accusing stare.

"Erik…" Timo's voice cracked, fragile as glass. "There's… something there."

Erik's heart pounded in his throat as he inched forward; his knees trembled with each step. The sight was surreal—a grotesque figure stripped of life, as if time had exiled its flesh long ago.

"It really is there," Erik whispered, adrenaline surging through him.

For several agonizing seconds, they stood, caught between morbid fascination and unyielding horror. Outside, the rain continued its relentless drumming on the metal roof—a strangely calming counterpoint to the terror within.

"We… we need to call the police," Erik said in a thin, wavering voice.

Timo staggered back. "Yes… immediately."

Erik fumbled for his mobile phone. As Timo pressed his back against the wall to steady his ragged breathing, Erik reported the scene. After a brief call with the emergency center, he tucked the phone away, his hands still shaking.

"They're sending someone. We're to wait here and not touch a thing."

Timo nodded silently, eyes fixed on the lifeless form as if it were a magnet. The oppressive silence was finally interrupted by the piercing blue lights of arriving patrol cars, their beams cutting through the rain-soaked gloom.

The surreal tension of the warehouse slowly gave way to the clinical reality of the police presence. As the flashing blue reflected ghostlike images on the wet metal walls, the sound of tires crunching on soaked gravel heralded the arrival of authority.

A police car halted at a respectful distance from the warehouse entrance. Two officers stepped out, unfurling barrier tape as they approached.

"Good evening. Emden Police. Have you made an emergency call?" one officer asked, his tone calm yet firm. "Tell us exactly what happened."

Erik cleared his throat, his voice trembling. "At the back… we found a mummified corpse." His words betrayed his inner turmoil.

Timo added in a brittle tone, "In a bricked-up cellar room. We just removed a few bricks, then..." The officers exchanged a glance. The younger one pulled his collar up against the chill, while the older reached for his radio.

"Are you sure it's a corpse?" the older asked, professional skepticism lining his words.

Erik nodded silently.

"Okay," the officer said as he pressed the intercom button. "We need immediate assistance. Stay calm and don't touch anything."

Shortly after, another vehicle—a civilian police car—rounded the corner. Detective Lena Berg and her partner, Bodo Zimmermann, emerged, both their faces set in focused determination and quiet tension.

"Erik Meyer?" Lena asked, scanning the two men. "And you're Timo Reinders, correct?"

Erik shifted uneasily. "Yes. This is Timo. We... we found this."

A patrolman stepped forward, gave Lena a brief rundown of the situation, and pointed toward the dark opening in the wall. "This is the entrance. The cellar is pitch black— we only have torchlight."

Bodo exchanged a concerned look with Lena, brushing rain from his jacket. "Have you touched or altered anything since discovering the body?"

Timo immediately shook his head. "No. We only removed some bricks and then called the police."

Lena quickly scribbled a few notes. "It's good you called immediately. Forensics are on their way. We'll need a detailed description later."

Erik pulled a packet of cigarettes from his pocket, but his hands trembled too much to light one. Bodo noticed and said, "You can wait over there in the shelter. We'll be right with you." Relieved, the two men retreated, visibly shaken yet glad to hand off the burden.

Alone for a moment, Lena lingered by the dark opening. A cold, moldy breeze wafted out, carrying with it the heavy scent of damp decay and long-forgotten memories. In that instant, a faint whisper—almost imperceptible—rippled through the darkness, and her heart raced. Her hands curled into fists, and her breath caught in her throat.

"Lena?" Bodo's gentle touch on her shoulder broke her reverie.

Forcing a weak smile, she replied, "It's just this place—the confinement, the odor… it feels like the walls have swallowed everything." Bodo nodded. "Every case is unique, yet sometimes it feels all too familiar." "No," she whispered, "never."

Determined, Lena added, "Forensics should be here soon. Until then, let's take a look around." Raising her torch, she led Bodo into the pitch-black cellar.

The dusty floor crunched under their steps as the beam of light danced over walls shrouded in creeping shadows. A thin layer of dust blanketed every surface—as though no one had disturbed this space for decades, apart from the brief work of the two men at the wall.

In the far corner, a mummified body sat on a worn wooden chair—ancient as the building itself. Its hands were bound with rotted ropes, and its head tilted slightly, as if locked in a silent vigil.

Lena inhaled deeply, her pulse pounding in her ears, and focused the beam on the faded clothes. A shiver raced down her spine—not only from the chill but from the disquieting thought of how long this person had been abandoned.

Bodo knelt carefully, letting his light slide across the dusty floor. "No fresh tracks," he murmured. "No one's been here for years."

As Lena's senses absorbed the haunting surroundings— the creak of the floor, the subtle rustle of dust—the physical tension in her body mirrored the storm raging outside. Her heart hammered, her fingers trembled, and a deep-seated ache welled up inside her. Then, footsteps echoed from behind. Markus Weber, a forensics technician, entered with his team.

"Lena, Bodo," he said quietly, "we're setting up the spotlight to reveal more." Within minutes, a cold, clear light filled the space. Dust particles shimmered in the beam, and the corpse's features became ghostly: parchment-like skin, sunken eyes, and decay etched in every line.

"It's remarkable how well-preserved the body is," commented Corinna Stein, the forensic specialist. "The dry environment and poor air circulation likely led to its mummification. We'll secure it after documentation."

As Corinna and Markus worked, their eyes drifted over rusted tools, tattered manuals, and empty crates—silent witnesses to a long-forgotten era.

Bodo gently placed his hand on Lena's shoulder. "Are you alright?" She managed a nod, though her eyes betrayed the turmoil inside. For a moment, memories surged—a familiar cologne, the warm timbre of her father's laugh, the well-worn bracelet he always wore—each detail a poignant reminder of what she'd lost. "Just memories…" she whispered, the pain nearly overwhelming.

"We'll get through this," Bodo assured softly.

Later that night, as Lena and Bodo returned to their car for a brief respite, the relentless rain drummed on the windows. Shortly after midnight, Lena's mobile phone rang, its shrill tone slicing through the darkness. The caller ID flashed "Corinna Stein," and Lena's pulse spiked as the cold night suddenly felt much more personal.

"Corinna? Do you have any results?" Lena asked, her voice unsteady.

"Initial indications, yes," came the muffled reply from the lab. "The ring found on the mummified body bears the engraving: 'Karin – For Dad.' We also discovered a name on an old metal plaque attached to the jacket lining—Broder." A sickening twist of emotion gripped Lena. Broder. It was a name that had surfaced earlier in the investigation. She closed her eyes as memories of her father's gentle voice, the comforting scent of his cologne, and that cherished bracelet flooded back.

"Do you mean… the body could be Mrs. Karin Broder's father?" she whispered, barely able to process the thought.

"It seems very likely. We need further tests—DNA samples won't be analyzed until tomorrow. But the engraving is clear: 'Karin – For Dad.' It's more than mere coincidence."

Lena's heart pounded in her ears as countless questions surged: How long had he been missing? Why was no one searching? And how was she to tell a daughter that her father might have perished in a dark, hidden cellar?

Bodo, sensing her mounting distress, reached out and gently touched her arm. "Are you okay?" She hesitated, then said quietly, "Corinna thinks it might be Karin Broder's father." Bodo raised an eyebrow.

"Do you think it's the same name we…" Lena pressed a finger to her lips. "I'll speak with her in a moment, okay?" She turned back to the call.

"Thank you, Corinna. What do you suggest?"

"I recommend you contact Karin Broder as soon as possible. An official DNA match will take time, but if she can share details—any unique features, past medical interventions, or personal jewelry of her father—it would help. She might also know if he was ever reported missing." "Understood," Lena murmured. "I'll handle it. Please keep me posted."

After hanging up, Lena sat motionless, staring out through the rain-beaten windshield. Inside, her body trembled with a mixture of dread and determination. The thought of having to break such devastating news to a stranger in the dead of night made her stomach twist, especially with the victim's identity still uncertain.

Bodo switched on the interior light.

"You have to call her, don't you?"

Lena ran her hand through her hair, her pulse thundering.

"Yes. But I hate this part of the job. I can secure a crime scene and grill a suspect, yet nothing prepares you for delivering human tragedy." Gently,

Bodo squeezed her hand.

"Shall I take it?"

Grateful, she shook her head. "I know you would. But I'm the lead investigator. Besides, the person on the other end may be too distraught."

With trembling fingers, Lena scrolled through her contacts until she found Karin Broder's number—a number that once belonged to a routine call months ago when the name meant little more than a peripheral detail. Now, it carried the weight of unimaginable loss.

Taking a deep breath, she pressed the dial button. The call seemed to stretch on interminably before a sleepy, slightly irritated "Yes?" finally broke the silence.

"Mrs. Broder? This is Inspector Lena Berg. Please excuse the late call, but it's urgent."

A rustling, then a soft clearing of the throat was heard.

"Inspector Berg? What's happened at this hour…?"

Lena's throat tightened, but she forced herself to speak calmly:

"We discovered a mummified body at the old Emden shipyard this evening. While we haven't confirmed its identity yet, we found a ring engraved with your name. There is a strong suspicion that it may be your father."

For a long, heart-stopping moment, there was only silence—punctuated by the distant hum of a heater or ventilation. Then, in a voice thick with emotion, the reply came:

"That… can't be. My father disappeared without a trace twenty years ago. The police never had any leads… How… how could this be?"

Lena felt her own throat tighten as she fought to maintain her professionalism.

"Mrs. Broder, I understand this must be a shock. We will do everything we can to confirm the facts. Tomorrow, we'll come by to discuss the details—DNA tests and all. I know this is hard, but please try to get some rest."

A trembling

"Yes, of course… oh my God,"

came through before the line went dead.

Lena slowly set the phone aside, her eyes fixed on the dark interior of the car as her heart hammered with the weight of responsibility. She felt as if she had just delivered the worst possible news to a stranger. Bodo's concerned gaze met hers.

"You did the right thing," he murmured softly.

Tears welled in Lena's eyes as she recalled the comforting scent of her father's cologne, the soft timbre of his voice, and that cherished bracelet that now seemed like a relic of another life. The memory was so vivid it almost made her feel his presence beside her.

"Thank you,"

she whispered, barely managing a weak smile.

In that moment, Lena knew the true investigation was only beginning. If the body really was Karin Broder's father, the questions loomed large:

Who had locked him in that cellar—and why?

Was this a long-forgotten missing persons case turned murder, or was there an entirely different story behind it?

Looking at the police tape sealing off the hall—a hall now silent and shut tight—she sensed that answers lay buried deep, waiting to be unearthed with great effort.

As the last beams of the forensic lights danced outside in the rain, Lena leaned her head against Bodo's shoulder, a silent vow forming in her heart. The coming day would test their limits, but there would be no turning back.

Outside, the rain began again—first as a gentle drizzle, then as a torrential downpour. Like a stubborn companion, it sang its monotonous song as Lena steeled herself for the painful task ahead: calling Mrs. Karin Broder and unveiling a truth that might shatter a lifetime of memories.

It wouldn't be easy. But one thing was certain: for the unknown soul trapped in that dark cellar for decades, the truth had to—and would—be brought to light, no matter the cost.

# Chapter 4

The fog clung to the shipyard like a living thing, slithering through the cracks of abandoned buildings and settling thickly over the desolate surroundings. Lena Berg descended the creaking metal stairs with deliberate care, each step sending a dull echo through the silence. The air was thick with damp, oil, and the stale scent of weathered concrete. The flickering beam of her flashlight skimmed across the stained walls, its unsteady glow making the shadows seem restless.

Every sound stretched unnaturally, reverberating as if the cellar itself resented her presence.

Lena paused at the bottom, inhaling deeply in an attempt to steady her nerves. *What am I doing down here?* she murmured, though she already knew the answer. Something was pulling her forward—a quiet, insistent force pounding in her mind like an unrelenting heartbeat. This place held secrets, buried and waiting.

Her footsteps were muffled on the damp ground as she moved toward the corridor where Heinrich Broder's body had been found. The darkness felt almost sentient, curling around her legs like invisible tendrils. Her grip tightened around the flashlight, its trembling light exposing fine cracks in the concrete—veins of a long-dead thing, frozen in time.

A shiver crawled through her spine, but she pushed forward. *It's just a cellar,* she told herself, but the words rang hollow. The air was too thick, the silence too expectant.

She knelt at the spot where loose bricks had been removed the day before. Her fingertips brushed over the rough surface, pausing at a narrow gap. Clenching the flashlight between her teeth, she slid her hand deeper into the crevice. Cold, brittle paper met her touch. Heart hammering, she carefully withdrew it and unfolded the fragile sheet.

The message sent ice through her veins:

**"Everything ends in the shadow."**

Below the words, an ornate feather had been meticulously drawn.

Lena's pulse quickened. This wasn't a careless doodle—it was a warning. A whisper from the past.

A sudden crash shattered the silence.

Her flashlight slipped from her grasp, spinning wildly across the floor as a bucket clattered against the concrete. A flickering shadow darted across the walls, stretching and twisting in the erratic glow. Whipping around, Lena scanned the room, but there was nothing—nothing but the swirling mist seeping through a broken basement window.

She swallowed hard, retrieving the flashlight with shaky fingers. *Pull yourself together,* she muttered. But the unease clung to her, heavy as the note in her hand.

Carefully, she tucked the paper into a protective sleeve inside her jacket. One last sweep of the room. Nothing stirred. Still, the weight of unseen eyes pressed against her back.

*"Everything ends in the shadows,"* she thought, the words tolling in her mind like a prophecy—or a threat.

The ascent to the surface felt endless, the metal steps groaning under her weight. When she finally emerged, the shipyard lay submerged in silence, the fog swallowing the world whole.

The meeting room buzzed with quiet urgency. Files, notes, and half-empty coffee cups cluttered the long table. Corinna Stein typed rapidly on her laptop, Jan Müller sifted through a file, and Robin Ahlers stood at the window, arms crossed, staring into the milky wall of fog beyond the glass.

Lena placed the protective sleeve on the table. "I found this in the cellar," she announced, keeping her voice steady despite the tremor inside her.

Silence fell instantly. Robin stepped closer.

"What does it say?"

Lena took a slow breath. *Keep it together.*

"Everything ends in the shadows," she repeated, voice hushed. "And a feather. It's deliberate—a message. But why hide it down there?"

Corinna picked up the sleeve, inspecting the fragile paper. "It's old—almost handmade. But the writing looks newer. Someone wanted it to seem more aged than it actually is."

"Or it was only recently hidden there," Jan remarked, setting his file aside. "The killer could've had access to the cellar. Or someone else—someone who wanted to mislead us."

Lars Lammerts, seated at the head of the table, looked up from his notes. "Let's not get too caught up in symbols. Sometimes a piece of paper is just a piece of paper."

Lena met his gaze. "And sometimes it's much more than that," she countered. "This was hidden. It's meant for us."

A beat of silence followed, broken only by the rhythmic tapping of Corinna's keyboard. Lars sighed. "Either way, we need to question the family. They might know more than they're letting on."

Robin suddenly turned his laptop toward them. "I found something in the archives.

An old, incomplete case file from 2004—financial irregularities. And it mentions a note with the same message."

Corinna straightened, eyes narrowing. "Two notes. Twenty years apart. Both with the same words?" She shook her head. "That's not a coincidence."

Jan exhaled sharply. "This could be a setup. Someone wants to drag us back to 2004."

Lena nodded slowly. "Which means we need to find out *who* had access to those files—and why they're incomplete."

As she finished speaking, her phone vibrated against the table.

A private number.

Heart pounding, she picked up. "Berg, Emden Police."

At first, only static.

Then—

A voice. Distorted. Deep. Crawling from the receiver like something alive.

**_"Everything ends in the shadow."_**

The call cut off.

Lena sat frozen, the phone still pressed to her ear.

Robin cursed under his breath, running a hand over the back of his neck. "What the hell was that?"

Lena lowered the phone slowly. "The same message," she murmured. "Anonymous. Distorted."

Corinna shot her a wary glance. Jan stood abruptly, as if movement might help him process the situation.

"We're being watched," Corinna said, voice barely above a whisper.

"Or someone's trying to manipulate us," Jan countered, his unease palpable.

"Maybe both," Lena admitted. But one thing was certain—there was no time to waste.

As the team launched into urgent discussion, Lena leaned back against the wall, her fingers instinctively pressing over the sleeve in her jacket pocket. The words from the note echoed in her mind, louder than before.

She had crossed a threshold—deeper into the secrets of the shipyard, deeper into Broder's past.

And there was no turning back. Through the window, the fog thickened. This was just the beginning.

# Chapter 5

The rain pounded relentlessly against the car roof, drumming a steady rhythm as Lena stared out at the slick, mirror-like road. The wipers moved with a steady, almost impatient beat, as if mimicking the pulse in her temples. Beside her, Bodo sat in pensive silence, his expression unreadable. Outside, the night crackled with unspoken tension.

Lena's thoughts wandered to Katrin Broder. Even after all these years, the sight of her father's remains would shake her. What was boiling beneath the surface of her controlled façade?

Bodo broke the silence. "How do you think she'll react?" His voice was measured, but his eyes betrayed a quiet concern.

Lena exhaled slowly. "Some freeze when old wounds are reopened. Others lash out—or break apart." She glanced at him. "We need to tread carefully."

Through the misty downpour, the Broder villa emerged like a looming specter—an austere monument wrapped in high stone walls, its depths concealed by a shifting veil of rain. Well-manicured trees and impeccably trimmed hedges stood like silent sentinels before whatever secrets lay hidden within.

Lena pulled her coat tighter as she stepped out. A strange weight pressed against her chest—an unspoken warning lingering in the air.

Together, she and Bodo ascended the steps to the massive wooden door, its ornate brass knocker glinting under the porch light.

Bodo rapped three times. Each knock rang out like a distant echo, a prelude to the unknown.

A soft rustling behind the door. Then, with a slow, drawn-out creak, it swung open.

An older woman stood in the frame, her silver hair neatly pulled back, her cool eyes assessing them with quiet suspicion.

"Yes?" Her voice was crisp, distant.

Lena stepped forward, flashing her badge. "Lena Berg, Emden Criminal Investigation Department. This is my colleague, Bodo Zimmermann. We'd like to speak with Mrs. Katrin Broder."

The woman's gaze flicked to the ID, her nod barely perceptible. "Come in."

Inside, the house greeted them with a silence more telling than words. The marble floor gleamed beneath the glow of a stately chandelier—elegant, yet impersonal. A faint scent of polished wood and something older, more elusive, clung to the air. It was a place that had once been grand, but now felt like a relic of the past, quietly decaying beneath its pristine surface.

Lena's gaze lingered on a large oil portrait of a woman with sharp, aristocratic features. A relic of another time, watching. Waiting.

"Follow me," the woman instructed.

Mrs. Hoffmann, Lena assumed. The housekeeper's voice was steady, but there was something else beneath it—something barely perceptible. A tremor, quickly swallowed.

They moved through a long corridor lined with portraits. Painted eyes followed their steps, their expressions frozen in time, their secrets locked within the silence of the house.

As they walked, Bodo spoke, his tone almost casual. "Mrs. Hoffmann, how long have you worked for the family?"

A pause. Her fingers curled slightly around the hem of her apron. "Almost half my life," she murmured without turning. Then, as if snapping back into place, she continued forward with renewed purpose.

Moments later, they arrived before a set of heavy double doors.

"Wait here. I will get Mrs. Broder," she announced before vanishing inside, leaving them alone in the vast living room.

The space was refined but restrained. Plush carpets, dark wooden furniture—wealth without ostentation. But beneath the careful arrangement, there was something else. Something restrained. Something unsaid.

Lena's eyes drifted to the mantelpiece, where a photograph rested. Heinrich Broder with his children. Katrin, poised even as a young girl, already carrying the weight of a name that demanded perfection.

A quiet click. The door reopened.

Mrs. Hoffmann entered first, followed by a tall, elegant woman.

Katrin Broder.

She moved with an effortless grace, her light-colored dress as unassuming as her expression. Cool. Controlled. Unreadable. She took her seat without ceremony, her back straight, her gaze unwavering.

Lena and Bodo followed suit, the tension in the room tightening like an invisible noose. The rhythmic ticking of a grandfather clock filled the silence, marking time in slow, deliberate beats.

Lena broke it first.

"I called you last night. I hope you've had time to collect yourself. We have a few questions—not just about recent events, but about the days leading up to your father's disappearance."

Katrin's expression remained impassive. A flicker, barely there. A breath that hesitated before it met the air.

"Some truths," she murmured, almost absently, "are too painful to speak aloud."

Her voice was soft. Detached. But something in the way she said it sent a whisper of unease down Lena's spine.

Bodo's voice was even, but there was a quiet intensity beneath it. "Sometimes, things that once seemed unimportant become crucial later. Anything you remember could help."

Katrin considered this. Slowly. Carefully.

"My father had enemies," she admitted. "Shortly before he vanished, he was... tense. I remember a phone call. He was angry. But he never said who it was with."

Before Lena could press further, Mrs. Hoffmann returned, carrying a tray of tea. She set it down with careful precision, but her eyes—just for a fraction of a second—betrayed something else. Concern. Or perhaps fear.

Katrin barely acknowledged the gesture. Lena leaned forward, her voice measured.

"On the phone yesterday, it sounded like you were being cautious. We are here to find the truth. If you trust us, we can help."

The words lingered in the space between them.

Katrin inhaled, the movement almost imperceptible. Then, colder than before, she repeated:

"Some truths are too painful to speak aloud."

The air shifted. A subtle drop in temperature, or maybe just Lena's own awareness of it.

Goosebumps prickled her arms.

"We will need you to officially identify your father's remains," she said at last. "Let us know when we can accompany you to the coroner's office."

Katrin's nod was barely a movement. "Tell me when. I'll be ready."

Lena studied her carefully. "We also need to speak with your staff. Especially Mrs. Hoffmann."

A flicker of reaction—so brief it could have been imagined.

The housekeeper hesitated. Her fingers tightened ever so slightly around the tray. "I… of course. If it's necessary."

"Tomorrow at the precinct would be best," Bodo added, his voice calm but firm.

A silence stretched. Then, with a clipped nod, Mrs. Hoffmann murmured, "As you wish."

Lena didn't miss the way her shoulders stiffened. The hesitation, small but telling.

As they stepped outside, the house loomed behind them, its windows dark save for a single flickering light on the upper floor.

A shadow passed behind the glass.

Bodo glanced at her. "What do you think?"

Lena didn't answer immediately. She studied the house, the way it swallowed the light, the way it seemed to watch them as much as they watched it.

"Katrin Broder is hiding something," she said finally. "And Mrs. Hoffmann knows more than she's letting on."

Bodo nodded. "Then we dig deeper."

Lena started the engine. In the darkness, only the pale glow of the villa remained—a silent warning against the night.

# *Chapter 6*

The first rays of sunlight slanted through the large windows of Lena's house on Gatjebogen, bathing the kitchen in a warm, amber glow. Outside, the leaves rustled in the gentle wind, carrying the crisp scent of an autumn morning into the house.

Lena stood at the window, a steaming cup of coffee in her hands, watching as the golden light illuminated the trees, their leaves ablaze in shades of orange and yellow. It was a peaceful picture, but her thoughts were far from calm. The case occupied every corner of her mind.

Behind her, dishes clinked softly. Bodo set the plates on the table with deliberate care. "I tried not to scramble the eggs too much," he said, sliding a plate toward her. There was a hint of pride in his voice. "No guarantees, though."

Lena turned, managing a faint smile. "More than I could have done today." She sank into a chair as Bodo refilled her coffee cup. "Thanks."

He studied her closely. "You barely slept, did you? Broder?"

Lena sighed, wrapping her hands around the warm ceramic. "He was missing for twenty years, and now... now he's lying in a cellar as if he never belonged anywhere else." She exhaled slowly. "The deeper we dig, the more questions we find instead of answers."

Bodo nodded, his expression steady. "That's our job—to find answers. And you'll put the pieces together. You always do."

"Maybe," she murmured, taking a bite of the eggs. The taste barely registered. "Today's not going to be easy."

Bodo reached across the table, resting a hand on hers. "We'll handle it. Together."

A small smile ghosted across her lips. "I'll grab doughnuts for the team on the way. Tradition is tradition."

"Robin would never forgive you if you didn't," Bodo said with a smirk.

Lena chuckled softly. "He has a weakness for the ones with icing. I think he's been counting the days."

"Then let's not keep him waiting," Bodo said, rising to clear the table. "I'll warm up the car."

Lena reached for her jacket as a cool breeze drifted in through the open window. She closed her eyes for a moment, drawing in the crisp morning air before exhaling slowly.

"Let's start the day."

The drive to the bakery passed in comfortable silence. The streets were bathed in golden light, the morning sun painting warm hues across rooftops. Leaves swirled in lazy spirals as the wind carried them along.

Lena watched the shifting patterns of light and shadow on the façades, but her mind was elsewhere.

Katrin Broder.

Why was she so evasive? Was she hiding something, or did she genuinely know nothing? Perhaps she feared revealing too much. Had Broder confided in her that night? Had he shared something that cost him his life?

A quiet unease settled in her chest.

Back at the precinct, the team gathered in the meeting room. The air smelled of coffee and ink, files stacked high across the long table. Lars stood at the head, his gaze sharp.

"Corinna, you have the floor."

Corinna straightened in her chair. "Toxicology confirms it—arsenic was the cause of death. But we also have something crucial. We extracted DNA from a tooth." She exhaled. "There's no doubt. The body is Heinrich Broder."

Silence. Bodo folded his arms. Lena felt her stomach tighten. Across the table, Robin exchanged a glance with Lars—unspoken understanding passing between them. They had all suspected it, but confirmation was different. Final.

Lars cleared his throat. "We had two key interviews yesterday. Katrin Broder appeared controlled, almost indifferent. But when she mentioned her father's phone call, she hesitated. Her hand stopped midair before she set it on the table. She averted her gaze—like she was afraid we'd read the truth in her eyes."

Robin leaned forward. "Do you believe her?"

Lena shook her head. "Not entirely. She was evasive when we pressed for details."

Lars nodded. "Mrs. Hoffmann claimed Broder wanted to settle old scores. She mentioned a meeting with a stranger shortly before he disappeared—but conveniently, she didn't know any details."

He scanned the room. "Jan and I will question them again. Robin, go through Broder's contacts. Lena, Bodo— you're speaking with Thomas Broder." Lena gathered her notes. In the hallway, Bodo slowed his pace. "Think Katrin will show emotion this time?" Lena sighed. "Hard to predict. But we have to be ready."

As they crossed the parking lot, her phone vibrated.

A message.

**Sender: Unknown.**

*Stop digging or someone else will disappear.*

Lena's pulse stuttered. She held out the display to Bodo. His jaw tightened as his eyes flicked over the words.

"That changes everything," he murmured.

# *Chapter 7*

The morning lay heavy over Emden. The damp air carried the earthy scent of wet leaves, while the first light of dawn refracted in the puddles along the street. For a brief moment, the city seemed to hold its breath.

Inside the car, silence hung thick.

Bodo focused on the road, guiding the vehicle through the slick streets. The hum of the engine was their only companion, a monotonous backdrop to his thoughts. Beside him, Lena sat hunched over the case files, her fingers absently tracing the edges of the pages—a silent reflex, a sign that her mind was already deep in the conversation ahead.

Bodo stole a glance at her before breaking the silence.

"Do you think she'll cooperate?" His voice was calm, measured, but the tension beneath it was unmistakable.

Lena flipped a page, scanning the contents as if the answer might be hidden somewhere in the ink. "That depends on what she's willing to admit to herself."

A pause.

The soft click of the turn signal punctuated the moment as Bodo steered into the driveway of the forensic center. The building loomed ahead, its angular glass façade catching the pale morning light. Inside, only the truth awaited.

Bodo parked. His hands remained on the wheel for a beat before he exhaled, switched off the engine, and turned to Lena.

"Let's do this."

Karin Broder was already waiting outside.

Her coat was pulled tightly around her shoulders, as if shielding her from more than just the morning chill. The delicate pearls on her ears seemed oddly out of place—like a last grasp at an elegance that had long since faded.

Bodo studied her closely. The way she clutched the strap of her handbag, her fingertips skimming over the leather in slow, rhythmic strokes. No trembling, no overt signs of fear. But he could feel it.

He took a step toward her, his gaze steady. "Good morning, Mrs. Broder."

Karin lifted her head, meeting his eyes for only a fraction of a second before looking away. "Morning," she murmured.

A reflex. Not a real greeting.

Lena stepped forward, her voice carrying a professional warmth. "Thank you for coming."

A hesitation. Then a nod. "I had no choice."

The words were cool, controlled. But Bodo caught the faint tremor beneath them—an almost imperceptible strain in her voice, a shield held up just a little too tightly.

He opened the door for her. She stepped inside without another word.

Dr. Julia Müller approached, a clipboard tucked under her arm, her glasses slipping slightly down her nose.

"Are you ready?"

Bodo exhaled a quiet snort. "Are we ever?"

Julia's lips twitched, but the moment of amusement was brief. Her expression turned serious as she turned to Karin.

"Mrs. Broder, we can begin whenever you're ready."

A slight rise and fall of Karin's shoulders. "Then... let's get this over with."

The identification room was sparse. Functional. Unforgiving.

Cold air clung to the walls. The sterile glow of the neon lights cast sharp, merciless shadows over the metal table—on the white sheet that concealed a figure beneath. A lifeless echo of the past.

Julia stepped forward.

"Take all the time you need."

She pulled back the cloth.

The moment stretched.

Karin Broder froze. Her lips parted slightly, as if about to speak—but no sound came.

Her gaze didn't linger on the face. Not on the sunken features of the dead man. It went straight to the ring.

A signet ring. Simple. Old. A fragment of another time.

Her fingers clenched the edge of her handbag, as if grounding herself in the present. Her shoulders rose slightly before she pressed her lips together, exhaling in a slow, controlled motion.

Bodo caught it—the subtle flicker of her lashes, the faintest twitch in her jaw.

A fracture in the mask.

"Yes."

Her voice was too even. Too practiced.

"That's him."

Bodo narrowed his eyes slightly. It wasn't the confirmation that unsettled him. It was the silence that followed.

Julia gave a short nod and gently replaced the cloth. "Thank you, Mrs. Broder. You did well."

Karin inhaled deeply, her gaze lingering on the covered body for a moment longer. Then, she closed her eyes briefly, as if sealing something away. When they opened again, the calm was back.

"Can we move on?"

No tears. No escape. Just an unwavering need to stay in control.

Bodo glanced at Lena. She had noticed it, too.

They moved into the adjacent room.

The toxicology reports were spread across the table.

Julia picked up the top page, her voice even.

"The analysis confirms it. Mr. Broder died of arsenic poisoning."

The moment the cracks deepened.

Karin's eyes remained fixed on the paper before her.

Her fingers tightened against the table's edge—just slightly. A minuscule flex of her jaw. Her breath, just a fraction shallower.

Bodo saw it. He waited.

"Arsenic?" His voice was quiet. Probing. Julia nodded. "Still detectable, even after all these years. It was administered over an extended period."

A barely perceptible twitch in Karin's jaw. She swallowed. Slowly. One hand released the table, hesitating midair, as if she needed to remind herself that she could still move.

"Who..." A stall.

"Who does that?" Bodo watched as her gaze locked onto a single point in the room. An anchor. Something to hold onto.

There it was.

The crack.

Lena's voice was steady, deliberate. "That's exactly what we're going to find out." The words fell like a closing door. When they stepped outside, the sun had risen higher in the sky. But its warmth no longer reached them. The past had awakened.

And it wouldn't disappear again.

# *Chapter 8*

Marie Hoffmann entered the police headquarters with tense shoulders, her fingers tightening around the straps of her bag. The sterile scent of disinfectant lingered in the air, and the cold neon light cast harsh reflections on the floor. A low, steady hum vibrated through the walls.

The investigators were already waiting in the interrogation room.

Robin Ahlers leaned casually against the table, a steaming cup of coffee in his hand, while Jan Müller sat ready with his notepad. Lars Lammers, as always, kept his expression unreadable, but his watchful demeanor left no doubt—he was taking in every detail.

Marie sat down, her fingers fidgeting with her sleeve. "I don't know what else to say. I told you everything back then."

Robin nodded, his tone measured. "We know that, Mrs. Hoffmann. But sometimes, memories surface later. Time can bring clarity."

Marie pressed her lips together. Her fingers drummed lightly on the tabletop, her gaze flicking to the door—as if to reassure herself that they were truly alone. "It was… just a feeling. But I think Broder was afraid."

Jan raised an eyebrow. "Afraid of what?"

Marie inhaled deeply.

"At some point, he received a black folder. I don't know what was in it, but it changed him. He became… different. Suspicious. He barely spoke about the shipyard anymore."

She hesitated, then added, "I once saw him draw the curtains in his office before opening it."

A silent exchange passed between the investigators.

Lars' hand remained motionless on the table, but something in his posture shifted slightly, as if a missing puzzle piece had just fallen into place. He leaned forward, his gaze sharpening.

"Did someone pressure him?" His thumb brushed absently against the edge of the table—an unconscious tell that he had just picked up on something crucial.

Marie hesitated. Again, her eyes darted toward the door, as if expecting someone to walk in at any moment. Then, in a whisper, she said:

"Sorokin. I saw him with Broder several times. Always outside, never inside the offices. Once, they were standing on the quay—Broder clutching the folder like his life depended on it. He was on edge for days afterward."

Robin straightened slightly, his fingers drumming absently against his coffee cup.

"Did you ever hear what it was about?"

Marie shook her head quickly. "No, but… he told me once that he'd made a mistake. That it was about money."

She hesitated. Then, lowering her voice even further, she added, "And then there was this other man…"

The pause stretched.

A name on the tip of her tongue, but something held her back—as if saying it out loud would make it real.

"Timofej Fedorov," she finally murmured. "He's on your radar too, isn't he?"

Jan's pen moved swiftly over the notepad. "What do you know about him?"

Marie lifted a shoulder in a tense shrug.

"Not much. But he was always around when Sorokin was. And I heard Broder whisper his name on the phone once. After that, he looked at me like I'd overheard something I shouldn't have."

A brief silence settled over the room.

Then Lars gave a slow nod.

"That helps us. Thank you, Mrs. Hoffmann."

Marie exhaled audibly, as if releasing a breath she hadn't realized she was holding. There was relief in her expression, but the tension hadn't fully left her eyes.

"If you find Broder…"

She hesitated, choosing her words carefully.

"Tell him he can trust me. If he's still alive."

Robin met her gaze, his nod slow but cautious. His eyes, however, held quiet skepticism.

Marie opened her mouth as if to say something else, then stopped herself. A moment later, in a whisper, she added:

"He always said you have more to fear from the wrong friends than from enemies."

# *Chapter 9*

After Marie had left the room, an eerie silence remained. Lars and Jan sat motionless, the newly revealed information hanging in the air like the distant echo of an approaching storm. Finally, Lars leaned forward, pressing his hands flat against the table as if trying to ground himself.

"Jan, this is bigger than we thought." His voice was calm, but his eyes betrayed something far from composed. "Sorokin, Fedorov, and this black folder… This isn't a coincidence. Broder knew something—something that made him a target."

Jan let the words settle for a moment before flipping through his notes. "These financial traces… they don't just point to a bad deal. There's more to it. Something tied to Broder's decisions."

Lars stood and walked to the window. Outside, the wind swept the colorful autumn leaves across the streets of Emden, making them dance—a silent signal, an imperceptible warning. "Sorokin's threat wasn't just pressure. It was an ultimatum."

"Marie has given us more than she probably realizes." Jan closed his notebook. "She showed us that Broder was afraid. Not just for himself, but for something he couldn't let go of."

Robin was already waiting in the meeting room. The dull glow of his screen bathed his face in a pale light. Without a word, he projected a document onto the large monitor.

"Timofej Fedorov." He pronounced the name as if testing its weight. "Well known in the world of illegal arms trafficking. Arrested in Thailand in 2008, extradited to the US. Had ties to international conflict zones."

He tapped on the next file. The series of numbers on the screen looked harmless—but the abyss lay between them. "Between 2006 and 2008, large sums of money flowed from Broder's shipyard to a company called Danube Trade Limited. Registered in Cyprus. Linked to Fedorov."

Lars narrowed his gaze. "Amount of the last transaction?"

"May 2008. Five hundred thousand euros."

A brief silence. Then: "Money laundering?"

Robin leaned back. "Maybe. Or arms dealing. Fedorov often used struggling companies as a cover. When Broder was in trouble…"

Lars turned slowly. "And Sorokin? Where does he fit in?"

Robin switched the document. "He's not directly part of Fedorov's network. But he's the one pulling the strings. There are signs he's been operating in this environment for a long time."

He hesitated, choosing his next words carefully. "He was in Emden multiple times. Had smaller, regular contracts with Broder's shipyard. A classic pattern for concealing transactions."

Jan rubbed his chin thoughtfully. "Then maybe Sorokin was the middleman. The one who brought Broder and Fedorov together."

"Or more than that," Robin's voice was quiet but insistent. "Maybe Broder made a deal that didn't go as planned. Maybe he ended up with something he wasn't supposed to have."

Lars' face hardened. "What if he was trying to get out? Maybe he realized too late who he had gotten involved with."

Robin shook his head slowly. "If he had gotten out, would he still be alive?"

Silence. Then Lars took a deep breath. "We need to check Broder's background again. Someone knows more. The only question is: who?"

Robin gave a curt nod. Jan closed his notebook. When they left the meeting room, the air felt heavier, as if an unseen presence had stepped inside.

The door clicked shut. And with it, the last certainty that what they were looking for had already found them.

A quiet vibration broke the silence of the corridor. Lars paused and pulled out his phone. An unknown number. He answered.

"Yes?"

A soft breath on the other end. Then a distorted voice, barely intelligible:

*"You're digging too deep. Stop now—or there's no turning back."*

The line went dead.

Lars remained still, his phone still pressed to his ear. Seconds passed before he slowly raised his eyes to Jan. There was something dark in them, a realization sinking deep into his thoughts. He pressed his lips together and inhaled, as if trying to absorb the moment.

Robin took a step closer, his voice low. "Was it Sorokin?"

Lars lowered the phone, his expression unreadable. "Maybe. Or someone working for him."

The silence stretched, thick with unspoken thoughts. Then Jan finally stated the obvious. "We're not stopping."

Lars nodded, slow and deliberate. "No. Now more than ever."

# Chapter 10

**2003**

*The autumn sun bathed the Faldernpoort in a warm, golden light. Yet beneath this soft glow lay an imperceptible tension—like the silence before a storm.*

*Katrin Broder stepped out of her father's jet-black car. The soft click of the door faded, barely audible in the stillness of the early evening. She paused briefly, letting her gaze sweep over the hotel's façade—a harmonious blend of Frisian tradition and sleek modernity. A symbol of stability. But she knew that stability could be deceptive.*

*Beside her stood Heinrich Broder—tall, austere, immaculately dressed. With a precise movement, he adjusted his cuffs.*

*"Stay by my side, Katrin."*

*His tone was calm, but there was no request in his voice— only an order.*

*Katrin hesitated. Her gaze flickered to his face—hard, motionless, unyielding. A silent resistance stirred within her. Not open defiance, but something deeper. A flicker inside her. She imperceptibly clenched her fists, then immediately relaxed them again. He couldn't notice.*

*"I want you to meet Alexei Sorokin. It's important—for the future." A name. A shadow. She nodded. But something inside her tightened.*

*The hotel embraced them in subdued elegance. Dark wood, polished surfaces, the delicate aroma of freshly brewed coffee. Conversations drifted through the room like a muffled murmur, accompanied by the soft crackling of the fireplace. A painting hung above it—a sailing ship, powerful on the surface yet always at the mercy of the depths.*

*Guests had gathered in the conference room. The buffet was sumptuous, the scent of freshly baked bread mingling with the aroma of expensive wine. Heinrich approached Ono Marthens, a man whose smile was as inviting as it was calculating.*

*"Heinrich! Welcome. And this must be Katrin." Marthens' hands briefly rested on hers. "The next generation of Broders, I presume?"*

*But before Katrin could answer, the atmosphere in the room shifted.*

*A man entered.*

*The conversations ebbed away, as if the air had suddenly grown heavier.*

***Alexei Sorokin.***

*He moved with effortless precision. Tall. Slim. His deep blue suit fit perfectly—not merely worn, but a second skin. His stature was upright, his demeanor imbued with a quiet authority that required no forcefulness.*

*His eyes—cool, penetrating grey—swept over the room with measured calculation. Then they settled on Katrin.*

*A barely perceptible smile.*

*"Mr. Broder." His voice was deep and smooth. He extended a hand toward Heinrich—a greeting with the controlled dominance of a man who always maintained the upper hand. Then he turned to Katrin.*

*"And this must be your daughter. Katrin, isn't it?"*

*His handshake was firm. His palm warm. Her fingers felt slightly damp.*

*"Nice to meet you, Mr. Sorokin."*

*"Please—Alexei." His smile deepened, but his eyes remained cold. "Your father has told me a great deal about you. Especially about your interest in art. I find that... fascinating."*

*"Thank you." The words came too quickly. Felt foreign. "I'm trying to broaden my horizons."*

*"An admirable trait." His voice dropped a shade. "Sometimes—if I may—a fresh perspective opens entirely new worlds."*

*Before she could respond, Heinrich steered the conversation toward the shipyard. But Katrin couldn't ignore how Alexei continued to study her.*

*Was it curiosity? Or something else?*

**Later in the evening.**

*The room had emptied. Voices had faded into distant murmurs. The scent of red wine and candle wax hung thick in the air.*

*Katrin stood at a high table, taking a moment for herself.*

*Then she felt him.*

*Alexei stepped beside her. "A successful evening." His voice was calm, almost gentle. But beneath it lay something else.*

*She turned to him. "My father places great importance on tradition. It's the foundation of his work."*

*Alexei took a sip of wine. His gaze lingered on her.*

*"Foundations are important." He let the words settle between them. "But sometimes... they need to be renewed. New ideas. New paths. Wouldn't you agree?"*

*A harmless conversation. And yet, not.*

*Then it happened.*

*She hadn't noticed him move. Hadn't seen him reach into his pocket. Hadn't even heard a sound.*

*But suddenly, there was something on the table in front of her.*

*A business card.*

*Black. Plain.*

**Alexei Sorokin.**

*Nothing else.*

*Katrin blinked.*

*She hadn't seen where he had taken it from. Hadn't noticed him place it there. A quiet shiver ran down her spine.*

*Alexei leaned back, watching her with that composed smile.*

*"If you ever seek inspiration—or a conversation about art."*

*He held her gaze a second too long. Then he picked up his glass. Drinking. Waiting.*

Katrin slowly reached out. Her fingers brushed the smooth surface of the card.

They were trembling.

Why?

A puzzle, she thought. One I don't want to solve—but have to.

"Thank you," she said quietly.

Alexei studied her. Then he nodded. A step back. A brief pause.

Then his final words: "Sometimes… true art lies not in the obvious, but in the hidden."

He smiled.

Then he turned away. And the warmth disappeared with him. An invisible curtain of cold settled over the room.

Katrin's breathing was shallow. The candles seemed to flicker less brightly. She reached into her pocket and felt the business card under her fingertips.

This evening was the beginning.

A game had started. And she didn't know if she would ever understand the rules.

# *Chapter 11*



*2003*

*The Broder villa lay in deceptive silence. The afternoon sun cast sharp shadows through the high windows as Alexei Sorokin entered. His movements were smooth, his expression polite yet unreadable. Heinrich extended his hand, but Thomas kept his distance, arms folded, gaze watchful.*

*"Welcome, Alexei," Heinrich said. "I'm sure you'll be impressed by what we've prepared."*

*Alexei smiled. "I have no doubt about that, Mr. Broder." His gaze shifted to Thomas, who regarded him impassively. "And I'm sure your son will bring interesting perspectives to the table as well."*

*"We'll see," Thomas replied coolly.*

*Before the atmosphere could grow any tenser, Katrin entered the room. A folder in her hands, her posture calm and composed.*

*"Alexei," she greeted him with a brief smile. "I hope my father hasn't made you too many promises."*

*"I trust the Broders know what they're doing," Alexei replied, his voice measured. His gaze lingered on Katrin a moment longer before shifting back to Heinrich.*

*Thomas watched the exchange in silence. An unpleasant feeling spread through his chest.*

*It wasn't the first time he had wondered how much Katrin really knew.*

*The roar of machinery and the sharp scent of lubricating oil filled the shipyard. Heinrich led Alexei through the production area, Thomas trailing behind, arms still crossed.*

*"This line here," Alexei began, motioning toward the machines, "is a classic—solid, reliable. But it's also a hindrance. Modernization could cut your production time in half."*

*"And double the financial outlay," Thomas countered. "Who's going to pay for that? Us? Or do you have a plan?"*

*Alexei paused, his gaze resting briefly on Thomas before a slow smile appeared. "Financing is a question of trust, Mr. Broder junior. And trust starts with choosing the right partners."*

*"Or knowing what those partners have in mind," Thomas muttered.*

*Heinrich shook his head. "Thomas, we've discussed this. Alexei is offering us an opportunity we can't afford to miss."*

*"Maybe we should talk about what he gets out of it,"* Thomas replied, eyes fixed on Alexei.

*Alexei smiled again, but his eyes remained cold. "Sometimes, Mr. Broder, true strength lies in letting go of the old. It takes courage to accept progress."*

*Thomas sat in his office late that night. In front of him lay the contracts Alexei had presented.* **Danube Trade Limited**—*the name kept appearing, tied to payments funneled through Cyprus and the Cayman Islands. Consultancy services, allegedly. But nothing about these documents felt genuine.*

*He picked up his phone and typed in the company's address. The result was sobering: an empty mailbox, a blank website.*

*A knock at the door made him flinch. Katrin entered, a cup of tea in her hands. "You look like you're chasing ghosts," she remarked casually.*

*"Maybe I am." Thomas lowered the documents. "Danube Trade Limited," he murmured, looking up at her. "Does that name mean anything to you?" Katrin hesitated for a fraction of a second, then shook her head. "Why are you always looking for problems, Thomas?"*

*"Because problems tend to hide themselves," he replied. Katrin placed the cup on his desk and stepped closer.*

*"Maybe you should just listen to Alexei. Sometimes solutions are simpler than you think." He scrutinized her, brow furrowed. "Or more complicated than they seem." Katrin smiled, but when she turned away, Thomas noticed her fingers sliding restlessly over the cup.*

*He rubbed his temples. Next to the payment details, he spotted a handwritten note:*

**Release by A. Sorokin.** *He stared at the words.*

*Why was this note here? Was it a mistake—or a deliberate move? Suddenly, the light from his desk lamp flickered, and a soft creak made him freeze. Slowly, he walked to the door and opened it.*

*An envelope lay on the floor.*

*He bent down, picked it up, and hesitantly opened it. Inside, he found a single note, written in clear, curved handwriting:*

**Trust is an investment. Be sure you can afford it.**

*The* **Danube Trade Limited** *logo was embossed at the bottom. Thomas lowered the note and looked back at the documents on his desk. A cold shiver ran down his spine.*

*He knew Alexei was watching him.*

*And he knew he couldn't win this game alone.*

# *Chapter 12*

**2024**

The sun struggled against the haze that cloaked Emden on this crisp autumn morning. The muffled horn of a distant freighter drifted through the air, while the cool breeze carried the metallic scent of the harbor. The streets lay under a veil of grey mist, as if the city itself was holding its breath.

Lena Berg sat behind the wheel of the company car, her hands resting loosely on the steering wheel. Beside her, Robin Ahlers stared out of the window, his thoughts as foggy as the landscape outside.

*"It's strange how the city has changed,"* he murmured eventually, absentmindedly twirling a biro between his fingers. *"There used to be something majestic about the Broder shipyard. Now it just looks… abandoned."*

Lena nodded without taking her eyes off the road. *"The shipyard may be derelict, but the secrets it holds are still very much alive."*

The car came to a stop in front of the massive entrance gate of the Broder shipyard. The company logo, once a proud emblem of industry, hung askew, corroded by rust. The air was thick with the scent of wet metal and old oil. Somewhere in the distance, a loose metal sheet rattled in the wind.

Lena switched off the engine and glanced at Robin.

*"Ready?"*

He shrugged. *"As ready as I'll ever be."*

Thomas Broder's office was housed in the main building of the shipyard. The reception area was plain, almost barren, with furniture that bore the undeniable marks of time. An older employee led them down a long corridor, its walls lined with yellowed photographs and aged documents—silent witnesses to an era long gone.

Thomas was waiting for them in a sparsely furnished office. His suit was rumpled, and the tiredness in his eyes betrayed sleepless nights. Yet, he straightened up and extended a firm handshake as they entered. Outside, the faint hum of machinery mixed with the distant clang of metal on concrete.

*"Mrs. Berg. Mr. Ahlers. What can I do for you?"* His voice was formal, measured—but far from welcoming.

Lena took a seat on one of the rigid chairs, while Robin remained standing.

*"We're investigating the circumstances surrounding your father's disappearance,"* Lena began. *"There are indications that old documents on the shipyard grounds might be relevant. We were hoping you could grant us access."*

Thomas' expression hardened. His left hand twitched slightly at the edge of the table.

*"My father had many secrets. What exactly do you think you'll find?"*

Lena picked up on the underlying tension in his voice. She wondered if his defensiveness was rooted in knowledge—or in fear.

Robin took a step forward.

*"Maybe you missed something back then. Or maybe you chose to overlook it."*

The words lingered in the air, heavy and unspoken, until Thomas let out a sharp exhale.

*"I don't have any answers. My father kept everything to himself."*

A knock on the door cut through the silence.

A young woman entered, elegantly dressed, her demeanor poised yet reserved.

*"Mr. Broder, the documents for the new project."*

Her Hungarian accent gave her voice a soft, melodic quality.

Thomas gave a curt nod. *"Leave them here."*

Aniko Kiss placed the documents on the table and hesitated for a fraction of a second. Her gaze met Robin's—just long enough for a barely perceptible smile to flicker across her lips before vanishing again.

A smile just for him?

Robin felt the heat rising in his face. Did Aniko suspect something? Her glance unsettled him. Had she deliberately looked at him longer than necessary? Or was he just imagining it?

Lena, ever observant, registered the moment with quiet scrutiny.

*"Mrs. Kiss,"* she asked calmly, *"do you happen to have access to the old archives?"*

Aniko looked momentarily surprised before nodding hesitantly.

*"Yes, I could take a look. If it helps."*

A sharp glance was thrown in her direction—barely noticeable, but enough to make her press her lips together briefly.

*"That won't be necessary,"* Thomas cut in abruptly. His fingers drummed nervously against the tabletop. *"Old documents are irrelevant."*

But Lena wasn't deterred.

*"Perhaps you can't be sure of that, Mr. Broder,"* she replied, her voice calm yet unwavering. She turned back to Aniko.

*"Would you accompany us?"*

A beat of silence. Then Aniko quietly agreed.

*"Of course."*

Thomas pushed back his chair abruptly. His fingers fidgeted with his wristwatch before he hastily placed it on the desk.

*"If you have no further questions, please excuse me. I have an appointment."*

His voice was clipped, his movements hurried as he strode toward the door before anyone could object.

Aniko hesitated for a brief second, then cast Lena an apologetic look.

*"I can check and let you know,"* she said softly before leaving the room.

Lena watched her in silence, unable to shake the feeling that Aniko knew more than she was letting on.

The drive back to the Police Department  was filled with quiet contemplation.

Robin stared out of the window, then ran a hand through his hair.

*"Do you think he's scared? Or just trying to keep us at a distance?"*

Lena cast him a brief sideways glance before nodding slowly.

*"Maybe both. Fear can make people do exactly that."*

She could still feel the unease radiating from Thomas. A faint drip echoed on the concrete in the deserted shipyard, amplifying the oppressive atmosphere. His nervous gestures, the restless drumming of his fingers— it all pointed to something he was trying to keep hidden.

Robin frowned.

*"They're hiding something,"* he muttered finally, eyes fixed on the road ahead.

*"Or they know more than they're admitting,"* Lena added. *"Thomas is clearly trying to block us from something."*

When they arrived at the station, Lars Lammerts greeted them with a grim expression.

*"We found something in Heinrich Broder's files,"* he said without preamble.

Lena felt her pulse quicken.

*"What exactly?"* Her voice was composed, but her eyes sharpened.

Lars handed her a folder.

*"Suspicious transactions. It could be money laundering."*

Lena's heartbeat skipped. She exchanged a glance with Robin, who nodded slightly.

The puzzle was beginning to take shape.

*"Then let's dig deeper,"* she decided. *"The truth is buried in those shadows."*

Robin let out a soft chuckle but there was no amusement in his eyes.

*"Then we'd better bring a damn good torch."*

# *Chapter 13*

The first rays of sunlight filtered through the slightly parted bedroom curtains, sending gentle beams dancing across the old wooden bed. From the kitchen drifted the aroma of freshly brewed coffee, its quiet machine hum underscoring the early morning stillness. Lena lay for a moment with her head against Bodo's chest, savoring the tranquil calm before the day's endless questions and puzzles came rushing in again.

"Robin was glowing like a traffic light yesterday," Lena began with a faint smile that did little to mask the tension slowly creeping in. "When Aniko mentioned the archives, he could barely keep his composure."

Bodo pulled her closer. "He's unbeatable when it comes to computers, but women… that's where things get interesting. I'm betting Aniko has her own way of handling him."

Lena's brows drew together momentarily. "I feel like she wants to help us but is being extremely cautious. That folder—it almost sounded like she was showing us a secret path without risking too much herself."

"Or she's testing how far she can trust us," Bodo replied, running his fingers over the handwritten notes they'd spread out on the table the previous evening. "That folder is more than just a clue—it's the key to something big."

When they left the house, fog had settled over Emden's streets like a thick veil. In the distance, muffled city noises merged with the rhythmic drumming of raindrops, which had already begun leaving their first wet traces on the pavement. Jan Müller was waiting in front of the police headquarters, immersed in his morning ritual: crouching beside his old BMW R90/6, carefully polishing the chrome. The soft squeaking of his cloth, the rustle of falling leaves, and the distant honking of car horns blended into a strange tapestry of sound.

"You take better care of that machine than most people do their own cases," Bodo called out, while Lena paused with a quiet smile.

"You've got to set priorities," Jan replied dryly, straightening up. "But don't worry—I'm ready. Lars has a few surprises for us today, and you're right on time."

"I'm not too fond of surprises," Bodo muttered as they climbed the steps to the station. Lena cast one last glance at the fog shrouding the city in a mystical haze.

Inside the Bureau's meeting room, a concentrated silence reigned. Lars stood at the whiteboard, his red marker circling and connecting names—Broder, Sorokin, and the ominous black folder—revealing their tangled relationships.

Robin was hunched over a file in the corner, while Corinna Stein scrolled through her tablet with elegant swipes of her finger.

"Glad you're here," Lars said without preamble. "We've got news. Mrs. Hoffmann's statements from yesterday might finally untangle this case. The black folder isn't just a clue—it could be the key to everything."

Lena sat down, pulled out a notepad, and began scribbling eagerly. "She said Broder always seemed visibly tense after Sorokin's visits. Apparently, the folder's contents weighed heavily on him."

"Robin, that's your task," Lars continued. "Stick close to Aniko. I want to know everything she knows. And Jan—those archives at the shipyard are now your construction site. There may be more hidden there than we'd like."

His expression grew more serious. "Then there's the city administration. Early signs point to something being off there—a thread of conflict that might lead us astray if we don't unravel it carefully."

Once the meeting ended, tasks were assigned. Lars gave Lena and Bodo a scrutinizing look before saying, "You two talk to Sebastian Broder. His workshop is a good place to catch him outside his usual environment. Surprise us. But be on your guard—he won't volunteer everything."

"Understood," Bodo replied, while Lena organized her notes. They both knew that speaking with Sebastian could raise more questions than answers, but it was a risk they were willing to take.

Outside, the sky had grown darker, and a cold wind whistled through the streets. Lena pulled her coat tighter as she walked to the car. Once inside, Bodo placed the notes carefully on the dashboard, fastened his seatbelt, and settled in.

"What do you make of this black folder?" Lena asked, eyes on the rain-slicked road.

"I think it's more than just a clue. If Sorokin really put pressure on Broder, it could be the key to exposing the whole network," Bodo said, gazing thoughtfully out the window.

Behind them, the familiar streets of Emden receded as the landscape turned grim: flat fields lined with leafless trees, silent windmills, and rain falling steadily on the wet asphalt. The glow from streetlamps seemed almost ghostly in the gloom.

At the end of a narrow road stood Sebastian Broder's Gulf house, flanked by empty fields and a row of barren trees. Next to it was his workshop, with wood shavings scattered in front of the door and tools lining the walls. Through dirty windows, a half-finished table was visible. The air smelled heavily of fresh pinewood as Lena and Bodo stepped out of the car.

"Charming place," Bodo remarked dryly when Sebastian opened the door. The man's angular face looked more tense than usual. He clutched a screwdriver in one hand, tapping his foot nervously, his gaze darting away from Lena.

Just as he was about to say something, a deep rumble of thunder shook the workshop's windows, and a sudden gust rattled the panes—nature itself reflecting his inner turmoil.

For a fleeting moment, he rubbed his hands together, shot an uneasy look out the window as though he felt someone watching, then mumbled something unintelligible. He changed the subject by hesitantly opening the door. "Criminal Investigation Department?" he asked curtly, not quite inviting them in.

"Lena Berg, Emden CID. This is my colleague, Bodo Zimmermann. We'd like to talk to you about your father," Lena explained calmly.

With a motion that felt almost reluctant, Sebastian opened the door a bit wider. "Come in."

The workshop was simple but full of life. Tools hung on the walls, their handles gleaming from frequent use, and on a small table lay a half-finished chest of drawers. The warm, almost welcoming atmosphere stood in stark contrast to Sebastian's edgy demeanor.

"What's this about?" he asked, sitting down on a chair and crossing his arms. He still gripped the screwdriver too tightly, fiddling with his sleeve.

Lena chose her words carefully. "Your father wanted to speak with the police before he disappeared. He said he had important information. Do you know what that might have been?"

Sebastian avoided her gaze. "I was already here by then—I had nothing more to do with his company."

"And that was right when the company was coming under increasing pressure," Bodo added. "Coincidence?"

Sebastian stared at the workbench in silence, his hands shifting uneasily, a fine sheen of sweat forming on his forehead. "It was no secret that place was a powder keg. Everyone was at each other's throats. I wanted out before I got dragged down with them."

Lena didn't relent. "Did your father ever mention being threatened or feeling under pressure?"

"He was always under pressure," Sebastian replied flatly, his fingers tracing the edge of the table as he cleared his throat repeatedly.

Suddenly, a shrill ring broke the tense silence. Sebastian flinched, almost dropping the screwdriver. He scrambled for his phone. His expression darkened as he turned away. "Hello?..." After a brief, halting pause, he added quietly, "No, now really isn't a good time. Later."

For an instant, his eyes darted around the room, as if searching for hidden listeners, before he ended the call. Lena offered him a business card. "If you think of anything else, please contact us."

Sebastian took the card, glanced at it briefly, and then left it unanswered on the table. With his foot still tapping nervously and his gaze shifting away, he followed them to the door.

A heavy silence filled the car as they climbed in. The windshield wipers thumped against the wet glass, the distorted light from the streetlamps dancing across the slick road. Bodo was the first to speak.

"Did you notice how tense he was when that call came?"

"Yes," Lena replied softly, her knuckles whitening around the steering wheel. "And his excuse was flimsy at best."

"He's definitely hiding something," Bodo said thoughtfully. "We might learn more soon—Robin and Jan should dig deeper into these new clues."

Meanwhile, back at the office, Robin was preparing his materials for a meeting with Karin Broder when his phone suddenly vibrated. He pulled it from his pocket, glanced at the display, and felt his heart beat faster. He paused, running a hand over his lips while tapping a finger on the edge of the table. An odd sensation swept over him—he felt an urgency he couldn't explain.

Aniko knew more than she let on, and something told him she was in danger.

"Robin Ahlers."

"Good afternoon, Mr. Ahlers," Aniko began, her voice gentle but tinged with noticeable caution, each word almost hesitant. After a brief silence, she continued, "I… I found something in Heinrich Broder's files."

Robin sat up straighter, focusing intently. "What exactly did you find?"

"There's a note mentioning 'a decision that isn't sufficiently covered up'—" Her voice wavered on the phrase "covered up," followed by a long pause, then she went on, "—and that Thomas should conceal it."

"That sounds important," Robin said, jotting it down. "Where are you right now? I can come over immediately."

A moment of hesitation. "That's… not a good idea. We should meet somewhere neutral, so we don't attract unwanted attention."

Robin frowned, writing down the rendezvous details. "Is an hour from now good for you?" "That's perfect. See you then," she concluded, her tone slightly warmer but still laced with underlying nervousness.

While Robin continued gathering information at the Police Department , Lena carefully navigated the car through the autumn landscape. The rain intensified, drumming incessantly on the roof, its drops bending and refracting the light from the streetlamps on the soaked roads. Bodo studied the documents in silence. The fields outside blurred by, and the pale, otherworldly glow of the setting sun cast everything in a haunting light.

"Did you notice how edgy he was during that phone call?" Bodo asked, breaking the silence without looking away from the window.

"Yes," Lena replied softly. "And his excuse was anything but convincing."

"He's definitely hiding something," Bodo repeated, lost in thought. "Hopefully we'll get more details soon—Robin and Jan are on it."

Back at the station, just as Lena and Bodo were documenting their impressions of Sebastian Broder's behavior, Lars burst in with urgent news:

"A man just showed up—claims the police are making a huge mistake. He says he knows what really happened to Heinrich Broder."

# *Chapter 14*

The meeting room at Emden CID was all but silent. Only the faint buzz of the whiteboard and the occasional rustle of papers disturbed the tension. Lars stood by the door, watching closely as he showed their visitor in.

The man, in his mid-sixties, wore a threadbare coat that hung loosely from his narrow shoulders. His hands trembled slightly as he pulled it tighter around himself. His eyes darted around the room, as if trying to ensure no one else was listening.

"Mr. Vogel," Lars said by way of introduction. "Former safety officer at the Broder shipyard."

He gestured toward a chair, but Vogel hesitated. His gaze flickered to the door, then to the windows. Only after a moment did he finally lower himself onto the seat, pressing his hands flat against the table as though he had to force his own nervousness into submission.

"Thank you for coming," Lars continued, taking a seat at the table. Lena leaned against the wall with her arms crossed, while Bodo stood by the window, the Emden skyline visible behind him.

Vogel drew a long breath, his Adam's apple bobbing as he swallowed. "I'm not sure this is such a good idea… but I couldn't stay silent any longer."

Lars kept his tone calm yet insistent. "You're safe here. Tell us what you know."

Vogel ran both hands over his face, as if trying to steady himself. "I worked at Broder's shipyard for years. Heinrich Broder was a difficult man—strict, but predictable. Then, in the months before he vanished… he changed."

Lena straightened, eyes narrowing with interest.

"Changed? In what way?"

Vogel's voice was barely more than a whisper. "He became paranoid. He kept muttering that certain things had to remain hidden. He brought in new security measures—especially for one storage room on the shipyard grounds. No one was allowed in there except him and a handful of others."

Lars scribbled notes with quick, sharp strokes, each mark reflecting the tension in the room.

"Do you know what was kept in that storage room?"

Vogel shook his head slowly.

"Not exactly… but once, I stayed late. I was working overtime and saw him leave that room carrying a black folder under his arm. He didn't notice me, but… he looked as if someone were following him—or as if he was terrified of being seen."

Lena tilted forward slightly.

"Did you ever ask him about it?"

Vogel let out a bitter, hollow laugh.

"You didn't just talk to Heinrich Broder. Not when he was like that. And in those last few weeks… he was afraid of someone."

Lars studied him closely. "Afraid of whom?"

Vogel opened his mouth, then closed it again. His eyes roamed the door and the walls, as though searching for hidden microphones. "I saw too much back then," he murmured. "Saying more puts me at risk."

Lars leaned in. "Mr. Vogel, if you stay silent, you could be putting other people at risk. Do you really want that?"

Vogel stared at his own hands, his fingers working against each other. His breath came faster, and when he finally spoke, his voice was rough. "If you truly want the truth… then start with Thomas. He knew more—a lot more."

Lars narrowed his eyes. "Thomas Broder? What exactly did he know?"

Vogel moistened his lips, which had gone dry. "Check the security protocols," he said, his voice barely audible. "You might find something there. But… some secrets only bring disaster."

Before Lars could reply, Vogel stood abruptly, his eyes filled with urgency—almost panic. "You think you're searching for answers. But some truths cost more than they're worth."

His hand was already on the doorknob when Lars tried to stop him. Vogel shook his head, and a moment later he was gone.

That afternoon, Lena parked outside the Emden public prosecutor's office. A cool, damp heaviness clung to the autumn air, and the sterile atmosphere of the stairwell seemed to amplify her unease.

Dr. Roland Becker sat behind his imposing desk, frowning as he flipped through a stack of files. "Mrs. Berg, what can I do for you?" he asked, polite but distant.

Lena took a seat, leaning forward slightly. "I need access to Sebastian Broder's phone records. There are indications he's being threatened. The call he got during our interview could be crucial."

Becker pressed his pen harder against the paper, as if to keep his hands occupied. "I can't release any data without a court order."

Lena pressed her lips together, swallowing a spark of frustration.
"Dr. Becker, this is a murder investigation. We know Sebastian Broder is withholding information."

Becker sighed, his gaze flickering in an unspoken internal struggle.

"I understand your position, but without direct evidence of an active crime, my hands are tied."

Anger flared in Lena, but she fought to keep it under control.

"Thank you for your time," she said curtly.

Outside, she inhaled the cool air, then pulled out her phone.

"Well?" Bodo's voice crackled through the line, brimming with expectation.

"Nothing," Lena said sharply. "Becker won't budge. No approval, no data. We'll have to do this differently."

Bodo let out a resigned sigh. "And that means…?"

Lena started the engine, her gaze lost in the darkening street. The moment felt like the calm before the storm. "It means we put pressure on Sebastian. He knows more than he's admitting. And we're going to make him talk."

A brief pause. Then Bodo's dry tone: "I'll get the coffee ready."

Lena ended the call. Rules were meant to provide security—but sometimes there were bigger things at stake. And she was willing to take that risk.

# *Chapter 15*

Robin left Karin Broder's villa feeling conflicted. Their conversation had been polite yet noticeably distant. She carried herself like someone well aware of her own influence, but her answers remained vague. Time and again, she pointed out that Thomas knew everything about his father's business—almost as though she wanted the focus squarely on him. But Robin realized she was only giving him what she felt safe sharing: no solid information, no tangible clues.

He climbed into his car and took a deep breath. Outside, the late-afternoon light had taken on a warm, golden hue. The city's brick facades glowed in the reflection of the still canals, and a light breeze carried the scent of rain and damp leaves. Starting the engine, Robin pulled away. Traffic was sparse, and the familiar cityscape should have been calming. Yet his thoughts kept circling back to that conversation. Was Karin Broder hiding something? Or was she simply trying to steer the investigation in a particular direction?

He finally parked behind the former town hall—now the East Frisian State Museum. From there, it was just a short walk to the Grand Café at the Citygarten, where he was meeting Aniko. She had asked him to come; apparently, she'd found something important.

Upon entering the café, he was greeted by a comforting warmth, suffused with the aroma of freshly brewed coffee and sweet pastries. Soft lighting created an intimate atmosphere.

His eyes roamed the room until they settled on Aniko, seated in a quiet corner. She looked as elegant as ever, but there was a new tension in her posture. Her shoulders were rigid, and her gaze flicked nervously around the room as if checking for unwelcome observers.

"Robin," she said. Her Hungarian accent gave his name a softer sound, though her voice was quieter than usual—laced with uncertainty.

"Hello, Aniko," he replied, a slight smile on his face. He recalled their first meeting—how her presence had momentarily thrown him off balance. That wouldn't happen this time. "May I?" he asked, gesturing toward the chair across from her.

"Of course." She slid a brown envelope across the table. "I've found something. It might be important."

Robin sat down and opened the envelope. Inside were several old documents, neatly organized. He pulled out a handwritten note and read it aloud under his breath: "'Secure project—keep documentation incomplete.'" He frowned. "Where did you find this?"

"I'm digitizing the old company files,"

Aniko explained, taking a sip of her cappuccino. Her fingers gripped the cup more tightly than necessary.

"This page was stuck  between some trivial reports. I almost missed it, but the wording caught my attention."

Robin skimmed the other pages.

"Someone deliberately left gaps in the paperwork—maybe to hide something."

Aniko leaned forward, though her gaze drifted to her hands rather than the documents. She toyed with a ring on her finger, a habit Robin recognized as a sign of her nerves.

"I'm not sure about this, Robin,"

she murmured, voice barely above a whisper.

"Ever since I started digging into all this, I've felt like someone's been watching me. Maybe it's just my imagination, but…" She trailed off. "I'm scared."

Robin regarded her seriously.

"Aniko, if you feel unsafe, you have to tell me. I don't want you putting yourself in danger."

She met his gaze, and he saw more than fear—he saw an inner conflict tearing her in two. She trusted him, perhaps more than she wanted to admit. But was that enough? Could she truly help the police without risking her own safety?

Robin slipped the documents back into the envelope.

"You did the right thing. If Thomas really knows more than he's letting on, this could be our key. But if you're uncomfortable, we should proceed carefully."

A fleeting smile crossed Aniko's face, though it looked forced.

"I'll keep digging. If I come across anything else, I'll let you know."

"That would be great," said Robin. Then, more softly,

"Thank you, Aniko. You've been a big help."

A faint blush warmed her cheeks.

"I just want to do what's right."

Still, the anxiety lingered. What if she made a misstep? What if she went too far?

They sat in silence for a moment. Robin could sense her tension but knew better than to press her. At last, she set down her cup and stood.

"I need to get back to the shipyard. But… if you have any more questions, you know where to find me."

Robin rose as well. "Of course. Thank you again, Aniko."

She said goodbye with a soft

"Goodbye, Robin."

But as she approached the exit, she froze. Her shoulders tensed, and her eyes flicked toward the door.

She stood there for a moment, as if she recognized someone outside—or feared being recognized.

Then she straightened, turned away, and left the café in hurried steps.

Robin watched her go, a knot forming in his stomach. Was he imagining things? Or did Aniko have every reason to be afraid?

He sank back into his seat, eyes fixed on the envelope. The documents provided new leads—and raised new questions. The incomplete records looked like a deliberate attempt to conceal something. Exactly what was being covered up? And just how deep did Thomas's knowledge go?

He had a feeling this discovery would change the course of the investigation. Aniko had handed him a crucial clue, yet her fear weighed on his mind. He would need to look out for her.

After paying, he stepped into the cool evening air. Walking to his car, he felt the chill wind on his skin. His thoughts weren't just on the documents, but on Aniko and the way she'd looked at him. Sliding into the driver's seat, he set his jaw in determination. Time to check these new leads back at the station.

# *Chapter 16*

Jan sat at his desk in the Police Department , eyes fixed on the files. The puzzle pieces seemed to be falling into place, yet with every new clue, the solution slipped further away.

Then his mobile phone vibrated on the tabletop. He reached for it—out of habit—but something made him hesitate.

**Sebastian Broder.** A name he hadn't expected to see this late at night.

He answered. "Müller."

Silence on the other end. Then came an irregular, ragged breathing. At last, in an almost whispered voice:

"Mr. Müller… I think I'm in danger."

A tightness gripped Jan's chest. "What do you mean? What happened?"

"There was someone… outside my house." Sebastian's words came fast and choppy, as if he had to force them out under some crushing pressure. "They asked about my father… about me. I wouldn't let them in, but they said… I know too much."

Jan's jaw clenched. "Are they still there?"

"I… I think so."

Then, in the background, a noise. Muffled. A scraping sound, followed by the clink of breaking glass. "Sebastian?" A crack. Then a dull thud. A muffled groan. Silence. All that remained was the monotone beep of a disconnected call.

Jan stared at his phone. For an instant, it felt like someone had thrown him into deep water without warning. Had that been Sebastian's last call?

His muscles tensed. He snapped out of it, sprang to his feet, and bolted toward the briefing room. The chair he'd been sitting on crashed to the floor behind him, rattling against the desk.

Lars and Bodo caught sight of him immediately. They knew at once something was wrong.

"Sebastian just called," Jan said hurriedly. "He sounded panicked. Someone was there, threatening him. Then I heard a crash, a groan—and the line went dead."

Lars was already reaching for his jacket. "Bodo, you're with me. Jan, stay here and be ready in case he calls back."

**Route to Rhauderfehn** Night pressed low over the fields, and the blue lights of the police car cut through the darkness. The siren sliced the silence of the country road like a scalpel.

Lars's fingers gripped the steering wheel tightly. His eyes stayed fixed on the road, but Bodo could see the muscles in his jaw working.

"Sebastian sounded terrified," Bodo muttered.

Lars answered only after a pause. "Or worse."

It was a quiet murmur, but it made the car's interior feel a few degrees colder. "It sounds like someone wants to make sure he stays quiet."

They reached the entrance to Sebastian's Gulfhof and immediately saw the first sign of violence—a shattered windowpane. Splinters of glass lay scattered like frozen shards in the glare of the headlights. Lars's expression hardened, though he said nothing. Instead, his hand moved to his holster.

Bodo tensed. "No noise, no movement inside."

"Let's hope it's not already a crime scene," Lars said grimly as he moved forward.

He was the first to enter. The wooden floor groaned under his boots, as if warning them of approaching disaster. A faint smell of cold smoke and something metallic hung in the air.

Inside—silence.
But an eerie silence, one that spelled trouble.

In the living room, they found an overturned chair and a fresh bloodstain on the floor. Then they saw a dark trail leading toward the workshop.

Bodo followed it, heart pounding. Inside the workshop, they found Sebastian. He was slumped against the workbench, his shirt soaked with blood, his fingers clenched around the fabric. His skin was so pale it seemed almost translucent in the sparse light, and his breathing came in shallow, rasping gasps.

Bodo hurried to him. Sebastian's eyes fluttered restlessly, as though trying to flee from some horror only he could see.

Then Sebastian's gaze caught on something: a rolled-up piece of paper. Bodo picked it up and unrolled it. A chill rippled down his spine as he read: **"Everything ends in the shadows."** Below the words was a meticulously drawn feather.

Lars stepped up beside him, his expression dark. "This is the third time now," he said, voice low and taut. "The first time, it was a cryptic note. The second time, a pointed hint. But now… now it's a message."

Bodo stared at the paper in his hands. "This isn't a coincidence anymore." His voice sounded rough. "Whoever's behind this wants us to understand. The only question is who—and what they're trying to say."

Lars let his gaze sweep around the workshop. "The pattern's too precise to be random." He knelt by. Sebastian, whose eyes were unfocused and glassy. His lips trembled, then he whispered, "The… feather… always… follows."

His words were barely audible. Then he slumped forward again. Bodo and Lars exchanged a look.

"'The feather follows,'" Bodo echoed. "Sounds like we're dealing with someone who's always one step ahead." Lars's face was unreadable. "Or someone who wants us to think exactly that." Silence fell between them, broken only by the quiet hum of a flickering neon lamp overhead.

Lars reached for his radio."We need an ambulance."

Outside, the night air was cold enough to make their breath visible. Bodo stared at the broken windowpane. "This was a warning," he said quietly, voice steady.

Lars turned to him. "They wanted to make sure he'd keep quiet."

Bodo set his jaw. "And if he never says another word?"

Lars tucked the radio back into his jacket and looked up, his gaze calm but his voice anything but. "Then we'll find the truth ourselves. But one thing's certain: they see us coming—and they're already waiting."

# *Chapter 17*

Late-autumn sunlight filtered through the tall windows of the precinct, casting sharp shadows across the massive conference table. The steady ticking of the wall clock and the low hum of the whiteboard underscored a tension that no one dared to name.

Lars Lammerts stood at the whiteboard, his grip tight on a red marker. The tension in his shoulders spoke of the heavy burden of unanswered questions. With a deliberate stroke, he connected the names **Heinrich Broder** and **Thomas Broder**. Beneath them, in bold lettering:

**"Everything ends in the shadows."**

"Karin Broder keeps insisting Thomas must know every detail of his father's business—sure of it, but still vague," Robin Ahlers said, leaning his elbows on the table and studying the words. "It's like she's trying to mislead us or protect someone."

Leaning against the wall, Lena Berg arched a skeptical eyebrow. "Do you think she's hiding the truth?"

"Not exactly," Robin replied hesitantly. "But she's holding back more than she's revealing—like she's got something to hide."

Meanwhile, Bodo Zimmermann was lost in thought, fiddling with a ballpoint pen. Its rhythmic clicking echoed like a heartbeat in the hushed room.

"This is the third time we've seen something like this—first in Heinrich's documents, then in that workshop, and now again. Always that damn feather."

Lars's gaze lingered on the stark words.

"Whoever leaves these messages wants us to find them. But what's the purpose?"

The question hung in the air. Robin exchanged a pensive look with Lena.

"Maybe we should ask Karin directly. Her reaction could be the key."

"Not yet," Lars decided firmly.

"We don't have enough to go on. Lena, Robin—talk to Thomas. See what he knows about this clue."

Lena pushed away from the wall, her eyes drifting one last time to the phrase **"Everything ends in the shadows."**

"What if this message is both a warning and a clue?"

she asked quietly.

"It might be that Karin holds the real answers, not Thomas."

Just then, Karin Broder's name briefly flashed across a nearby phone screen. Without comment, Bodo pushed the device aside.

Lars inhaled deeply, lifted the marker, and announced,

"We'll figure these messages out, one step at a time. The feather is our key to whatever dark secrets lie beneath all this."

### *Flashback – 2004*

*Night had fallen over the Broder shipyard, wrapping the crumbling halls in a somber hush. Long shadows stretched over decaying walls. Moonlight bathed the desolate site in an eerie glow, a light that hinted at both hope and despair.*

*Heinrich Broder sat in a dimly lit office, surrounded by piles of papers, files, and a flickering computer screen labeled, officially,* **"Shipbuilding Materials."** *But Heinrich knew there was far more in these deliveries than simple construction supplies. Standing before him was Mr. Vogel, the shipyard's security officer. His grim expression and anxious eyes spoke volumes.*

*"Should I log the cargo the usual way?" Vogel asked softly. Heinrich's gaze was cold as ice.*

*"No. Let the drivers through without questions—and no one asks why."*

*After repeating his instructions, Heinrich opened a drawer and pulled out a leather-bound notebook. For a moment, he seemed to steel himself against a danger he could already sense. Then he shut the notebook and slipped its key into his pocket.*

*Amid the computer's monotonous hum, a headline flickered on the screen:*

**"Spanish Authorities Tighten Controls After Madrid Attacks."**

*Heinrich felt a chill course through him. A slight tremor in his hand betrayed an inner turmoil he was determined to hide.*

*A knock on the door jolted him out of his thoughts. "Come in," he called, keeping his voice steady, though he could feel the storm gathering within. Karin entered, her footsteps measured, her demeanor unwavering.*

*"I wanted to talk to you," she said calmly. "Thomas is concerned about this shipment. Maybe you should make it clear that he shouldn't interfere in matters that aren't his."*

*Heinrich's eyes darkened, and for an instant, raw fear flickered behind his stern façade.*

*"Thomas needs to focus on his own responsibilities. What I do is none of his concern."*

*"I'll talk to him,"* Karin replied,

*"but don't underestimate him—he won't just stay silent."*

*"Then make sure he understands his place,"* Heinrich muttered, as doubt gnawed at him from within.

*Outside, a truck rumbled through the main gate, its headlights piercing the darkness and throwing dancing shadows on rusted gates and overgrown tracks. Stacked on its loading bed were unassuming crates—ones that concealed deadly secrets. Heinrich stood at the loading area with Timofej Fedorov, a tall man whose sharply defined features spoke of silent resolve. He motioned for the driver to stop.*

*Nervous, the driver handed Timofej an envelope, which he accepted with a curt nod.*

*"Shipbuilding materials, at least on paper,"* Heinrich said quietly, eyeing the crates that held far more than harmless raw materials.

*"A portion of this shipment's heading to Spain,"*

*Timofej added casually, flicking away a cigarette.*

*The name **Sorokin** hung in the air like an ominous specter. Heinrich's eyes betrayed a flicker of doubt that he quickly repressed.*

*"And if we've crossed a line?"* Timofej asked softly, turning to Heinrich.

*"Then we cross it together,"* Heinrich answered coolly, though his hands trembled for a split second. *"The risk is Sorokin's to bear."*

Once the truck vanished into the night, Heinrich headed back to his office. The flickering headline on his computer screen served as a haunting reminder of the danger ahead. The hum and ticking grew ominous until another knock on the door cut through his thoughts.

Thomas entered, visibly worn out, the signs of a sleepless night etched on his face. Without preamble, he said,

*"The crates are in storage. Have you thought about what we're really doing here?"*

Heinrich leaned back, folding his arms as he tried to project calm. Inside, however, uncertainty and fear churned.
*"Do your job, Thomas. My business is my own."*

*"That's not enough anymore, Father,"*

Thomas countered, disappointment rather than anger in his voice.

*"When did we stop deciding things for ourselves? Or are you letting Sorokin steer the ship now?"*

Heinrich rose slowly, meeting his son's gaze. His voice was sharp and controlled.

"You have no idea what it takes to keep alive something everyone else has abandoned."

"Maybe it wasn't worth saving,"

Thomas shot back, his eyes searching Heinrich's face, which for a moment revealed genuine fear and uncertainty.

"Look at what we've become. Is this really your plan?"

A heavy silence stretched until Thomas said quietly,

"I hope you know what you're doing, Father."

Then he turned and left, the door closing with a hollow thud that deepened Heinrich's solitude.

Alone, surrounded by documents and the unceasing tick of the clock, Heinrich felt his thoughts swirling like storm clouds. A tremor ran through him at the memory of the leather-bound notebook—its sealed contents meant more to him than he dared to admit.

Later, in an abandoned warehouse, the smell of oil and dust mingled with the metallic tang of the machinery. Heinrich opened a heavy door and stepped inside. A single lamp flickered overhead, casting long shadows over neatly stacked crates. He let his hand slide across the rough wood of one whose seal was loose. With a soft crack, he pried it open, revealing its contents: assault rifles wrapped in plastic, with explosives packed beneath—lethal cargo.

As he shut the lid, sweat beaded on his palms, a silent witness to his growing dread. A sudden noise made him start.

Timofej Fedorov emerged from the darkness, his casual stride and inscrutable smile only adding weight to Heinrich's troubled thoughts.

"Relax, Heinrich. I just came to check if everything's ready for tomorrow. You know Sorokin—he doesn't like surprises."

"It's ready,"

Heinrich replied, trying to keep his voice steady despite the uncertainty creeping in.

"You seem tense. That's not like you,"

Timofej noted, stepping closer.

"I've got it under control,"

Heinrich insisted, though his eyes told another story—control was slipping through his grasp.

*"Control is an illusion, my friend. Do you really think these crates are only for us? These shadows reach farther than you imagine."*

*Heinrich clenched his fists, and for a moment, the anguish in his gaze was unmistakable.*

*"I don't need a lecture. We'll make the delivery."*

*"Sorokin wants results—no doubt about that,"*

*Timofej added. A long silence followed, during which Heinrich's internal battle raged. Finally, Timofej said,*

*"I'll see you tomorrow. Get some rest, Heinrich."*

*Left alone in the darkness, Heinrich's gaze fell on a single sheet of paper resting on a crate. He picked it up, hesitating before unfolding it:*

**"Everything ends in the shadows."**

*Beneath it was the ornately drawn image of a feather. A chill ran through him, and in that moment he realized his grip on control had long since failed. Heart pounding, he slipped the sheet into his pocket—tomorrow would change everything.*

# *Chapter 18*

**2024**

Outside, the darkness felt impenetrable. The wind rattled the windows, making them shudder, while the trees in front of the house cast eerie shadows across the façade. The storm carried with it a peculiar restlessness, as though the night itself was trying to deliver a warning.

Lena Berg sat in the kitchen, an empty cup in her hands. The coffee inside had long since gone cold, yet she kept clutching the mug as if she could somehow reclaim its lost warmth. On the table before her laythe note with its cryptic message:

**"Everything ends in the shadows."**

Those words echoed in her mind, an ominous prophecy pressing heavily on her chest.

"Lena?"
Bodo's voice was soft but insistent. He stood in the doorway, arms loosely folded, his gaze resting on her. "It's nearly three in the morning. You should be asleep."

"I can't." Her voice was rough, drained. She never took her eyes off the note. "This pen, this phrase—it's like someone is trying to tell us something, but I can't see the pattern." Bodo stepped closer and placed a comforting hand on her shoulder. "You'll see it more clearly in the morning. Sleep helps."

Lena snorted. "You're a terrible liar."

A faint smile tugged at the corner of Bodo's mouth. "Probably. But I'm all you've got."

Reluctantly, Lena let him guide her out of the kitchen. Even once she was in bed, though, the words continued to reverberate in her head:

**Everything ends in the shadows.**

The first pale rays of sunlight fought their way through the thick fog, sending faint beams skimming over the canal. Lena stood at the window with a steaming cup of coffee, watching the mist curl lazily above the water.

"This is my favorite version of you."

Bodo entered the kitchen, hair tousled, eyes weary. His voice still held the warmth of sleep.

Lena turned. "Which version is that?"

"The one who's completely focused. The one who won't let go until she finds the truth."

"How poetic," she said, taking a sip of coffee. "I hope you're right. That feather and that phrase are driving me crazy." Bodo stepped closer. His gaze was steady and determined. "We'll figure it out—together. Even if we have to search every inch of that damned shipyard."

Lena met his eyes before looking back out the window.

"Sometimes I wonder why you're so unshakable. Like you really believe everything will turn out okay."

Bodo shrugged. "Maybe because I believe in you."

A faint heat rose to Lena's cheeks. She quickly turned to stare at the fog again. "You're impossible, Bodo."

The note and the pen lay on the table, surrounded by the files Aniko had uncovered at the shipyard. Lena ran her fingers over the paper, rereading the words for what felt like the hundredth time.

Robin projected a list of transactions onto the wall. "These payments went to Danube Trade Limited, a company registered in Cyprus. The paperwork says it was for machinery, but the sums are absurdly high."

"And the reinforced storage room?" asked Jan Müller, flipping through the documents.

"It's painting a clear picture," Lena said slowly. "The feather, the transactions—something valuable was hidden there. But what, exactly?"

"What about Thomas Broder?" Lars Lammerts folded his arms across his chest. Lena leaned back in her chair. "He claims his father handled everything alone. But Vogel's statement and these files say otherwise. Thomas is in deeper than he's letting on."

Robin nodded. "And another thing: Sorokin's name appears multiple times. The feather could be his calling card—a symbol of his control."

Lars's tone was resolute. "Time to confront Thomas with the facts."

Rain pounded the windshield as Lena parked outside the Broder shipyard. The building looked abandoned, its walls moss-covered, the company sign's letters faded and peeling.

"Doesn't look like anyone's invested in this place for years," Robin remarked dryly.

Lena pressed her lips together. "Thomas will just put up a fight, like always."

Inside, an older man led them wordlessly to Thomas's office. The air smelled of stale coffee and damp paper. Thomas sat behind a large desk, his expression cold.

Aniko stood beside him, her shoulders rigid, clutching a folder so tightly that her knuckles whitened. Lena stepped forward. "Mr. Broder, we need to talk about the documents your assistant gave us."

Thomas's face darkened. "You did WHAT?"

Aniko flinched. "I… I had to," she murmured, barely audible. "It was the right thing to do."

Lena's voice hardened. "Your assistant has shown more responsibility than you have."

Thomas's jaw clenched. "Those documents prove nothing!"

Robin stepped in. "They prove you know more than you're letting on. And Sorokin's name keeps popping up. Care to explain that?"

Aniko looked at Robin with a mixture of uncertainty and gratitude. He met her eyes in silence, the tension in the air crackling.

Suddenly, Thomas leapt up. "Some things shouldn't be brought to light!" he snapped before storming out. The door slammed behind him.

For a moment, the room was still. Then Lena exhaled, trying to remain composed. "He's hiding something."

Robin clenched his fists. "And he's scared."

Aniko's gaze fell. Her hands trembled, but then she straightened her shoulders. "Then we need to push him even harder." Outside, the rain kept falling in sheets, and the shadows grew ever darker

# Chapter 19

A single desk lamp cast a pale glow over scattered files in the half-lit meeting room at Emden Police Headquarters. The bitter scent of freshly brewed East Frisian tea mingled with strong coffee, but nobody was drinking. Tension weighed heavily in the air.

The team sat in expectant silence as Lars entered, eyes narrowed and brow furrowed. He dropped into an old chair, massaging his temples, then slammed a fist on the table.

"Damn it!" he growled. "We're missing vital links—too many gaps. We need evidence, and we need it now!"

From among the papers, Lena picked up a black feather, flawless and almost unnaturally vivid. Her pulse quickened as she turned it over. Written in elegant calligraphy beneath it were the words:

**Everything ends in the shadows.**

Her voice was calm yet resolute. "We know Thomas has been holding back. Karin Broder's housekeeper hinted there are still countless questions. Let's go see her immediately."

Robin slid his tablet across the table, tapping a standout line. "Look at this: in 2004, six months before Broder disappeared, there was an anonymous transfer of two hundred thousand euros from Cyprus, routed through a shell company. All signs point to Sorokin."

Lars folded his arms, glaring at the data.

"A single payment isn't enough to put him away—no matter how much it stinks of money laundering. I want names, documents—something solid!"

Bodo, who had been standing quietly in a corner, spoke up.

"Lena, Robin—head to Karin Broder's. She knows more than she admits, and Thomas is in deeper than we thought."

With a curt nod, Lars waved them off.

"Go. Bring me real evidence for once!"

Lena took the wheel, guiding the squad car off the Police Police Department lot. They crossed an old bridge spanning the railway tracks, as a freight train thundered past below, its metallic clatter echoing in the early morning light. The sun's rays struck the rails, turning them silver.

As soon as they'd cleared the bridge, Lena noticed a dark SUV hugging their rear bumper. It wasn't aggressive, exactly, but it never wavered. A prickling unease crawled across the back of her neck.

She flipped on her indicator, slowed down, then turned onto a side street. Seconds later, the black beast followed, making an abrupt lane change that dashed any hope of shaking it. Bodo shifted in his seat, meeting Lena's eyes in the rearview mirror.

"No way that's a coincidence," he muttered.

When they finally pulled up to the imposing villa, the SUV continued on, though not without lingering in the distance. Lena and Bodo approached the heavy wooden door, and Lena rang the bell decisively. After a moment, Marie Hoffmann, the housekeeper, appeared, her expression guarded.

"Mrs. Broder isn't receiving visitors," she said in a faintly defensive tone.

"That doesn't change anything," Lena replied, coolly. "Please tell her we're here."

Marie disappeared inside, clearly reluctant. Minutes later, the door to a lavish living room swung open. Karin Broder whirled around, still holding her phone to her ear. Her knuckles stood out white against the device.

"What do you think you're doing?"

she demanded, voice taut. A flicker of fear and defiance passed over her features before she continued in a near-whisper, "Some truths cost more than you're willing to pay…" Then, hastily, "I'll call you back."

She ended the call and took a shaky breath. "I don't have time for your theatrics."

Lena folded her arms. "Before Heinrich disappeared, he and Thomas had a major argument. What was it really about?"

Karin avoided her gaze, running a trembling hand along the edge of a heavy table. Her voice was ragged, almost regretful.

"Thomas handled all the business with my     father. He wanted out, but Thomas wouldn't let him—or couldn't. There was manipulation, intrigue, power plays…"

"Why?" Bodo asked gently, trying to pierce her guarded exterior.

Karin let out a weary sigh, her words soft and strained.

"It was about Sorokin. My father always warned me: you don't just deal with people like that. But Thomas thought he could handle it. Appearances can be deceiving—and sometimes you only realize it when it's too late."

A heavy silence followed as Lena and Bodo turned to leave. In the hallway, Marie Hoffmann stopped them with a timid glance, her eyes darting to the stairs as though making sure no one else could hear. In a near-whisper, she said,

"Sometimes, while going through old files, I find subtle notes—details not in the official records. Some of them belonged to Sebastian. You might want to ask him, discreetly."

Lena nodded, taking in the hint. "Thank you."

Back at the Police Department , Lena and Bodo reported to Lars. He leaned back, thoughtful.
"If these hidden notes turn out to be diaries, they could be the proof we need. Find out if Sebastian Broder still has them."

Lena moved to the window, looking down at the Police Department 's parking lot. It lay deceptively quiet. Her eyes settled on a gray SUV, parked motionless, almost menacing. Then she spotted a subtle movement inside— a faint glint      behind the tinted glass, as though someone had aimed a camera or a scope her way.

Her heart lurched, and she yanked the door open, rushing outside. But the SUV's engine revved, tires squealing as it peeled away. It roared across the asphalt and disappeared around a corner.

"Damn!" Lena's voice was thick with anxiety. "Who the hell was that?"

# Chapter 20

*Flashback: 2004, Shipyard*

*The shipyard lay under a star-filled sky, cloaked in an unnatural silence. The cold glare of the floodlights cast grotesque shadows across gleaming steel frames, giving the containers a deceptive sense of order. Between the buildings stretched darkness—an emptiness that threatened to swallow everything.*

*A heavy scent hung in the air: cold metal, machine oil, mingling with the damp chill of the nearby water. In the distance, a seagull screeched—or was it a cry? The steady groan of a crane heightened the impression that the shipyard was moving in slow motion—an inanimate machine under cover of night.*

*Then came footsteps, quiet yet purposeful.*

*Thomas emerged from the shadows, hands buried deep in his pockets, his gaze hard.*

*"You're getting out."*

*No question mark, no emotion. Just a statement that sliced through the silence. Heinrich turned to face him slowly, the floodlights carving sharp contours into his features.*

*"I've looked away for too long. Sorokin has held this shipyard—and us—under his thumb for ages. I'm tired of being his puppet."*

*Thomas stepped closer. As a beam of light grazed his face, a fleeting shadow crossed his features.*

*"Sorokin doesn't let anyone walk away."*

*"I'll take that risk."*

*A short, bitter laugh. Resigned.*

*"It's not just your risk, Father." Thomas's voice was barely above a whisper, yet each word was heavy. "Do you really think you can disappear and leave me behind?"*

*Heinrich's eyes narrowed. "Then come with me."*

*A twitch along Thomas's jaw—an inner struggle, betrayed only by subtle tension in his face.*

*"I… I can't." The silence between them pressed like lead.*

*Then, quietly, "Or is it that you don't want to?"*

*A gust of wind rustled a nearby tarp. Thomas went on, his words a slow, inevitable blade:*

*"Sorokin needs us. And I won't be the one to disappoint him."*

*Suddenly—a movement in the darkness.*

**Karin Broder.**

*She moved calmly, almost gliding. The floodlights skimmed her face, momentarily obscuring her thoughts. "Is this really your plan?"*

*Her voice was gentle, almost affectionate—but something cool lingered beneath the surface. Heinrich's face hardened.*

*"This is a family matter, Karin."*

*A thin, melancholy smile curved her lips.*

*"That's exactly why I'm here." Her gaze flicked between father and son, as though searching for fine cracks in their resolve. Thomas raised his eyebrows.*

*"And you think you understand what this is all about?"*

*"You only see what's obvious." She shook her head softly. "I see what's hidden underneath." Her tone was calm, almost tender—but there was a flicker in her eyes that had nothing to do with compassion.*

*"This shipyard isn't just a business. It's our legacy. If you two keep tearing each other apart, there'll be nothing left." Heinrich studied her, seeking an answer he couldn't find. Then he turned back to Thomas.*

*"So, you've made up your mind."*

*Thomas's shoulders remained rigid.*

*"Yes."*

*A brief silence followed. Then Heinrich said simply, "Then pray you're trusting the right people." With a curt nod, he turned and disappeared into the darkness.*

*Karin remained. Her gaze followed him, but her thoughts stayed hidden. After a while, Thomas broke the silence. "And you? Whose side are you really on?"*

*She held his gaze, her smile barely more than a hint.*

*"On our family's side."*

*She took a step toward him.*

*"But sometimes, you have to stretch out both hands to protect what's yours." There was a glimmer in her eyes— not merely loyalty, but something else, something Thomas couldn't yet grasp.*

### Heinrich's

*The desk lamp threw long shadows across the polished wooden surface. Outside, the wind beat against the windowpanes like a warning.*

*An opened envelope lay before him: two hundred thousand euros. The money from Cyprus. Heinrich's fingers trailed over the banknotes—a sum worth far more than its nominal value.*

*With steady hands, he opened his notebook and began to write: "The shipyard is no longer ours. Maybe it never was. We've been nothing but pieces on Sorokin's chessboard."*

*He paused, the pen hovering over the page. "Thomas believes he can control the game. He's wrong." A deep breath. Then he went on: "Karin… Her eyes see too much, but her words reveal little. Is that her shield—or her means of manipulating us all?"*

*A noise made him look up. Outside, through the closed windows, came a faint clatter. Heinrich's hand froze on the page. His chest rose and fell more quickly as he listened.*

*The wind? Or something else? For a moment, he remained perfectly still, the sound of his breathing the only thing in the room. Then he closed the notebook, slipped it into a drawer, and turned the key with a quiet click.*

*Outside, the shipyard lay in the grip of night—dark, inescapable. And somewhere in that darkness, a decision was taking shape that would change everything*

# *Chapter 21*

**2024**

Lena sat on her well-worn but reliable leather sofa—a silent witness to countless nights when darkness and secrets seemed inextricably intertwined. She sat with her legs bent, one trembling hand clutching a cup of coffee that had long since gone cold. Outside, the wind lashed mercilessly against the window, rattling the frame and carrying with it the heavy smell of wet asphalt and salt. The pale glow of streetlamps cast fleeting shadows on the walls, as if half-forgotten memories were trying to surface.

Sleep had become a distant dream for Lena—her thoughts spiraled into a relentless maelstrom of questions and doubts. Images of Karin Broder and Thomas replayed in her mind—Thomas, whose role shifted endlessly between perpetrator, accomplice, and pawn. Her heart hammered in her chest, as though she were in a room filled with flickering candles, each one extinguished by an invisible gust of wind.

Suddenly, she heard a soft scratching in the darkness. Lena froze, holding her breath to listen. Seconds stretched into an eternity as a siren wailed in the distance—only to be drowned out by the howling storm. Her gaze drifted over the battered bookshelf and settled on an old photo: Lena and her father, taken at a pivotal time shortly before he enrolled in the police academy. His piercing, demanding gaze seemed to convey a silent warning through the years:

**"Don't let yourself be blinded. Be careful not to slip into something from which there is no return."**

A chill crept up her spine, and she gripped the cup tighter.
*What if I'm already in too deep?* she wondered.

A sudden gust of wind rattled the window's glass. For a fleeting moment, she thought she saw a figure reflected there—a dark silhouette, motionless, lurking. Her pulse spiked, and she blinked rapidly—but all that remained was the pallid glow of streetlamps and the unfathomable blackness of night.

Lena closed her eyes and sighed. Sleep remained elusive, haunted by the shadows of the past. Tomorrow, she would return to the abandoned shipyard—the place where Heinrich Broder had left his dark footprints. Perhaps there, she would find answers that would illuminate not only the case but also her own life.

A few hours later, she stood beneath the dull neon lights of the Police Department 's briefing room. The air was thick with stale coffee and the pungent tang of printer toner—reminders of countless nights spent poring over leads.
Lena massaged her temples as she set a freshly printed search warrant for the shipyard on the table.

"You swore you'd never end up like your father—caught in a vortex of unsolved cases and lonely nights. But isn't that exactly where you've landed?"

She murmured quietly, her finger tracing the edge of the document as though trying to soothe her gnawing doubts.

"Dr. Becker signed off on the warrant yesterday. We're authorized to search the shipyard." Her voice was calm but resolute.

Lars Lammers leaned back in his chair, his gaze sharp and questioning. "And you think we'll actually find something there?"

Lena raised an eyebrow.

"Someone's been using that site—at night. There's more going on than we realize."

Just then, a metallic click from the corridor carried into the room—a sound that didn't belong in such a secure place.

"Everyone—by the door, now!"

Lars's command cut through the tension, his eyes suddenly alert as his hand darted to his holster like a predator sensing prey. Lena held her breath, every nerve in her body straining to detect the slightest movement.

In the darkness, only the soft drip of water was audible—until, abruptly, a sharp metallic snap, cold as a blade slicing through silence.

A shadow flickered across the room. And before Lena could react, it was as if a starting gun had been fired.

The drive to the shipyard passed in eerie quiet. The steady whir of tires on wet pavement sounded muffled, as though the entire city was holding its breath. Dense fog crept over the streets, swallowing the glow of streetlamps and shrouding the surroundings in a pale gray. Seated upright in the passenger seat, Lena felt her senses sharpen with every passing meter. The old shipyard—a relic of another era—looked untouched for decades, yet someone had definitely been there. Someone who wanted to erase all traces.

Lars brought the car to a stop with a soft squeal of the tires. The outlines of the abandoned buildings loomed against the night sky, rusted metal supports lending the scene an ominous presence. The air was heavy with the smells of oil, saltwater, and decay.

Lena pushed open the rusty main gate, which groaned under her grip. Her gaze swept across the dimly lit halls—until she froze.

Off in the distance, barely visible through the fog, was an SUV—dark, bulky, half-concealed behind one of the old sheds, like a ghostly sentinel.

She felt her heart quicken. In one fluid motion, she reached for her phone to snap a photo. But by the time she unlocked the screen and looked up, the vehicle was gone. A knot formed in her stomach, and a sense of foreboding took hold. Her rational mind insisted the fog was playing tricks, but her instincts screamed that they weren't alone.

Inside, the sprawling hall smelled damp and stale, as though time itself had claimed dominion here. The stench of rusty metal and old machine oil mingled with the drip of water from leaky pipes, echoing in a lonely chorus. Her flashlight swept over corroded containers and faded markings, the remnants of what had once been a bustling production floor. Then she spotted the crates—large, coated in dust, yet obviously empty. Approaching them, she realized that the faint symbols on the sides weren't ordinary shipping labels but unmistakable military markings.

Lars stepped up beside her, eyeing the boxes suspiciously.

"So why are they empty now?" he asked.

Corinna bent over one of the rear crates, running a swab along its worn interior.

"Hold on a second…" she murmured, lifting the cotton tip into the light. Lena moved closer, noting the thin white residue clinging to the crate's inner wall.

"What's that?" Jan asked warily, while Corinna held the swab steady.

"My guess is explosive residue—probably C4,"

she said quietly.

Suddenly, a foreboding crunch echoed through the hall, making them all jump. Lena held her breath, every sense on high alert for the faintest sound. Then, in the stillness, a sharp metallic click—cold and precise, like a blade against the darkness. A shadow flickered across the room. A sudden flash of light, a heavy thud, and a muffled cry— and in that instant, all hell broke loose.

# Chapter 22

The streetlamps cast their glow over the dark canals, turning them into molten gold and giving Emden the appearance of a magical labyrinth—a city balanced between silence and secrets, deceptively peaceful while truth simmered behind closed doors, demanding to be brought into the light.

It was a stark contrast to the meeting room in the police headquarters. Cold neon lights banished every shadow, leaving no space for ambiguity. The whiteboard resembled a web of names, numbers, and location markers—a network riddled with gaps waiting to be filled.

Bodo leaned back in his chair, fingertips pressed together. Lars stepped up to the table and let his gaze travel around the group.

"Jan?"

Jan Müller placed a battered file on the table.

"I went through the old records from the Broder shipyard. Between 2002 and 2004, the term 'strategic cargo' shows up repeatedly. Smuggling, maybe weapons, maybe chemicals, maybe something else entirely."

A moment of silence followed. Then Jan went on,

"And those tracks we found in the hall—yesterday we came across weapon crates. C4 residue on them."

Corinna gave a terse nod.

Lars's expression hardened.

"So, it's more than just money laundering, after all."

He tapped a brittle document with faded ink.

"According to this, Thomas Broder was supposed to take over after his father died. The shipyard was probably just a front for illegal deals. And the worst part? Looks like Hermann Voss—who now works for one of Sorokin's companies—was involved."

Robin frowned, his gaze drifting to a map that showed money flows snaking through half of Europe.

"What about the nighttime truck deliveries?"

Jan shook his head. "No oversight at all—just internal directives from Heinrich and Thomas. And they were often on-site themselves."

Lars ran a hand over his face, as though he could wipe away the grim puzzle pieces of the past.

"Then we start here."

He jotted down the next tasks on the whiteboard:

- **Robin**: Analyze financial flows
- **Jan**: Search city archives
- **Lena**: Investigate family connections
- **Bodo**: Tap contacts—someone out there knows more

A knock at the door made everyone turn.

Lars raised an eyebrow. "Yes?"

An officer stepped in, holding the door ajar.

"Aniko Kiss is here. Says she has something for us."

Lars hesitated, exchanged a glance with the others, then gave a curt nod. "Send her in."

Aniko walked in with cool determination. She carried a stack of brittle papers, her fingers clenched around the yellowed sheets. A muscle in her jaw twitched as she handed them over.

"I found these in the shipyard's safe,"

she said, her Hungarian accent giving her words an unmistakable edge.

"Maybe they'll shed some light."

Jan crossed his arms. His gaze remained steady, but a flicker of suspicion passed through it.

"Aniko—can you guarantee these documents are authentic?"

She tensed for a fraction of a second, then met his eyes.

"I have nothing to hide. But that doesn't change the truth."

Tension in the room mounted.

"That's enough," Lars interrupted sharply.

"Robin, take Aniko home."

Robin hesitated, then nodded.

Outside, the rain-slicked streets gleamed in the lamplight. As they drove through the city, the wind swept damp mist across the cobblestones. The canals reflected the glow of streetlamps—Emden seemed tranquil. Deceptively tranquil.

Robin pointed at the Kunsthalle Emden, its façade dramatically lit.

"I come here often when I need to think," he said quietly, almost pensively. "Reminds me that something always remains, no matter how chaotic things get."

Aniko followed his gaze.

"Yes. It's different from my home. But in a good way."

They continued driving. The New Delft, the old harbor's core, lay silent in the night. The masts of sailboats rose like silhouettes against the sky.

"Hungry?" Robin asked after a while.

Aniko grinned.

"Let me guess—you already reserved a table somewhere?"

**Da Sergio**, Hermann-Neemann-Street. An old warehouse, large windows reflecting the harbor's shimmering waters. The aroma of fresh pasta and warm bread filled the air. Robin chose a table overlooking the Delft.

"Why did you become a cop?"

Aniko asked after a moment. Robin took a sip of wine, letting the question settle.

"Because someone has to bring the truth to light."

A short silence followed.

Then the atmosphere changed. Lena and Bodo appeared in the doorway. Lena took half a step forward, her gaze drilling into Robin—cool, measured. Her voice was calm but biting.

"You do seem to find company quickly."

Robin started to respond, but Lena lifted a hand to stop him.

"She's still a key figure in this case. We'll discuss it tomorrow."

Her eyes flicked to Aniko, then back to Robin.

"But for now, you're taking her home." It wasn't a request.

Robin paused for a moment, then nodded curtly.

Lena turned and left without another word. Outside, the wind pushed tendrils of mist through the streets. Together, Robin and Aniko stepped into the night, but as Robin was about to climb into his car, he froze. A black BMW idled on the roadside—engine running, headlights off.

He forced himself to stay calm, though his pulse quickened. The car didn't move, but it was there, lurking. Waiting. This case was far from over.

# *Chapter 23*

The morning sun streamed through the half-open curtains, bathing Lena's flat in Gatjebogen in a warm, golden light. The aroma of freshly brewed coffee blended with the cool morning air drifting through the tilted window. Yet the events of the previous evening still reverberated in Lena's thoughts—memories that stirred both annoyance and concern.

In the kitchen, she stood at the stove wearing a thin dressing gown, turning eggs in a pan. Bodo entered quietly, his footsteps muffled by the soft carpet. Without a word, he placed his hands on her hips and pressed a gentle kiss to her shoulder.

"Early riser, huh?" he murmured in his deep, soothing voice.

Lena glanced away from the pan for a moment.

"Robin really got under my skin yesterday—such reckless behavior."

Bodo answered with a mild smile.

"He's still green. Mistakes happen, but some decisions can have dire consequences." A fleeting look in Lena's eyes betrayed her inner turmoil—the thought that she should have warned Robin more sternly weighed on her like an invisible shadow.

The smell of coffee drew them in, and soon they were seated at the kitchen table, sharing a brief moment of peace before the day's challenges announced themselves.

No sooner had Lena left the flat than she was swept into the bustle of police headquarters. The corridors buzzed with activity—stern faces, hurried footsteps, and curt orders that sparked through the air. There was no space for hesitation here.

With determined strides, she entered Lars Lammerts' office, Bodo by her side. Behind a meticulously organized desk—flanked by family photos and a lone houseplant that lent the stark room a trace of warmth—Lars looked at her.

"Morning, Lena. What brings you here?"

Without preamble, she said, "It's about Robin. Last night, he took Aniko to Da Sergio. That risky move isn't just unprofessional—it jeopardizes our entire investigation."

Lars's brow furrowed in concern. "Did he explain his reasons?"

"He thought he could gain her trust—but it was damn dangerous."

A heavy sigh escaped Lars as he asked, "Has he been in touch today?"

Lena shook her head silently.

"No. And that worries me."

Bodo added tersely, "His phone's off. I've tried to call him several times."

"So now we have two problems—his unauthorized action and his sudden disappearance,"

Lars summed up, pulling out his phone.

"We'll deal with this properly. Track him down at his flat. Lena—don't take any unnecessary risks. If you see anything suspicious, secure the scene immediately."

With Lars's words echoing in their minds, Lena and Bodo drove to Robin's flat in Transvaal—a nondescript apartment block with its shutters closed. His car was nowhere in the parking lot. Lena pressed the doorbell, but there was no response. She radioed in:

"Carpenter to Control Center. Inquiry regarding missing person—Robin Ahlers. Checked his home address, no response so far."

"Received, Ms. Berg. Keep us updated,"

came the terse reply.

Bodo studied the dark windows. "He's not here."

Lena nodded. "Then there's only one other lead."

Their next stop was Aniko's home in Wolthusen. From a distance, Lena could see a plain two-story building whose white façade glowed almost eerily in the morning light. A blue Polo—Robin's car—was parked in front. Lena hit the brakes abruptly.

"That's his car."

Bodo got out carefully and approached the vehicle. The driver's door was ajar. A quick look inside made his stomach clench: there was a dark stain on the passenger seat—blood. A cold chill of dread washed over him.

Lena crouched down, pulled on disposable gloves, and started examining the interior with a flashlight. "Blood," she muttered softly, catching the musty smell of old leather and a hint of sweat.

Bodo immediately grabbed the radio.

"Carpenter to Control Center. Location: Wolthusen. Possible trace evidence—blood in the vehicle. Requesting forensics."

"Understood. Secure the area. Forensics en route," came the reply.

Lena's heart pounded as she approached the house. The front door was locked, but she heard a muffled, unsettling sound inside—a faint scraping, mingled with the pungent odor of sweat and old wood emanating from the creaking floorboards. She drew her weapon, flashed Bodo a warning look, and radioed again:

"Carpenter to Control Center. Possible break-in or coercion on the premises. Two people unaccounted for. We're securing the area."

Before going in, she signaled for Bodo to check the rear of the building. After he muttered,

"Back's clear," Lena counted down in a whisper: "Three… two… one…"

With a firm grip, she pressed down the handle. The door creaked open. A shadow darted through the dim corridor, and suddenly something slammed into her back. She stumbled, feeling her balance give way.

She heard the attacker's ragged breathing, the boards beneath his feet crunching as he ran. Lena raised her weapon, but the masked figure was too fast. A flicker of movement—then he was gone.

In the adrenaline-fueled chaos, the corridor itself seemed to tremble. With one last powerful shove, the perpetrator vanished into the darkness. A low hum broke the silence.

A small device lay vibrating on the cold floor, its screen flickering ominously. Bodo picked it up. Lena stepped closer, her heart hammering, and the display glowed briefly—a symbol resembling a stylized eagle, followed by an almost illegible message:

**"Help... Robin..."** Then the screen died in a bright flash.

Suddenly, frantic shouts and a loud radio call echoed through the house.

"Police! Hands up!" Lena's voice rang out firmly in the corridor, while footsteps and a crashing sound stoked the tension further. Bodo cursed under his breath, scanning the empty room.

Then, as if the chaos had peaked, an engine roared outside—headlights flared through the dusty air and jagged windows.

"Backup is on the way," crackled the radio.

Lena ground her teeth. The moment had passed—the perpetrator had escaped, leaving behind blood, disorder, and that eerie, cryptic message that still flashed before her eyes.

One urgent question remained: **What had Robin found out?** And what dark scheme was unfolding in the shadows?

# *Chapter 24*

A dense morning fog shrouded Emden in a thick cloak as Lena Berg stepped out of the patrol car. The damp air weighed heavily on the city, laced with the scent of wet leaves, cold asphalt, and a faint trace of engine oil—metallic, sharp. A chill prickled down her spine.

Robin's car was parked at an odd angle in the driveway—positioned in a way that immediately drew Lena's attention. She slipped on a pair of gloves, approached, and peered through the window. Her breath caught. The passenger seat was pushed all the way back, and resting precisely in the center was a single object: a mobile phone, untouched, deliberately placed.

A young forensic specialist appeared, clipboard in hand, gloves still pristine.

"No sign of a struggle in the car. Some scratches on the exterior, but nothing indicating forced entry."

Lena nodded. Her gaze drifted from the phone to the house's dark façade, its open door radiating an eerie invitation—like someone wanted this exact effect. She stepped inside, cautiously, unsure what danger might lurk beyond those walls.

The flat appeared undisturbed. No overturned furniture, no shattered items—only a subtle tingling at the back of her neck, a warning born of years on the job. Bodo joined her, taking in the scene with a practiced eye.

"If someone broke in, they sure cleaned up after themselves."

But Lena's attention snagged on a small detail: a chest of drawers in the living room, its top drawer pulled open just a crack. Fresh scratches on the wood suggested someone had pried it open recently. She moved closer, carefully eased the drawer forward, and it slid out without a sound.

"Someone was looking for something," Bodo muttered.

A crumpled sheet of paper slipped from the stack of invoices and notes—yellowed, covered in hastily scrawled writing. Lena picked it up and held it toward the faint light.

"Bodo…this isn't the original."

He stepped in, jaw tightening, eyes darkening.

**12 April 2004 – I have the feeling someone's following me. The shipyard's not safe anymore. Maybe I'm being paranoid, but if I'm right, soon it'll be too late.**

Lena's heart clenched.

"That's Heinrich Broder's handwriting." The next line read: **If something happens to me, it won't be an accident. They mustn't get their hands on this.**

"Damn," Bodo whispered.

Suddenly, the entire flat seemed to quake—a dull thud shattered the silence. A massive figure stood in the bedroom doorway.

"Bodo!" Lena shouted—too late.

The blow struck his temple. His head snapped back, followed by a hollow thump. Silence. A stifled gasp. Lena's training kicked in as she reached for her gun.

"Police! Stay right where you are!"

The attacker moved with lightning speed, twisting around and dashing toward the back door—his motions too precise for a common burglar. Bodo lay motionless, blood glistening on his temple, his heartbeat pounding in Lena's ears. She couldn't lose him.

Without hesitation, she tore after the intruder. Outside, the cold morning air bit at her face. The thick fog turned the alley into a maze of shifting shadows and flickering streetlights.

"Berg here! Suspect heading toward Pastor-Friedrich-Street! Need backup ASAP!" she radioed.

The assailant knew the area, veering into a narrow, unlit passage to the left of the driveway.

Lena followed, her footsteps echoing on the gravel. She stumbled over a piece of rusty metal, nearly losing her balance; her hand struck the slick pavement in a jolt of pain. She pushed herself upright and looked ahead: the suspect was now about ten meters away.

She closed the distance with each stride, eyes locked on the dark silhouette cutting through the fog. Then, in an instant, the figure spun around. He wrenched a rusty pipe from its holder and flung it at her. Lena dodged aside, the pipe grazing her jacket before clattering away. The man then hurled himself through a metal door, which slammed shut behind him with a metallic clang.

Lena shoved the door open—darkness swallowed her, and the suspect was gone. An engine roared. Tires screeched. A dark van careened around the next corner and disappeared into the fog. Lena's foot collided with a crate, sending another spike of pain through her leg. She cursed under her breath as her radio crackled:

"Lena, backup's en route. Where are you?"

Gasping for air, she answered, "Suspect escaped. But we found something—a copy of Heinrich Broder's diary."

Lars Lammerts' calm yet urgent voice resonated through the line: "That's more than we had. Report back to the Police Department immediately."

A chill rushed through Lena—Bodo. She pivoted and ran back.

As she turned onto Berend-de-Vries-Street, the first emergency lights reflected off the wet pavement. Bodo lay on the ground, pale, blood seeping from his temple. He winced, struggling to rise.

Lena dropped to her knees beside him. "Your head…"

"It's ringing like the ship's bell on the Gorch Fock,"

he groaned, "but I'm alive." He exhaled shakily, then forced a wry smile. "Let me guess—Lammerts wants us back at the Police Department right now?"

Lena nodded, her worry plain.

Bodo pressed a trembling hand to his injured forehead. "Then let's get moving. Just…give me a second for some ice…if I can."

The dense morning fog still clung to Emden, as though the city itself were holding its breath. Finding Broder's diary changed everything. This was no ordinary case—it was more than just a lead. It was a warning, an open declaration of war.

Under the subdued glow of desk lamps in the open-plan office, the atmosphere felt almost comforting compared to the tense quiet outside. The faint scent of stale coffee and printer toner hung in the air—details few people noticed. Bodo sank into his chair with a groan, accepting an ice pack from a silent colleague and pressing it to his throbbing temple. The attack had clearly rattled him.

Lars Lammerts, already waiting, turned his attention to the papers in Lena's hand. "Sit," he said curtly, no warmth in his tone. Lena draped her jacket over a chair and spread out the copies. Lars scanned the text, then looked up—his eyes cold, his expression resolute.

"This…" He tapped the page with his knuckles. "This isn't just some private note. It's a damn warning."

Lena nodded.

"And someone wanted to stop us from getting it."

Bodo leaned forward. "They planned that ambush. They knew we'd be searching Aniko's place. Must've been watching us."

Lars leaned back, gaze dark. "If Broder wrote that he was being followed, it connects back to the shipyard—where he was last seen. And now we've got another attack."

Lena took a steadying breath. The puzzle pieces were starting to fit, but the overall picture remained murky.

"Forensics find anything else?" Lars asked.

"Nothing concrete," she said, "but there's oil residue—machine oil."

For a moment, no one spoke. Then Lars's eyes sharpened. "Could tie to the shipyard or some heavy-machinery warehouse."

Bodo nodded. "So we know where to look next."

Suddenly, Lena's work phone buzzed—a muffled, unsettling vibration. Everyone went silent. She glanced at the screen. One line:

**Stop digging or soon you'll be digging for the deuces.**

A chill spread through Lena.

"The deuces?" she repeated, looking at Bodo and Lars. Wordlessly, she passed them the phone. Lars read the message, his eyes growing colder.

"This isn't just a threat—it's a declaration of war. They know exactly what we're doing."

Bodo squared his shoulders, his gaze fierce despite the pain. "Whose number is it?"

Lena checked. Her stomach twisted. It was Aniko's number. A heavy silence fell. Bodo muttered a curse under his breath. "Either someone's got her phone or…"

Lena pressed her lips together, refusing to voice the grim possibility that Aniko—or Robin—might be dead. The air felt suffocating, tension looming over them like a drawn sword.

Lars stood slowly. His voice was calm, each word a warning. "We'll find out. But from here on, it's not just time working against us. Every step we take is under scrutiny."

Bodo arched an eyebrow.

"Then we lead them astray."

Lena looked at him.

"You're suggesting we set a trap?"

A thin smile flickered across Bodo's bruised lips. "Exactly. They think we're in the dark. We let them believe they're in control. When they feel safe—that's when we strike."

Lars nodded.

"First thing tomorrow. We'll focus on the shipyard, on our terms."

Lena exhaled slowly, her heart hammering in her chest. She knew they'd crossed a line. This was no longer a routine case—it was a deadly game, and one wrong move could be their last.

# *Chapter 25*

Lena sat alone in her office. The pale light from the desk lamp cast harsh shadows on the walls, draping the room in an unreal half-darkness. The stale smell of cold coffee lingered in the air. She hadn't slept. Couldn't sleep.

The message on her phone had burned itself into her consciousness:

**"Stop digging, or you can dig for the deuces."**

A sentence like a blade—precise, ice-cold. A game designed to feed her fear.

Robin had vanished. Aniko had vanished. And she hadn't been able to prevent it.

Her eyes fell on the report about Robin's car—the last trace: his vehicle, abandoned in front of Aniko's house. His phone destroyed. A silver feather placed on the hood—an undeciphered message.

Lena closed her eyes. She should have been quicker.

The door opened. Bodo entered, dark circles under his eyes, his gaze hard.

"You didn't sleep."

"No." He dropped into the chair opposite her.

"Stop beating yourself up."

Lena let out a bitter snort. "Robin is gone. Aniko is gone. And we have nothing."

"Nothing yet," Bodo corrected. "But we'll find them."

She stayed silent. Then she said quietly, "I was the last one to talk to him."

Bodo leaned back. "You didn't put him in this situation. The kidnappers did."

Lena ran both hands through her hair. "Maybe I should've…noticed something. Missed a sign. Maybe I was too slow."

Bodo met her gaze. "Or they think they're smarter than we are." A pause, then a hard, thin smile.

"That's where they're wrong."

The door flew open. Lars rushed in, face tense.

"No sign of Aniko's phone. No camera footage of what happened to them."

Lena clenched her fists. "Someone must have seen something." Lars's expression darkened.

"The only surveillance camera in the neighborhood? It failed that very night—expertly."

Silence.

Lena straightened, her eyes sharpening. "Then we've only got one lead left: Robin's car."

The morning air was bitingly cold, a fine drizzle veiling the city. The streets stood deserted.

Robin's car remained where it was. The driver's door was half open, as though he'd been about to get out—or had been pulled out.

Bodo tugged on gloves and shone his flashlight over the wet asphalt. "If they got him here, there might be something to find."

Lena stepped closer, leaned down—and her heart seemed to stop. An earring. Simple, gold, half-hidden in the gutter. She picked it up carefully. "It's Aniko's."

Lars came up beside her, his gaze watchful. "Think she dropped it on purpose?"

Lena turned the earring between her fingers. Her voice was quiet yet firm. "If she could—yes."

Her eyes roamed over the pavement. There had to be more.

Bodo pointed to a narrow alley behind a concrete wall. "If she was leaving clues just before she got taken, they'd be in there."

Lena gave a curt nod. "Let's go."

They followed the dark alley, flashlights cutting through the damp, slick ground. The rain had turned it into greasy mud.

Then—a faint glint in the beam of light. Lena froze.

A tiny piece of plastic. She knelt and lifted it carefully: a SIM card.

Lars exhaled. "Don't tell me that's…"

Lena turned the card in her fingers, a flicker of hope in her voice. "Could be Robin's."

Bodo pulled out his phone. "We'll have it analyzed. Maybe there's a last saved number. A message."

Lena took a deep breath. For the first time in hours, it felt like they weren't entirely in the dark. Robin hadn't been able to leave a message—but Aniko had tried. Now they just had to figure out where that trail would lead them.

# *Chapter 26*

The air in the meeting room was heavy—a mix of stale coffee, paper dust, and unspoken tension. Outside, the rain had been lashing against the windows just minutes before, but now all was quiet. Still, the sense of looming danger lingered.

Robin had vanished. And Aniko with him.

For hours, the team had combed through every clue, no matter how small. The nighttime surveillance footage from Aniko's street played on the screen. Corinna Stein, the forensic specialist, rewound the video.

02:37am

A black-and-white image. An empty street. Streetlights cast a cold glow on the wet pavement. Then—movement.

A dark van appeared. Silently. Deliberately. Like a hunter closing in on its prey.

Lena Berg stepped closer. "Stop there. Zoom in on the license plate."

Corinna tried. The image stayed blurred, the numbers unreadable.

"Tampered with," she said curtly. "Someone taped or painted over the plate. Not by accident."

Lars Lammerts frowned. "Amateur or professional?"

Corinna didn't hesitate. "Definitely professional. If it were just painted over, we could use infrared to reveal something. But a special film was used here—designed to fool surveillance cameras."

Lena pressed her lips together. "They knew exactly when to strike."

Bodo Zimmermann folded his arms. His gaze was cold. "So either Aniko was watched for days—or Robin was the real target."

Then Lars's phone vibrated.

An anonymous message. A single sentence:

**"Ask Thomas. He knows more."**

Silence.

Lars held up his phone. The words weighed heavily in the room. "This is either a clever trick—or someone's deliberately pointing us in the right direction."

**Ten minutes later**

Lena and Jan Müller stood outside Thomas Broder's flat. The corridor smelled of stale smoke and damp carpet. Behind the curtains—nothing. No light, no sound.

Jan knocked. Once. Twice. No answer.

168

"Damn," he muttered. "What if he really ran off?"

Lena pulled out her work phone and dialed Thomas's number.

It rang once. Twice. Then went to voicemail.

"He's not answering." She activated her radio. "Corinna, check the cell tower data for Thomas's phone. I need to know where he last logged in."

Seconds passed, then Corinna replied. "On it... Hold on... Okay. Last known location: B72. After that—radio silence."

Lena looked at Jan.

"The main road out of the city. Perfect place to disappear."

Jan met her gaze. "Or get intercepted."

**Back at headquarters.**

A tense hush filled the air. The team worked feverishly, but uncertainty gnawed at each of them.

Lars stood in front of the whiteboard. Names, places, leads—a chaotic puzzle that refused to come together.

"What do we have on Thomas?" Lena asked.

Corinna flipped through her files. "Massive financial troubles with the shipyard. For years. And then there's this payment: two weeks ago, Thomas received fifty thousand euros from an offshore account in Cyprus."

Lars narrowed his eyes. "Dirty money?"

Corinna nodded. "The company behind it surfaced in a money laundering case in Ukraine."

Bodo let out a low whistle. "Damn. First he's got money problems, then a big payout—and now he's vanished."

Lena let the idea sink in. "If Thomas is involved, why kidnap Robin and Aniko? What does he gain?"

Jan crossed his arms. "Or maybe he's being coerced."

Just then, Lena's phone rang. Unknown number.

She answered, "Berg."

On the other end—a distorted male voice. Calm. Precise.

"He's walking right into your hands." A click. The line went dead.

Lena stared at her phone, heart pounding. Then she slowly lifted her head. Her eyes flashed with resolve. She threw the door open. "Jan, call the Swart team—now!"

# Chapter 27

Robin awoke in darkness, thick and suffocating. His first conscious thought was pain—a dull pounding in his skull that smothered any coherent thought. A searing pressure stretched across his temples, as if his head were clamped in a vice. The floor beneath him was damp, cold, and reeked of moldy concrete.

When he tried to move, resistance stopped him—his arms were tied behind his back.

A sound pierced the silence—a slow, rhythmic dripping. It seeped through the void like a ghostly reminder that time had no meaning here.

His breath was shallow, his senses sharpening. He could feel the rough surface beneath him, the clammy air burning in his lungs. The scent of rust mingled with the stale dampness of a room that held no escape.

"Where... am I?" His whisper sounded strange—hoarse, unfamiliar. Panic crept in, but he forced it back. His fingers explored the floor—cracked concrete, uneven, cold. No warmth, no movement.

Alone.

Or not?

Beyond the blackness, something lingered. No sound, no movement—just a presence. A sensation deep inside him.

Aniko.

Gritting his teeth, he forced himself to stay still. His arms ached from the restraints as he rolled onto his side. A jolt of pain shot through his shoulders, but he ignored it. He needed to focus.

There. A noise.

Dull. Distant. Someone shifting against a wall?

"Aniko?" His voice was barely more than a whisper, swallowed by the dark.

No response.

The silence thickened, pressing in on him with every passing second.

Then—a breath. Short. Hesitant. But undeniably human.

Robin froze. His pulse hammered.

She was here. Somewhere.

Which meant they weren't alone.

Aniko woke to a sharp, pulsing pain in her temple. Her head throbbed, as if it had been slammed against a wall—maybe it had. Her breathing was unsteady, shallow.

The darkness was absolute, thick as tar, suffocating hope itself.

Slowly, she tested her limbs. Her arms were bound behind her, the restraints biting into her skin. Her fingers fumbled over the floor—damp, cold, rough. Concrete. She leaned back, feeling a wall behind her. Damp, cracked, lined with tiny crevices where the cold pooled.

A sting lanced through her temple as she moved. She reached up, fingertips brushing a sticky wound, crusted with dried blood.

What had happened?

Her stomach twisted.

The last memory—a dark car, Robin's worried face, a sudden jolt. Then—impact. Silence.

And now?

She strained to see through the blackness, but there was nothing. No light. No shape. Only void.

A sound made her tense. Droplets. A slow, deliberate drip somewhere in the distance. Like the steady pulse of this nightmare.

Her throat went dry.

She wasn't alone. She knew it. More than a hunch—a certainty.

Robin. Was he here?

Her lips formed his name, but no sound came out. Swallowing hard, she tried again.

"Robin?"

Silence.

Then—a shift. A breath.

He was here.

Relief flickered for a fraction of a second—then vanished, swallowed by the ice-cold truth.

They were trapped. Bound. Separated. Then—abruptly— a noise shattered the stillness. Footsteps. Heavy. Slow. Approaching. A bolt slid back, screeching, as if the door itself protested. A dull thud followed.

Silence. Aniko held her breath.

A voice. Deep. Cold. Calculating.

"Your people had better stop searching. Otherwise, they'll only find corpses." The words sank into the dark like a deadly promise. Aniko closed her eyes, though it made no difference. Her nails dug into her palms as her heart pounded wildly.

They had to get out.

Corpses.

The man had spoken the word with chilling indifference. No hesitation. No anger. Just a fact. Or a promise.

Robin clenched his jaw. His pulse thundered in his ears, his breath shallow. Fear was the enemy. Fear meant weakness. And weakness meant death.

He tensed his muscles, testing the restraints, searching for slack. The ropes were tight—but not unbreakable. He focused on every slight movement, every fraction of give.

Then—he heard it. A faint scraping sound. Barely there.

Not next to him. Distant. Another room? Aniko.

She was awake. She was fighting.

A flicker of hope sparked in him. They were not alone.

Then—footsteps. Faster. Heavier. The door screeched open.

A shadow loomed. And a voice—low, near, laced with danger:

# Chapter 28

Lena Berg sat in her office, fingers hovering over the keyboard. The screen displayed:

*"Robin Ahlers and Aniko Kiss have been found safe and sound. The investigation is continuing."*

A carefully orchestrated lie—exactly according to plan.

"Do you really think they'll fall for it?" Bodo crossed his arms as if shielding himself from the growing tension. Skepticism flickered in his eyes.

Lena met his gaze with unwavering determination. "If they believe the danger has passed, they'll get careless. And that's exactly our chance."

Lars Lammerts stepped up to the desk, his face as immovable as stone. "Then we go through with it."

With a decisive click, Lena sent the message out into the world—online press, local radio stations. The news was designed to make waves. Now, all that remained was to wait.

The office was dimly lit, the monitors casting a cool blue glow over their faces. The stale scent of cold coffee and electronics filled the air. A soft whirring from the server mixed with the distant drip of a leaking pipe.

Five minutes. Ten. Fifteen. Lena's eyes flicked to the clock. The seconds stretched unbearably. The silence thickened, pressing in on them like an unseen weight.

Bodo rubbed his chin. "Maybe they're too smart to take the bait."

Lars shook his head. "Or they know we're watching."

A tight knot formed in Lena's stomach. Had they overplayed their hand? Just as she opened her mouth to speak, her phone vibrated. A single message.

**"Interesting."**

Her throat went dry. "Damn it," she muttered. "They know we're expecting them."

The quiet tap of fingernails against the tabletop betrayed their tension. Had they made the right move—or had they just driven their enemy deeper into the shadows?

Then, unexpectedly, a new message flickered onto Bodo's screen.

A signal.

Lars stepped closer, voice calm but taut. "That can only mean one thing: they took the bait."

Lena nodded slowly, pulse quickening. "We've lured them out."

Bodo leaned forward, his voice low. "Or we've only driven them deeper into darkness."

Lena shook her head. "No. They think they're ahead of us. And that will be their mistake."

In a dimly lit room, illuminated only by a flickering neon tube, stale smoke hung in the air. A man stood with his back to the door, hands flat on the tabletop.
"They claim to have found them." His voice was calm. Almost amused.

The younger man beside him crossed his arms uneasily. "If that's true, then—"

"Then we're finished?" The older man let out a sharp, amused snort. "Nonsense."

He exhaled slowly, watching the smoke curl toward the ceiling. "They hope we'll panic. But if they think we'll relax…" He let the sentence dangle, reaching instead for a small device on the table.

A GPS transmitter. Its red light blinked steadily.

The younger man's brow furrowed. "Did you…?"

The older man shook his head. "No. But someone activated it."

For a moment, silence stretched between them. Then, slowly, he raised his gaze.

"Then we'll show them that we're always one step ahead."

Cold air, thick with the scent of salt and rust, swirled along Emden's southern quay. The looming shadows of abandoned warehouses stood like silent sentinels, their broken windows staring into the darkness like empty, lifeless eyes.

A gust of wind carried the acrid tang of seaweed and machine oil—ominous and heavy.

No light. No movement.

Corinna Stein pulled a flashlight from her jacket and swept its beam across the damp concrete. Dark stains clung to the floor.

"If they were here, they've covered their tracks well," she murmured.

Lena stopped. A chill traced up her spine. She exhaled slowly, barely above a whisper.

"It's a trap."

Bodo let out a quiet scoff. "For us—or for them?"

Lena's breath came shallow. It all fit too perfectly. Too neat. But they were in too deep now to turn back.

Lars moved cautiously through the empty space, his boots grinding against the dust-covered floor. The wind whistled through shattered windowpanes.

Then—he stopped.

"Here."

In a dusty corner, a crumpled sheet of paper lay abandoned.

Coordinates. A date. And a sketch—A black raven.

Lena frowned. Her breath caught.

This date…

Her voice was barely more than a whisper. "This is the day Heinrich Broder was reported missing."

Silence. Heavy as lead.

Bodo broke it with a low murmur. "That can't be a coincidence."

Lena's stomach tightened.

This wasn't a random clue.

It was an invitation.

She glanced at the others before pulling out her phone.

"We're turning the tables."

For a moment, tension pulsed through the air.

Lars nodded sharply. "Swart Team and undercover units?" Lena met his gaze. "I'll notify incident command. We'll secure the entire area. This time, we get them."

The weight of the moment settled over them. No turning back. No mistakes.

Lena's voice was steady, resolute.

"This time, we don't play by their rules."

A pause. "This time, we write them.

# Chapter 29

The air in the police department was stuffy, thick with the scent of coffee and the monotonous hum of neon lights—cold, unfeeling, almost mocking.

Robin had vanished.

Lena's gaze was fixed on the few scattered notes on the table—or rather, on the unsettling emptiness between them. The chair opposite her was vacant.

Robin's seat.

It had been for days.

Bodo stood in front of the evidence board, his jaw tight, fingers absentmindedly running along the rim of his coffee cup. A man searching for a pattern that refused to emerge.

The door to the meeting room swung open abruptly.

Lars Lammerts entered, his face set in determination, tension crackling in his movements. A printout in his hand.

*"We have a lead."*

Lena straightened as if jolted by an electric current. Lars placed the document on the table. A black panel van. Polish license plate.

The image showed a blurred surveillance shot from the harbor area. The vehicle looked anonymous, faceless—a phantom of metal and glass. But its significance was undeniable.

*"This was taken the night Robin and Aniko disappeared,"* Lars said, his voice edged with urgency.

Lena bent over the picture, eyes razor-sharp.

*"If we find this van, we find them."*

Outside, rain began to fall. The lights of Emden shimmered in the puddles like ghostly signals. Lena stood at the window, feeling the weight of unseen eyes. Watching. Perhaps at this very moment.

*"We have to trick them,"* she finally said, turning back to the team.

*"We'll leak a false lead to the press. Let them believe Robin was spotted in an abandoned house near the Knock."*

Bodo raised an eyebrow.

*"You want to flush them out."*

*"Exactly. If they think we're looking in the wrong place, they might make a move—and we'll be ready."*

Lars exhaled slowly. *"That's risky."*

Lena squared her shoulders, as if shaking off the weight of doubt.

*"Everything we do is risky. But if we don't act now, it might be too late."*

**Three hours later.**

Bodo and Corinna sat in an unremarkable car, parked on a dark side street. The false lead had been fed to the press. Now, they waited.

Bodo watched the street through the fogged-up window.

Then—his eyes narrowed.

*"There."*

Corinna followed his gaze. A lone figure appeared, pausing beneath a streetlamp. A phone was pulled out, a glance around—then the figure melted back into the shadows.

*"That wasn't random,"* Corinna murmured.

Bodo reached for the radio. *"Lena, we've got someone."*

The harbor air was thick with salt and oil, mingling with the damp cold of the rain. Corinna Stein and Jan Müller moved cautiously through the deserted docks, their flashlights slicing through the darkness.

A gust of wind sent a tarpaulin flapping against a container.Somewhere, a seagull screeched—a sound almost mournful. A warning.

Then—

*"Over here!"*

Corinna's voice echoed through the emptiness.

Bodo hurried to her. And then—his chest tightened.

A torn, bloodstained piece of fabric, caught between rusty metal.

Bodo stared, his pulse hammering.

For a split second, he was certain—it was Robin's jacket. The same color. The same frayed hem.

His heart stumbled. But as Corinna shifted the light, the truth became clear.

Not Robin's. Someone else's.

The blood along the edges wasn't fresh—too dark in the neon glow.

Bodo exhaled sharply.

*"Damn. This isn't good. "*His voice was hoarse.

Minutes later, Lena and Lars arrived.

Lena took the cloth, running her thumb over the dried surface.

Too fresh to be old. Too small to mean nothing.

Her heart drummed against her ribs.

*"If they're injured, we don't have much time."*

While Lena and Lars continued scouring the docks, Jan searched online records for the Polish van.

Then—

A hit.

*"The vehicle is registered to a shell company—tied to Eastern European human trafficking and illegal arms deals."*

Bodo's jaw tightened.

*"Shit."*

But that wasn't the worst part.

At the entrance of an abandoned warehouse, something had been left behind.

A symbol.

Drawn in chalk.

A black raven.

The lines were sharp, precise—almost artistic.

But the message was anything but beautiful.

Lars ran a hand over his face.

*"I've seen this before. Stralsund, in the '90s. The 'Black Ravens'—contract killers. They left symbols like this before they struck."*

Bodo crouched down. Something lay next to the drawing.

A feather.

Black as night, slightly curved, as if someone had idly twirled it between their fingers.

Lena rubbed the back of her neck.

*"Could be a marker. A message for their people."*

Bodo's gaze darkened.

*"Or a warning."*

A warning for us.

As the team raced against time to find Robin, Lena's phone rang.

The number—unknown.

She answered. A voice. Distorted. Barely more than a breath on the line.

*"You're getting too close."*

Lena stiffened. *"Stop looking. Or he dies."*

Icy silence.

Then—a soft chuckle. Barely audible. Distant.

A click.

The line went dead.

Lena stared at the phone, her grip tightening. A slow, burning rage coiled in her gut.

*"We're not stopping."* Bodo's eyes met hers.

*"This is getting dangerous."* Lena's smile was ice-cold.

*"It was never safe."* Outside, the wind howled over the docks. The hunt had begun.

# Chapter 30

The monotonous dripping in the darkness gnawed at my nerves like a rusty saw against bare flesh. Every sound echoed between the cold concrete walls, distorted, amplified—a slow torture to the ears.

The air was thick, heavy with humidity and fear, as if it had been trapped for decades. Every breath felt like a battle against something invisible, clawing at her throat.

Robin leaned against the wall. The handcuffs bit into his skin, his joints burned. His left arm was numb, a stabbing pain stretching from his shoulder to his fingertips.

He forced himself to stay calm.

Panic was the enemy.

**Think. Act. Survive.**

Aniko crouched opposite him. Damp strands of blonde hair clung to her forehead. Her breath came too fast, too shallow. Her blue eyes, usually alive with mischief, were wide, flickering in the weak neon light like frozen flames.

Her fingers fumbled across the floor—searching, feeling. Then—she stopped.

*"Robin..."* Her voice was little more than a tremor in the dark. *"Here. A screw."*

Robin blinked, scooting closer.

188

*"What?"*

*"The plate… it's loose."*

His gaze followed hers. A metal reinforcement on the wall—old, rusted. A screw hung by its last threads.

Hope flickered. Then reality crushed it.

No room for mistakes.

*"If we can get it out..."* Aniko whispered.

*"Then we have a chance."*

Robin tensed every muscle.

Aniko pressed her lips together, steadied her trembling fingers, and began to turn the screw. Millimeter by millimeter.

Her nails scraped against the corroded metal.

Every breath was too loud.

Every heartbeat an echo in the suffocating dark.

Robin made use of the time. Earlier, he had pulled a thin wire from the sole of his shoe. A tool. A possibility. A hope.

Carefully, he slid it into the lock of his cuffs.

The cold metal bit into his fingers. Focus. No mistakes.

Then—

Footsteps. Hard. Heavy. Right outside the door.

They froze.

A voice shattered the silence. Deep. Mechanical. Emotionless.

*"Sorokin doesn't want to take any more risks."*

A pause. Then—a soft click.

A gun. Safety off.

Aniko sucked in a sharp breath.

Robin felt his pulse slam against his ribs.

The screw was almost free. The wire slipped.

Robin gritted his teeth. One more try. Then—a muffled snap. The cuffs popped open. Robin exhaled, rubbing his wrists.

*"Hurry up."*

With a final, desperate twist, Aniko yanked the screw out.

The metal plate shifted.

Behind it— A dark shaft. Narrow. Moldy. But big enough. Robin's grip tightened on her shoulder.

*"You first."*

Aniko scrambled inside, pulling her legs up.

Robin followed.

The metal scraped against his arms, leaving fine, burning lines on his skin. Behind them— The door slammed open.

A harsh light cut through the darkness.

*"Damn it! They're gone!"*

A gunshot.

The bullet smashed into the concrete, leaving a glowing scar in the wall.

*"Faster!"* Aniko gasped.

They crawled forward, bumping into rusted pipes.

The shaft was damp. Stifling. A forgotten service tunnel.

Maybe an emergency exit. Then— Fresh air. Aniko pulled herself out, stumbling into a backyard. Robin followed, rolling to his feet, greedily sucking in the cold night air. Rain dripped from rusted containers. The ground gleamed wetly in the pale glow of a streetlamp.

**Free.**

Robin grabbed Aniko's hand. *"We have to—"* A shadow shifted. A man stepped out of the darkness. Broad-shouldered. Still. His eyes gleamed under the hood—two dead stars. In his hand—a pistol.

His voice was quiet. Almost gentle.

### *"Did someone give you permission to leave?"*

Robin reacted on instinct, shoving Aniko aside. Too slow.

The man was faster. A brutal punch to the stomach knocked the air from Robin's lungs. He doubled over, gasping.

Aniko screamed.

Strong arms seized her from behind. Another figure emerged from the shadows.

Robin reared up— Too late.

It was over. They were dragged back into the darkness.

# *Chapter 31*

The sky over Emden hung heavy like molten lead. The clouds pressed low, foreshadowing an inevitable catastrophe. A somber veil draped over the city, as if the night itself had held its breath.

Lena sat on a weathered wooden bench on the **Gatjebogen**, her gaze fixed on the dark water. The wind sliced across the quay, carrying the scent of salt, seaweed, and stale oil through the night. Waves crashed against the stone embankment—dull, restless thuds. Unstoppable. Like a warning.

**Three days.**

Three agonizing, endless days.

Robin and Aniko—gone. No trace. No sign of life. Just an abandoned car and a message on her phone, as cold as the wind cutting through her bones.

**It's not over yet.**

Lena pressed her fingers to her temples, desperately searching for something—anything—she had overlooked. Every thought led to a dead end. A grinding spiral of hope and fear.

Then—her phone vibrated.

She flinched. Pulled it from her pocket. **Lars.** Her heart clenched.

*"Lena,"* his voice was direct, sharp. *"We have a body."*

A shard of ice buried itself in her chest.

Not Robin. Not Aniko.

She jumped up.

Ran.

The night swallowed her footsteps.

The rain had eased, but the streets still glistened under the pale lantern light. Puddles collected in the cracks of the asphalt, reflecting the sky like broken mirrors.

Lena's hands gripped the steering wheel like a vice. The engine vibrated beneath her feet, a low, steady rumble that pulsed in sync with her heartbeat.

Bodo sat beside her—silent, watchful, his hands resting on his thighs.

*"Lena."* His voice was calm but firm. *"You need a break."*

She stared straight ahead, her shoulders rigid.

*"There's no time for that."*

Bodo didn't look away. *"That's exactly what he's counting on. That you'll make mistakes."* **Him.**

194

Whoever he was—he knew her. Played with her. Led her around like a pawn in his twisted game.

Her grip on the wheel tightened. The thought of failure gnawed at her. What if she had missed something crucial?

*"We didn't make mistakes,"* Bodo said quietly. *"But some-one wants us to believe we did."*

The traffic light ahead turned red.

She slammed on the brakes. The car lurched to a halt.

Rainwater streamed down the windshield in thick, sluggish streaks, city lights warping into ghostly shapes.

*"If it's Robin or Aniko..."* Her voice cracked. A cold shiver ran through her.

The thought that one of them could be dead choked her.

Bodo's gaze remained steady.

*"Then we find out who's responsible."*

The light turned green.

Lena floored the accelerator. **Pier 3** lay in semi-darkness. Rusted steel beams jutted into the sky like skeletal remains. Crumbling concrete peeled from the walls, old and brittle.

A police barrier fluttered in the wind, while the blue glow of patrol car lights cast fractured shadows across the wet pavement.

Lars stood at the warehouse entrance, shoulders tense, his face a stone mask. As Lena and Bodo approached, he exhaled sharply.

*"It's not Robin, "* he said at once. *"Not Aniko. "*

Lena gave a curt nod, but she didn't let relief in. Not yet.

She followed him inside.

Flashlights sliced through the darkness—

And revealed the body.

The dead man was kneeling, hands bound behind his back, head bowed as if frozen in silent prayer.

But the blood pooling around him told a different story.

Then—Lena saw his face.

His eyes. Wide open. Painted over in black.

A shiver ran through her.

Someone had turned him into a lifeless doll. A faceless imitation of a man who no longer saw, no longer knew.

Bodo stepped closer, his voice clipped. *"This is staged."*

Lena rubbed her arms, trying to shake the sudden chill creeping through her.

Something about him… Familiar.

*"An informant,"* Bodo murmured, recognition dawning. Lars gestured, and an officer handed him a small plastic bag.

Inside— A **memory card**.

A tiny, smeared drop of blood on its edge.

Lars turned the bag in his fingers, his expression dark.

*"This changes everything."*

Lena stared at the memory card.

**Why now? Why here?**

Her stomach twisted.

Someone had wanted them to find this. The air in the **police department's** technical room was dense, charged with tension. Corinna sat in front of her monitor, watching as the data loaded from the memory card.

Then—she froze.

Lars exhaled sharply. *"That can't be right."*

The video flickered onto the screen. A warehouse. Dark.

Light flickered. A figure in a long coat. The man turned toward the camera. His features—tired. Worn.

Marked by something he no longer controlled. **Thomas Broder.** The realization struck like a physical blow.

Lena felt the ground shift beneath her. Instinctively, she gripped the table's edge—anchoring herself to reality.

**Thomas.**

A name she had never expected in this context. And yet— It all made terrible sense. Her phone vibrated.

A message.

**You have seen him. He knew too much. You know it too.**

Lena stared at the words. A dark shadow coiled inside her, spreading like ink in water.

She swallowed. *"Do we still have time?"*

Nobody answered. Because the real question was—

**Was Thomas Broder already the next victim?**

## *Chapter 32*

Morning crept over **Gatjebogen**, but the sun had no chance against the thick, rain-laden clouds. A washed-out grey blanketed the city, the pale light struggling to break through. Seagulls shrieked over the harbor, their cries slicing through the sluggish silence.

The water lapped monotonously against the quay wall, carrying the sharp scent of salt, seaweed, and stale oil. A heavy mist clung to the wet cobblestones, mixing with the industrial haze drifting from the docks.

The streets shimmered with moisture. Puddles reflected the leaden sky.

A taxi sped through a dip, sending a spray of water into the air. Somewhere, a door slammed.

Then—silence.

An unnatural, lurking silence.

Lena lay in Bodo's arms. His skin was warm, his breathing steady. But her mind churned, restless.

She felt trapped. Like a prisoner in a windowless room.

**Thomas Broder.**

His name echoed through her thoughts, an endless refrain in the void.

He had vanished before he even reached the hospital. **Escape? Abduction? Or had this been the plan all along?**

Every possibility felt wrong.

If he had escaped—where to? If he had been taken—why now?

And if this had always been the plan… what else had she overlooked?

A chill ran down her spine, like a cold hand pressing against the back of her neck.

She drew in a sharp breath.

*"He's in deeper than we thought,"* she murmured. Her voice was rough from sleep.

Bodo was already awake.

His eyes, shadowed in the dim light, were sharp.

*"Everything points to him,"* he said quietly. *"Robin and Aniko's kidnapping. His escape. But why? What was he hiding?"*

Lena rubbed her forehead, as if she could smooth out the chaos in her mind.

But the noise in her head only grew louder. *"If he's really behind this—why the message? 'It's not over yet.' Someone wants us to believe he's guilty."*

Bodo shook his head.

*"Or someone wants him gone before we find him."* A dark unease settled deep in her gut.

It felt like running through a tunnel—only for someone at the other end to turn off the light.

Someone was pulling the strings.

And they were chasing shadows.

Lena threw back the duvet and reached for her jacket.

*"Let's go to the department. Maybe Corinna has something new."*

Outside, the city stirred awake.

The rain had eased, but the air was damp, heavy. Streetlights cast long reflections on the wet asphalt.

Workers in high-visibility vests stood at a corner, their breath rising in ghostly clouds. Cyclists glided past in silence, the beams of their bikes flickering across the brick facades.

Lena started the car. Turned on the radio. A burst of static. Then—a sharp crackle.

*"Emergency dispatch to Berg and Zimmermann—serious accident on **Johannes-Ehrling-Street**, near the **Knock** pumping station. Vehicle identified as a **BMW**. License plate confirmed: **Thomas Broder**."*

Lena's heart skipped a beat.

Her fingers clenched around the wheel.

**Thomas.**

Ice water flooded her veins.

A dull pressure spread through her chest, as if an invisible fist had closed around her heart.

Bodo turned to her, his gaze razor-sharp.

She grabbed the radio. *"Understood. ETA—three minutes.* Then she slammed her foot on the gas.

The car shot forward.

The engine roared. Tires bit into the slick road.

City lights blurred into streaked reflections as the rain turned the asphalt into a treacherous trap.

She ignored the traffic lights. The roads were empty.

Her pulse pounded louder than the engine.

When they arrived, their stomachs clenched.

The **black BMW**—Thomas' car—had slammed head-on into the stone embankment.

The rear still jutted onto the road, the front a twisted wreck.

The hood was crushed, as if struck by a giant's fist.

Cracks ran through the windshield like a shattered spider's web.

Blue lights pulsed against the wet pavement.

Firefighters and paramedics rushed around the wreckage.

A piercing screech cut through the night.

The hydraulic tool bit into the metal.

Seconds later, a medic shouted—

*"He's alive! Unconscious, but stable! We're taking him to the hospital!"*

Sterile light.

The sharp tang of disinfectant.

The monotonous beeping of machines.

Dr. **Heinemann** was already waiting. *"Ms. Berg. Mr. Zimmermann. You're here for Broder, I assume?"*

Lena nodded.

*"His condition?"* The doctor flipped through the file.

*"Traumatic brain injury. Internal damage. Critical but stable. He's in a coma. No prognosis yet."*

Bodo folded his arms. *"Anything unusual?"*

A pause.

Then Heinemann slid the file across the table.

*"There is… one thing."*

Lena's eyes scanned the report.

Then— She froze. Blood values.

**Irregularities.**

Her pulse kicked up.

*"What's this?"*

The doctor exhaled.

*"We found traces of nitroglycerin in his blood."*

**Silence.**

Bodo stepped closer. *"Which means—this was an execution attempt."*

Lena pressed her lips together. Suddenly, everything made sense.

The 'accident' had been staged.

Someone had ensured Broder left police custody—

Only to eliminate him.

*"Can I see him?"*

*"Briefly."*

The rhythmic beeping of the heart monitor was like a slow countdown.

Thomas lay pale, tubes running from his body. For a moment, Lena didn't see **him**.

She saw—

**Bodo.**

Memories surged.

His face, pale. Machines. Sterile light.

The moment she thought she would lose him. The helplessness. The fear.

A feeling that had nearly broken her back then.

Now, it washed over her again. Her fingers dug into her
jacket.

She inhaled sharply.

Forced herself back into the present.

Bodo's hand rested on her shoulder.

*"Lena?"*

She nodded, slowly.

Her voice barely above a whisper.

*"For a second, I thought it was you."*

His gaze didn't waver.

*"Then we'd better listen."*

# Chapter 33

The rain lashed against the meeting room windows, hammering with relentless fury, as if trying to erase the shadows of the past days. But nothing was washed away. The darkness lingered, thick and oppressive, sensing that something was terribly wrong.

Lena stood by the window, arms crossed, jaw tight. Her stomach was a clenched fist.

Four days. Four goddamn days.

Robin and Aniko had vanished—and they had nothing. Every lead slipped through their fingers like raindrops on a windshield.

A fist slammed against the table.

The wood shuddered, the sound rippling through the heavy silence.

"Bloody hell! What the fuck is this?" Lars' voice cut through the room like a blade—raw, sharp, desperate.

No one answered. Not because they disagreed. But because no one had an answer.

"Four days, Lena!" His eyes burned with frustration. "Four days of stumbling in the dark! I can't take it anymore! No clues, no ransom demand, nothing! What if they're already dead?"

Lena turned slowly, her gaze ice-cold. "They're not."

Her voice was steady, but inside, a storm raged. Doubt had no place here. Not now. Not ever.

Lars clenched his jaw. "And if they are? Tell me, Lena. What if we never find them?"

Silence. Thick as fog. Heavy as lead.

Then, the door creaked open.

An officer stepped inside, shaking rain from his coat. His face was grim, carved in stone.

"Lena. Lars." His voice was flat, reluctant. "I just came from the clinic."

Lena already knew what he was about to say before the words left his lips.

"Thomas Broder is dead."

The room froze.

"He succumbed to his injuries. The doctors did everything they could."

The words dropped like stones, pressing the air from the room.

No one said it. But everyone thought it.

That wasn't an accident.

Lars exhaled, rubbing his face. "Damn."

Lena's voice was too calm. Too controlled. "Forensics? Any findings?"

The officer hesitated. "For now? The injuries are consistent with a high-speed impact. But there are… irregularities."

A cold prickle ran down Lena's spine.

"What kind of irregularities?"

His lips pressed into a thin line. "I'm not allowed to speculate. But it looks like someone helped."

He didn't need to say more.

Sabotage.

Lena and Lars exchanged a glance. The doubt was gone. Someone had orchestrated Thomas Broder's death.

At the head of the table, Corinna stood rigid, her tablet clutched so tightly her knuckles had turned white.

"We have something."

All eyes snapped to her.

"Tell me," Lena said, her voice taut.

Corinna swallowed. "The vehicle's system. It wasn't tampered with on-site. The remote signal came from inside a building at the shipyard." A beat of stunned silence—then realization struck like a hammer.

Lars leaned forward. "That means our perpetrator either has direct access to the shipyard—or someone working inside does."

Corinna nodded. "And there's more."

She pushed a photograph across the table.

A metal fragment. Soot-covered. Splintered. Part of the tow hitch from the car that rammed into Broder's BMW.

Lena picked it up carefully. The jagged edge felt rough beneath her fingers. A dark stain—soot, or something worse?

"Dark SUV." Her voice was steady. "If we find the driver, we get our next lead."

Lars stared at the fragment. "That's our first solid trail to Robin and Aniko."

A pulse of raw energy surged through Lena.

"We're getting them back."

Then Corinna slid her tablet to the center of the table.

"I think you all missed something."

One sentence glowed on the screen.

**It's not over yet.**

The air thickened, the weight of those words settling like lead in Lena's chest.

A cold, unseen hand seemed to grip the back of her neck.

"Where did that come from?" Her voice cut through the room like steel.

Corinna hesitated. "It was sent to Broder's hospital computer. Exactly one hour before he died."

A slow, crawling shiver laced down Lena's spine. Then she noticed the attachment.

She clicked it.

An image appeared. Blurred. Rain-streaked.

Two figures. Behind a grimy window.

Lena inhaled sharply, her fingers tightening around the tablet as if she could pull them through the screen.

Robin and Aniko.

Lars shot to his feet. "Fuck! When was this sent?"

Corinna's voice was barely a whisper. "Two hours ago."

Lena yanked her phone from her pocket and punched in a number.

"Lars. I want the shipyard's access logs. Now."

The rain hammered down outside, cold, merciless.

But Lena didn't stop.

Someone had made a mistake. And it would be their last.

# *Chapter 34*

The pale light from the monitor reflected in Lena's tired eyes. She leaned back, massaging her temples.

Her instincts screamed.

Something was wrong.

For weeks, her team had pursued **Thomas Broder** as the mastermind behind the kidnapping of **Robin and Aniko**.

Now he was dead—

And with him, the whole puzzle fell apart.

The door opened.

**Corinna** entered, gripping a tablet tightly. Her gaze was serious, her posture tense. *"I checked his financial records again."* She hesitated briefly. *"Something doesn't add up."*

Lars and Bodo stepped closer.

Corinna turned the tablet around. A number glowed on the screen. *"Three weeks ago, a large sum was deposited into Broder's account. Shortly after, it was funneled into multiple offshore accounts."*

A pause. *"Someone was using him."* Lena's heart pounded harder.

A dull pressure tightened in her chest. *"He was a pawn."* Her voice sounded hollow.

Lars cursed under his breath. *"Damn. Then we've been chasing the wrong lead this whole time."*

The door **flew open** again. An officer rushed in—pale, tense.

Fingers gripping a **USB stick.**

*"We found something."* The **surveillance room** was dark.

Only the bluish glow of the monitors cast ghostly shadows on their faces.

Corinna inserted the stick. A file opened.

A **video**. Drone footage.

The camera glided over the **south quay**.

Abandoned harbor districts.

Rusting containers, decaying warehouses, dark, motionless water.

The moon glimmered off the damp cobblestones.

Lars' voice was barely a whisper.

*"That's the old cargo harbor. Nobody goes there anymore."* The camera panned.

Then—**movement in the darkness.** A **black SUV** rolled slowly over the cobblestones, stopping in front of an old brick hall.

Its headlights cast long shadows on the façade.

The driver's door opened. The video froze.

A **face**. Cold. Calculating. **Alexei Sorokin.**

Silence.

Absolute silence.

Lena took a slow, deep breath.

Her fingers tightened on the armrest. *"If Sorokin is here, it's not without reason."*

Bodo leaned forward, eyes locked onto the screen.

*"That's our best lead. We have to go there."*

Corinna rewound the footage. Zoomed in. The SUV appeared several times—briefly, never for long.

Two men **secured the hall**.

**Armed.** Then—

A **figure** emerged from the building. Out of focus.

Barely recognizable. But Lena **knew.**

She **felt** it. Her heart **stopped.**

*"That's Aniko."*

A shiver raced down her spine. Her stomach clenched.

**Robin and Aniko were there.** They had to be.

Lars pointed at the screen.

*"Here. The old entrance to the sewer system. That could be our way in."*

Bodo nodded.

*"If they're still alive, they're in the basement. That's where they keep hostages."*

Lena stared at the image. **Was this the place?** Or a **trap**?

One wrong move— And they'd walk straight into their own deaths.

She reached for her phone. Her voice was steady.

*"We need to make Sorokin believe we're looking elsewhere. Lure him out."*

Bodo smirked wryly.

*"Drive him into a trap—while we go in from behind."*

Lars frowned. *"If we screw this up—"*

Lena **cut him off**.

Her eyes **burned** with determination.

*"Then that's it."* Nobody argued. They all knew—

**This was their only shot.**

Lars left the room.

Made a call. Minutes dragged like hours.

Then—he returned.

His face, **hard as stone**.

*"Green light. But we have exactly one time window."*

Lena met Bodo's gaze.

Outside, rain lashed against the windows.

The **night was waiting.**

It was time.

# Chapter 35

The dungeon was a crypt of darkness and cold. Moldy dampness clung to the walls, seeping through the cracks, wrapping around Robin and Aniko like a second skin. The heavy stench of wet concrete, rust, and decay filled the air, suffocating, inescapable.

Robin sat with his back pressed against the rough stone.

His wrists burned—the shackles had torn into his skin.

Every breath ached, every movement scraped at the open wounds.

Somewhere in the darkness, Aniko's steady breathing cut through the void—quiet, controlled.

A defiant sign that she was still there.

Then— Footsteps. Voices. Upstairs, in the warehouse, a heated argument echoed through the beams.

*"We can't keep her here any longer!"*

A man's voice, sharp, panicked. An animal cornered.

*"It's the cops' turn now!"* Another voice followed. Calm. Dark. Dangerous.

*"Sorokin wants them alive."* A pause. *"For now."* A sickening thud. Something heavy slammed against wood.

Robin inhaled sharply. *"What if they talk? If they identify us?"*

Aniko held her breath.

Robin felt her shift—instinctive, like she could dissolve into the darkness. But there was nowhere to hide.

Only walls.

Only cold.

Only fear.

Then— The door flew open. Metal groaned as the heavy hinges gave way. A narrow blade of light slashed through the darkness, blinding Robin.

Tears burned in his eyes. Two men. Silhouettes against the harsh glow. One of them held a torch, its beam stabbing into Robin's pupils like a red-hot needle.

Robin squinted. Blinked. Showed nothing.

No pain.

No fear.

*"Get up."* Robin didn't move. A fatal second passed. *"I said—get up!"*

A hand grabbed his collar, yanking him upward. Pain ripped through his shoulders like shattered glass tearing into his muscles.

Then—the second man moved.

Silent. Calculated.

A knife flashed in the light. Cold. Precise. Deadly.

*"If your friends get too close, you're dead."*

His voice was smooth as glass. Cool. Emotionless. Final. Robin tensed. *"Leave her alone."* The man didn't even glance at him.

Instead—

He pulled out a phone and held it out to Aniko. *"Tell them it's fine. Tell them to stop looking."* Aniko didn't move. Her eyes met Robin's. A silent exchange.

A desperate understanding. They could do nothing— But they could guide.

*"Do it!"*

The knife pressed closer to her skin. Aniko inhaled. Slowly. Controlled.

Then— Like flipping a switch—

Her voice turned cold. Empty. Hollow. *"Lars… stop looking. It's no use."*

The kidnapper smiled. Sharp. Unsettling. He ended the call. The door slammed.

Darkness remained. Aniko slumped against the wall. Her breathing hitched.

Her body trembled— Not from fear— But from sheer tension.

Robin clenched his teeth.

*"We can't give up."* A silent nod. They both knew. They had spoken—

But Lars wasn't stupid. He knew Aniko's voice.

Her tone. He would know something was wrong.

But— Would he realize it in time? Robin's fists tightened.

Time was running out. And the next mistake— Would be their last.

The dungeon smelled of damp stone and death.

The wet walls swallowed every breath.Robin sat in a shadowed corner—but instead of remaining still, he pressed inconspicuously against the shackles, testing their give.

His gaze—hardened by pain, sharpened by defiance. Aniko lay beside him, her face torn between fear and resolve. Her eyes flickered— With terror. With unyielding will.

Then—

The door burst open. Two men stepped inside— Bringing the weight of danger with them. One grabbed Robin's collar. Pain flared, but he held still. The second man moved toward Aniko.

A phone in his grip. His gaze cold. Demanding.

*"Aniko. Speak."*

For an agonizing moment, time froze. A storm raged in her mind. Fear. Doubt. The desperate urge to protect the truth. One wrong word— Could mean death. Then— A voice crackled through the speaker.

Sorokin.

*"Aniko, I expect a clear answer. Where are the diaries? Or should I ask where Heinrich Broder is hiding?"* A cold shiver slithered down her spine. This wasn't just a demand. It was a death sentence. Her voice shook.

*"I… I know they're in the old archives. But I can't tell you exactly where…"* The words barely left her lips before— Sorokin's voice cut like a blade.

*"Your words alone aren't enough, Aniko. Show me proof. Or I'll make sure you and that pesky Robin pay the ultimate price."* The man beside Aniko grabbed Robin's shoulder— His grip brutal. A silent warning. Not just words. Pain.

Robin's eyes narrowed. A silent promise passed between them. We won't go down without a fight.

Aniko's inner conflict raged. Her voice trembled. *"I… I'll tell you. But you must promise—Robin stays alive."*

A low chuckle. Cold. Merciless. *"Your promises mean nothing, Aniko."*

*"Your words are your fate."*

*"One mistake—"*

*"And your world will sink into darkness."*

The tension snapped tight. Robin's fingers worked against the chains, subtle, determined. Each heartbeat— Each glance— Carried the weight of their fate.

The shadows pressed closer, thick and suffocating. As if they knew— That one second could change everything.

And Aniko's next words—

Would seal their destiny.

# Chapter 36

Lena felt her heartbeat quicken as Lars picked up the vibrating phone from the table. Unknown number. Her stomach knotted. Every call was crucial now—each one a potential turning point. But this one was different. It carried a weight that made the air in the office feel heavier, as if they were standing on the edge of something dark and inevitable.

Lars answered. A moment of silence. Then a voice.

"Lars... stop looking. It's no use."

Lena froze. Aniko.

But something was wrong. Her voice was too flat, too measured. Stripped of fear, stripped of anything real. Like an echo of herself, a version forced into existence by something—or someone—else.

Lars tried again. "Aniko?"

No answer. Just a quiet click. The line was dead.

For a moment, no one moved. The silence in the office thickened, pressing against them, stretching unbearably. It wasn't just the absence of sound—it was the weight of all the possibilities that came with it. Eyes turned to Lars, as if willing him to make sense of it.

Lena was the first to speak. "That wasn't her." Her voice was sharper than she intended, cutting through the tension.

Jan Müller frowned. "It was her voice."

"Yes, but not her." Lena's mind was racing, fitting pieces together at breakneck speed. "She was forced. Aniko is strong. She wouldn't sound like that unless she had no choice."

Lars exhaled slowly, rubbing his temple. "Robin didn't say anything."

Lena turned to him, the realization sinking in like cold steel. "Exactly. And that means?"

Lars' eyes darkened. "He kept quiet on purpose. Could be a sign."

Jan scratched his head. "I'll check the recording for background noise."

Lena clenched her fists. Every damn detail mattered now. Life or death was balancing on the edge of something fragile—something they might not see until it was too late.

While Jan worked, Lena moved to the window. The darkness outside felt alive, pressing against the glass. The harbor of Emden stretched beneath the cold glow of streetlights, the water barely stirring. Somewhere out there, Robin and Aniko were waiting. Fighting. Holding on. How much longer could they?

A keyboard clicked behind her. Jan turned. "Got something. Metallic echo. High ceilings. Large space."

"Warehouse?" Lars asked.

Jan nodded. "Listen to this."

He replayed the recording. A muffled humming. Then a metallic squeak.

Lena's stomach twisted. That sound. She knew that sound.

"A crane," she said, her voice barely above a whisper.

Jan's head snapped up. "Yes. And if we cross-reference with radio cell locations…"

His fingers flew over the keyboard, tension thick in the air. A map flickered onto the monitor.

"Here," he said, pointing. "An abandoned shipyard. Hasn't been operational for ten years."

Lars stepped in closer, jaw tightening. "Damn, that fits."

Bodo Zimmermann folded his arms. "Or it's a trap."

Lena's pulse pounded in her ears. Sorokin wasn't careless. If this was intentional, he wanted them there. He wanted control. He wanted to dictate the game.

But what if they did nothing? What if they hesitated too long?

She took a deep breath. The room was buzzing with tension, voices overlapping. Options were thrown into the air, weighed, dissected. Every plan had consequences, and none of them were safe.

"We need confirmation before we move in," Jan said firmly.

"I'll send a drone," Lena decided. Her fingers were steady as she issued the command, but her mind was already running through the scenarios:

- If they hesitated too long, Aniko and Robin would be dead.
- If they rushed in blindly, they'd walk into Sorokin's trap.
- If the lead was wrong, they'd lose precious time.

No perfect choices. No guarantees. Just risk and instinct.

The drone feed flickered onto the screen.

"There," Jan said, zooming in. Two vehicles. A van and an SUV.

"Any light sources inside?" Lars' voice was razor-sharp.

"No. But thermal imaging shows three people."

Lena narrowed her eyes. "We're looking for two."

Bodo's expression hardened. "One of them could be a guard."

"Or an interrogator," Lars muttered. The thought made Lena's stomach turn.

This was their best lead.

"Does the Swart Team confirm the footage?" Lars asked, turning to an officer speaking into his radio.

"Not fully, but it matches the pattern."

Lena exhaled. The time for second-guessing was over.

"We need to move," she said. "But controlled. No chaos."

Tactical plan:

- Silent entry from the rear.
- Swart Team with snipers for overwatch.
- A concealed unit ready for distraction if needed.

Lars ran a hand over his face. "If we mess this up, they're dead."

Lena met his gaze. "We won't." Then the radio crackled.

A distorted, barely-there signal. A voice. "Here… Ahlers…" Lena's breath caught.

Jan turned, eyes wide. "Robin?!" More static. A second of dead air.

Then nothing.

Lena's hands clenched so tightly her nails dug into her palms. "That was proof," she whispered.

Lars grabbed his radio. His voice was steel. "We go in. Now."

*Chapter 37*

The meeting room at the Emden police Department lay in oppressive silence. Only the soft humming of the neon lights broke the silence, as if they were the last people who dared to make a noise. The air was stuffy, charged with unspoken tension - as if the next word hung over life and death.

Lars Lammers stood at the head of the table, his arms folded and his jaw muscles tense. His rolled-up sleeves betrayed a latent impatience. Everyone in the room knew that he would love to throw himself into this mission. His eyes were fixed on the radio in the centre of the table. Silent. Dead. Without any signal.

Robin's last radio message was exactly thirty minutes ago.

Thirty minutes in which the world could fall apart. Thirty minutes in which two people were perhaps already fighting for survival.

Jan Müller sat in front of his laptop, his fingers flitting across the keyboard. Drone footage flickered on the screen in cool black and white, pixelated heat signatures flickered on the display.

"Three people inside," he said with mechanical precision. His voice was calm, but the glint in his eyes betrayed the tension. "Two close together. One distant. No movement outside."

Lena Berg leant forward, her brow furrowed. "No backup?" Jan shook her head. "Not visible."

Lars inhaled deeply, exhaled slowly. Time was slipping through their fingers like sand. Waiting was not an option.

"If we don't strike now, we'll lose them," he said. Nobody disagreed.

Lars' fingers ran over the map spread out on the table. The situation was clear: a warehouse, a limited escape area, a hint of opportunity.

**The plan was brutally simple.**

- Enter via the rear entrance. The Swart Team silently gains access to the hall.
- Snipers by the water. No suspect leaves the area.
- Blocking the escape routes. The vehicles are positioned in such a way that there is no escape.
- No negotiation. Hesitation could cost two lives.

Lars drew a line across the map with a red pen.

"We secure the area before we go in. Nobody fires unless it's absolutely necessary."

Lena looked at him. Her voice was quiet, a shadow of doubt in it.

"What if they use Robin or Aniko as shields?"

A moment of silence. Lars' jaw ground, the tension in his shoulders increased. A dark shadow flitted across his features. "Then we improvise."

Nobody asked for a plan B.

The convoy of emergency vehicles moved silently through Emden. No sirens. No flashing blue lights. Only the quiet, menacing hum of the engines echoed through the streets.

Lena sat in the passenger seat next to Lars, her fingers closed around the radio. Her gaze wandered over the sleeping city. She lay there peacefully, enveloped in the glow of the streetlights. Cobblestones glistened damply in the light. Behind closed shutters, people breathed quietly in their beds while two of them fought for their lives.

The old town hall towered darkly into the sky. On the Delft, the lantern lights were reflected on the still surface of the water. In the boats, masts creaked softly in the wind, while the smell of salt water and old oil impregnated the air. Lars turned down the dashboard light, plunging the interior into darkness.

"Do you remember our first observation in the shipyard?" he asked quietly. Lena nodded barely perceptibly, her voice a breath.

"Yes. It was routine back then."

Lars' gaze remained fixed on the road.

"Not any more." The dark outlines of the shipyard cranes rose on the   horizon. The halls drew closer, silent witnesses to the last minutes before all hell would break loose.

Swart Team officers scurried through the shadows, weapons unlocked, helmets pulled low over their faces.

Black silhouettes, part of the night, ready for what was to come. Lena got out of the car. The cool breeze from the harbour carried the smell of tar, rust and salt water. The ground beneath her boots was damp. The fog that crept over the area made the darkness thicker, more piercing. Lars stepped up beside her, his gaze fixed on the warehouse. The door was still locked.

Too quiet. Too quiet.

A shadow moved behind a window. A short, noisy sound from the radio. Distorted. Almost unintelligible. Robin's voice. "Don't..."

Then a muffled sound. Silence. Lena felt her heart skip a beat. A Swart commander approached her, radio in hand.

"All units ready."

His voice was calm, but the seriousness of the situation was written in his eyes.

"Your signal decides."

Lena closed her eyes for a moment. Robin. Aniko. Hang in there. Then she opened them again. Her gaze was clear. Her voice firm. "Access."

# Chapter 38

The night lay like a leaden veil over the site. Only the muffled sound of boots on wet tarmac broke the silence. Not a superfluous word. Not a single breath too many. Everyone knew what was at stake.

Lars lay flat on the ground, night-vision goggles pressed against his eyes. Three silhouettes glowed green on the display.

Two close together. The third—a little apart.

Robin. Aniko. Their guard.

Lena knelt beside Lars, her fingers wrapped around the cold steel of her gun.

Her heart pounded, but her hands stayed steady.

Precision.

Control.

No room for mistakes. A quiet crackle in the radio.

*"Snipers in position."*

*"Swart Team ready. Awaiting your command."*

Lars inhaled. The world held its breath.

Seconds stretched into eternity.

Then— *"Go."*

Shadows broke loose from the darkness.

Two groups—

One at the rear entrance. The other, ready to storm through the front. Then the night exploded. A deafening bang. Wood splintered. Metal groaned.

The battering ram tore the door apart, sending a shock-wave through the silence.

Chaos erupted.

Gunfire.

Muzzle flashes ripped through the darkness, shadows twitching like ghosts against the walls.

*"Cover!"*

Lena threw herself behind a crate, the rough wood biting into her shoulder. Her tablet screen flickered, the display shifting with her rapid movements. Three figures. Then—

A scream. Sharp as a scalpel through the noise. Robin.

Adrenaline exploded in her veins. She jumped up—
Ignoring the shouts behind her.

Three dark figures. A man raised his arm— A brief glint
of metal.

*"Stun grenade!"*

Lena shielded her face with her arm.

Then—

A dazzling flash.

A clap of thunder.

The shockwave ripped through the hall, rattling steel
girders like a dying beast. She lost her balance. The floor
rushed toward her— A dull impact.

Someone groaned.

Lena blinked, fighting against the searing white in her vision. Her ears rang, the world muffled.

Then—

She saw him. Robin. He lay sprawled on the ground,
clutching a crate. Dark splashes dripped onto the concrete.

Blood.

Lena gasped for air. Her body reacted before her mind did. She pushed herself up— A movement above Robin.

A gun pressed against his temple. *"Back off, or he dies!"* Lena's gun snapped up. Her voice, cold as steel.

*"Let him go."*

The kidnapper froze. His finger trembled on the trigger.

His eyes flickered—panic creeping in. A shadow moved at the edge of Lena's vision. A Swart Team operative—

Silent. Calculating.

Closing in.

The kidnapper knew it was over. His breath hitched. Then— A sudden decision. A jerk. A turn.

He ran.

*"Stop!"*

Lena sprinted forward. A shot cracked through the night. The sniper fired. The bullet whistled through the darkness— A metallic clang.

Sparks flew.

The kidnapper dove sideways. Not dead. Not hit.

Instead— He twisted, disappearing into the labyrinth of containers.

Lena cursed. He was fast. Ducking, weaving, vanishing into the maze of stacked steel crates and shipping containers. Shadows swallowed him whole. Footsteps echoed between the metal walls, bouncing in unpredictable directions.

A ghost slipping through the cracks. Lars' voice cut through the comms.

*"We need eyes on him!"*

*"Thermals can't track him through this maze!"* someone snapped.

*"Get the drone back up!"*

*"Too slow—he's already disappearing!"*

Lena skidded to a stop, her chest rising and falling hard. The sound of distant sirens drifted through the air. But the kidnapper was gone. For now.
Behind her—

Robin gasped. Lena turned. He sank to his knees, one hand pressed against his side.

Blood stained his shirt dark red. His voice—hoarse, broken.

*"Aniko…?"* *"Here."* Aniko stood at the edge of the hall, her hands still bound. Her eyes—wide, filled with unspoken emotions.

Lena yanked the key from her pocket, the handcuffs falling away in a sharp metallic clatter.

*"It's over."*

A lie.

The air still vibrated with tension. Gunpowder. Sweat. Fear. It hung thick in the room, pressing down on them.

Then—

A soft noise. Lars turned sharply. His gaze locked onto the floor.

A gleam in the dust. He bent down, picked it up. Turned it between his fingers.

Lena stepped closer.

*"What is that?"*

Lars' jaw clenched. *"A sign from Sorokin."* Lena's breath caught. He was still here.

And it was far from over.

# *Chapter 39*

Lena could still see it— Robin. Motionless on the floor. His shirt soaked in blood. His breathing shallow. Pain-clouded eyes, flickering on the edge of consciousness.

And Aniko—

Kneeling beside him, hands pressed against his chest, desperately trying to stop the flow of blood. Not a sound had escaped her lips. A silence heavier than any scream. Lena closed her eyes, rubbing her temples.

She couldn't let go of the image. Because she knew—if they lost Robin— They would lose Aniko too. Now— She sat alone in her dark flat. A glass of water stood on the table. Untouched. The night had kept her awake— Thoughts. Guilt. The gnawing fear that nothing would ever be the same.

Bodo was there. Of course he was. Leaning in the doorway, arms crossed, brow furrowed. His gaze rested on her— Not demanding. Just watching.

*"Have you spoken to her?"*

His voice was quiet. Lena shook her head. Bodo sighed.

*"She was with him all night,"* he said finally.

*"I was there briefly. She just sat there. Didn't say anything. Didn't sleep."*

Lena exhaled slowly. *"He's everything to her,"* she murmured. Bodo nodded. *"Yes."*

Silence.

A dangerous silence.

*"What if she stops talking?"* whispered Lena. Bodo stepped closer, his hand warm on her shoulder. *"Then we get her back."*

06:30 a.m. – Hospital

The pungent stench of disinfectant stung her nose. The bitter ghost of stale coffee lingered in the air. Cold steel. Pale neon light. A world that existed between life and death. Aniko sat next to Robin's bed. Arms wrapped around her body. Muscles tense. Neck painfully stiff. But none of that mattered.

Because— He is alive. That single thought had carried her through the night. But deep down— She knew. It wasn't over. What if—She had been too late? What if— Robin hadn't made it to the hospital in time?

What if— She hadn't reacted quickly enough? She hadn't cried. Not because she couldn't— But because she didn't know what came next.

The door opened. Lena stepped in. Aniko blinked. Slowly, she unfolded her arms. Her body felt strange—as if she hadn't moved in hours. *"What happens next?"* she asked, voice barely above a whisper.

Lena studied her. *"Robin will recover. But..."* She hesitated. Aniko felt it instantly.

*"What's wrong?"*

Lena exhaled. *"Thomas Broder is dead."*

Silence.

A sharp, cutting silence. Aniko's stomach clenched. The air in the room felt thinner.

Dead. She knew Thomas was involved in something dangerous.

But— Dead?

Her fingers tightened on the chair's edge.

*"How?"*

Lena sat down on the edge of the bed. *"*

*Tampering with the car. We suspect it was Sorokin."*

Sorokin. A shiver ran down Aniko's spine. Five days in captivity. The musty scent of the cellar. The voices.

*"Everything ends in the shadow."* She swallowed.

She ignored the trembling in her fingers. Her eyes locked onto Lena.

*"What happens to me now?"*

A brittle voice. She glanced at Robin. Then back at Lena.

*"My job... the shipyard... what do I do now?"*

Lena's gaze was serious.

*"Aniko... you can't go back to your old life."* Aniko's chest tightened.

*"What?"*

*"It's too dangerous. Sorokin has already killed once. We don't know if he's looking for you."*

*"But... my home, my job—"*

*"We're taking you to a safe house."*

The color drained from Aniko's face. *"I'm... supposed to go into hiding?"*

Lena nodded. *"At least for a while."*

Aniko shook her head slowly. This couldn't be true. She wouldn't be locked up.

Not in some strange apartment, under a false name, with a new address.

*"No..."*

*"It's the only way to protect you."*

Aniko's breathing quickened. Then— *"I have something else."* A whisper.

*"I saw Sorokin at Thomas's before the kidnapping."*

Lena froze. *"Are you sure?"*

Aniko nodded.

*"Yes. He was there—just before I finished work. And he wasn't alone."*

Lena leaned in. *"Who was with him?"*

Aniko swallowed. *"A woman."*

Lena and Aniko locked eyes.

*"Did you see her face?"*

Aniko shook her head. *"No. She was in the passenger seat. Just a shadow. But I know it was a woman."*

Lena's mind raced. A woman. Who? Why? Then—

*"And there's something else."* Lena's gaze snapped to Aniko. *"I overheard Sorokin say something about the Great Sea."*

Aniko hesitated.

*"A hiding place."*

Lena exchanged a look with Bodo, who had just stepped through the door. Bodo's voice was low. *"That could be our next lead."*

Lena nodded slowly. A hiding place. A woman in a car. And Sorokin. The puzzle wasn't complete yet. But the pieces were falling into place.

07:45 a.m. – Emden Criminal Investigation Department

Lena and Bodo entered the station. Aniko wasn't there. She was already in the safe house. She had no choice. And she knew it was the right thing to do.

But— It felt like being robbed of air.Lars threw a folder onto the table.

*"We've got Sorokin on drone footage."*

A grainy image appeared. A shadow, disappearing from a warehouse.

*"That's Sorokin,"* Bodo said quietly. Jan clicked further. Another image.

A crumpled piece of paper. Smeared with blood. Lena leaned in.

***"Everything ends in shadow."***

Below it— A signature.

Lena closed her eyes. Sorokin had killed Thomas. But why?

Bodo exhaled sharply.

*"So… we're going to the Great Sea next."*

Lars nodded grimly.

Lena set her jaw.

*"Then we have to beat him to it."*

# *Chapter 40*

The Presidium lay in eerie silence. Only the soft hum of the neon lights broke through the darkness, their cold light cutting sharp contours into the room. Outside, the rain lashed against the windows, a monotonous rhythm that dug deep into Lena's thoughts.

She sat alone at her desk, surrounded by a chaos of files, notes and yellowed pieces of evidence. The heavy smell of paper dust mingled with the stale vapour of old cigarettes. A thick folder lay in front of her. A monument of facts and figures. A trail that seemed to contain a single, incontrovertible truth.

**Thomas Broder. Main suspect.**

His death had shaken her. The manipulation of his vehicle - precise, merciless, final - had wiped him out within seconds. But there was something. A nagging feeling, a detail that left her no peace.

Her eyes travelled over the pages. Then she paused.

A tiny detail. Barely perceptible. And yet - a discrepancy.

One letter. **K.**

Again and again he appeared. Interwoven into the financial transactions, inconspicuous, hardly worth mentioning. And yet now, at this moment, it was impossible to overlook. Next to it, a name that lay like a dark shadow over the entire investigation.

**Sorokin.**

Lena's heartbeat accelerated. Had they been wrong? Had they thought Thomas Broder was the culprit, even though he was just a puppet?

The door opened.

Bodo entered, placed a folder in front of her and slowly sat down opposite her. His gaze was watchful, appraising.

"I've looked through the financial data and the surveillance footage again," he said quietly. "A few things don't add up. Thomas wasn't a mastermind, Lena. He was a victim."

The words echoed. She reached for her notes, flicking through them hastily. Her fingers glided over the entries.

**K.** The flow of money. Heinrich Broder's yellowed diary.

The pieces of the puzzle fell into place.

She raised her head. Her eyes met Bodo's. **"Karin Broder."**

He froze for a moment. Then he nodded slowly.

"She manipulated us," said Lena. Her voice sounded calm, but anger was flaring up inside her. "The supposed ignorance, the targeted clues - she steered us. She wanted us to suspect Thomas."

Bodo pulled the diary towards him and leafed through it. His brow furrowed.

"Here." He tapped a line.

"Just a small cog in a much bigger wheel..." Lena felt the hairs on the back of her neck stand up.

A shadow flitted across the glass wall of the office. Someone was moving outside - quietly, unobtrusively. Lena paused. Her fingers closed tighter around the file. Then she slammed it shut with a determined bang.

"We have a new focus,"

she said, her voice firm, unwavering. "We're no longer looking for evidence against Thomas. We're looking for the truth. About Sorokin. About Karin. And about what Heinrich Broder wanted to tell us with his last breath."

Bodo straightened up. "Then let's get started."

Outside, the rain beat against the windows as if applauding what was to come.

The rules changed that night. And Lena Berg was ready to drag the truth into the light - no matter what the cost.

## *Chapter 41*

The air in the office was stuffy, impregnated with the stale smell of old files, printer ink and cold coffee. Neon lights hummed softly, their pale light covering the solid oak table like a veil. Scattered on it: printouts, notes, yellowed photographs - fragments of a puzzle that was finally coming together at this moment.

Lena, Lars, Bodo and Jan sat round the table in silence. Everyone was lost in thought. But this time it was different. This time they had reached the turning point . The key was right in front of them.

A coincidence - or perhaps not - had led them to question Sebastian Broder again. At first he had lied, claiming not to have any notes from his father. But when Lena had shown him the photo of the handwriting, it had been over. The mask had fallen.

His fingers had trembled slightly as he led her into his workshop. The smell of fresh wood and machine oil was in the air, sharp and unmistakable. The heavy equipment stood still, but it wasn't the silence that made him nervous. It was what was hidden behind an inconspicuous wall.

A panel so perfectly fitted that it was barely noticeable. A soft crack. A narrow niche opened up. And there, between wood shavings and dusty spare parts, they lay. Eleven books. Bound in dark, almost  Black leather. The corners are chipped, the paper yellowed. Witnesses to a past that should be buried with all its might.

Now they lay on the table in front of Lena. She stroked the worn cover with her fingertips, feeling the weight of the years, the secrets. When she opened the first page, she was struck by a musty odour. Heinrich Broder's handwriting was meticulously precise, faded in places, but still legible.

She began to read.

"Control of the shipyard is slipping away from me. The shadows reach further than I thought. I have been made to understand that resistance is futile. I see their faces, but their names remain hidden. Sorokin ..."

An icy shiver ran down her spine. This wasn't a diary. It was a legacy.

Jan had already started scanning the pages. The gentle humming of his laptop broke the tense silence. Lars leant forward, stroking the notes with his fingertips as if he could extract the truth from them. Then he paused.

"Thomas - the little middleman. Just a cog in the wheel. The real threads come together somewhere else." Lena frowned. For weeks they had thought Thomas was the mastermind. But what if they had been looking in the wrong direction from the start?

Then she discovered it.

On the edge of a page, almost invisible: a scribble.

One name.

**Karin.**

A symbol next to it. A stylised feather.

Lars' face hardened. He exhaled audibly. "The feather..." he muttered. "Damn it. I knew I'd seen it somewhere."

He stood up, pulled a folder from the table and hastily flicked through the pages. Then - a yellowed photo. An old note. The symbol in the corner. The pen.

Lena held her breath. She had seen it before. It appeared again and again in connection with Sorokin. But this time it was next to Karin's name.

"That can't be."

But it could. And it changed everything.

Lars' expression darkened. "So we had the wrong focus then," he said harshly. "We were concentrating on Thomas, but Karin ... she was at the centre the whole time."

Lena turned the pages. Heinrich Broder had noted with frightening accuracy how the money flowed into the shipyard, how control was slowly slipping away. How Thomas was drawn into a game that was bigger than he had ever understood.

And how someone was pulling the strings in the back-ground. Someone who was far more powerful than Thomas. Bodo leant forwards, his eyes resting on a column of numbers. "These sums..." he said quietly. "This isn't a business for one person. This is much bigger."

Lars nodded slowly, his voice sounding sharper. More determined. "We thought Thomas was the head. But what if he was just a piece on the chessboard?" Lena's gaze flew over the lines. Then she got stuck.

A date. One day before Heinrich Broder's disappearance.

"I looked away for too long. The signs were there, but I didn't want to see them.  Karin was there when Sorokin arrived. I saw her. I heard her words. And I know now that I know too much."

Lena placed a hand on the yellowed paper. That was the reason why Heinrich Broder had to die.

Jan was already typing on his laptop. "I'm comparing the financial flows with the old surveillance data.  When we find out where the money went, we'll finally have proof."

Lars stepped up to the whiteboard. His fingers tapped on a picture of Karin Broder. "Then it's time to tear up the net."

**Silence.** Everyone in the room knew that there was no way back from now on.

# Chapter 42

Dusk settled over the Great Sea like a dark veil. The tranquil lake near Emden lay motionless, as if holding its breath. The deserted holiday homes stood on the shore, pale and lifeless, shadows of summers past. The last rays of sunlight struggled in vain against the gathering mist. Their reflections twitched on the surface of the water, distorted, restless - as if the water itself was resisting the impending darkness.

Seagulls screeched in the distance. Their call was lost in the gloom, swallowed up by the night. The clapping of the waves against the jetty sounded like a secret confession that no one was allowed to hear.

Karin Broder stood in the doorway of a remote holiday home. She wrapped her arms around her body as if she could ward off the cold. But it wasn't the wind that made her shiver. Her breathing was shallow and her fingers were trembling almost imperceptibly. The musty smell of the damp wooden beams mingled with a note that her stomach recognised before her mind did.

**Cigar smoke.**

It was as if someone had preserved the past in these walls. A sound in her head - the creaking of old floorboards, her father, irritable, impatient. Then a dull thud. A rattle. Silence. A  engine noise snapped her back to the present. Slowly, far too controlled to be accidental.  A black car glided silently along the narrow street, stopping right in front of the house. The door opened - frighteningly gently.

**Alexei Sorokin.**

Karin froze. Adrenalin shot into her stomach, choking off her breath. She had known he would come. But not so quickly. Not so silently.

He got out of the car. Calm, controlled. His coat immaculate, his hands deep in his pockets. His gaze was cold, but something lurked behind it - a quiet tremor, an unmistakable knowledge.

**He knew it.**

Karin forced herself to move. She walked towards him, slowly, as if each step was dragging her deeper into quicksand. Her hand searched for support, found the fabric of his coat. Her fingers clutched at it as if it were the last anchor in a world that threatened to swallow her up. "Alexei..." Her voice was barely more than a breath.

He let her be, scrutinising her motionlessly.

"I can't stay here. The CID is on my tail."

Sorokin tilted his head and gently pulled her to one side - away from the door, away from possible prying eyes.

His movements were effortless, natural.

"Calm down." His voice was quiet but unrelenting.

"You know I won't let you down."

She swallowed. The words could have been comforting. But there was something in his tone - a final, unsaid condition. Her fingers tightened around his sleeve.

"I... was there when my father died." A tremor in her voice, a break in the façade. "I could have done something. I let it happen."

Sorokin's face remained expressionless. No sympathy. No rebuke. Just a slightly raised eyebrow, as if her guilt was inconsequential.

"A conscience? Now?"

No mockery. No astonishment. Just a sober, devastating realisation.

"That won't save you, Karin."

The wind picked up, making a silver feather dance out of the beams. It tumbled, turned, fought against gravity. One last dance in the dying light of day.

Then she fell. Silently. For good.

Karin picked it up and turned it between her fingers. "See?" Her voice was brittle. "Nothing remains hidden."

Sorokin looked at her for a long time. His gaze unfathomable. Then he shook his head almost imperceptibly.

"We don't have time for omens, Karin."

His voice was harder now.

"Either you trust me - or you face your fate alone."

A sound cut through the night. **Sirens.** Close, unstoppable. Karin closed her eyes. The decision weighed heavily on her chest, pressing down on her like a wave crashing over sharp rocks.

"I trust you."  The words were little more than a whisper.

Sorokin did not wait. Without hesitation, he grabbed her hand and pulled her with him. "Then let's go. We'll get your things." They ran to the car. Karin stumbled, but caught herself at the last moment. One last glance across the water - the feather drifted away. Disappeared into the darkness.

Sorokin started the engine.

**The Broders' villa was only a few streets away.**

One last time.

Before the shadows of the past swallowed them up

# *Chapter 43*

The rain fell in heavy torrents, lashing against the tarmac and leaving silvery streaks across the windscreens of the parked cars. The darkness was heavy, oppressive, almost palpable. Streetlights cast dim light on the wet ground, but the city seemed lifeless, as if it had retreated under the force of the storm.

Katrin Broder hurried through the night, her pumps splashed in puddles, cold water splashed against her legs. She didn't feel it. Her heart was hammering in her chest, her breathing was intermittent. Every step felt like a desperate attempt to escape an inevitable catastrophe.

Sorokin was gone. No car. No message. Just silence.

He had dropped her at the crucial moment - like a worthless piece in a game that he had long since won.

With trembling fingers, she pulled her mobile phone out of her coat pocket. The number she had dialled countless times lit up in front of her. She pressed "Call" on . No dialling tone. Just emptiness.

"Damn..." The syllable evaporated in the patter of the rain.

She bit her lip, tasted copper. No time for doubt. No time for fear. There was only one way left.

With a jerk, she yanked open the door of her Audi A6, threw her bag onto the passenger seat and started the engine. The V6 roared to life with a deep rumble - a promise of power and speed. She wrenched the steering wheel round. The tyres screeched on the wet asphalt. Then she shot out into the night.

The silver-blue VW Passat Variant of the police ploughed through the pouring rain. Blue lights cut through the darkness with twitching flashes, reflecting in the rain-soaked streets like ghostly fingers of light.

Lena sat tensely in the passenger seat, her fingers clutching the radio. The windscreen wiper was working at top speed, but visibility remained miserable. Drops pattered onto the windscreen like small hammer blows, swallowing up contours and blurring the world.

Then - a movement. A shadow, far too fast.

"There, that's Katrin!"

Bodo reacted immediately, stepped on the accelerator. The Passat shot forwards. "Hold on tight."

Lena activated the radio. "Control centre, this is Berg. Suspect Katrin Broder is fleeing in a dark-coloured Audi A6 in the direction of the A31. We're in pursuit." The engine roared.

The tyres clawed into the wet asphalt. The speedometer climbed - 140. 150. 160 km/h. "She won't stop," muttered Lena.

Bodo nodded curtly. "Then we'll have to make them do it."

Katrin pressed down on the accelerator. The speedometer needle rose - 140. 160. 170. The rain lashed against the windscreen as if nature itself was trying to stop her. The tyres fought for grip, every steering impulse had to be precisely dosed.

The lights of the police car twitched in the rear-view mirror, distorted by the masses of water. "Just leave me alone!" she mouthed. No one could hear her.

With a risky manoeuvre, she pulled to the left, sped past a lorry and cut in again just in front of it. A dangerous game - one mistake and she would end up in the crash barriers.

But Bodo would not be shaken off. He knew this pattern. Panic. Desperation. The moment when the fugitive made the decisive mistake.

"She'll mess up one day," he said calmly. Lena pressed her lips together. "Or she'll have an accident."

Suddenly - a sign. village Tümmel exit - 500 metres.

Katrin knew that she couldn't stay on the motorway forever. She had to get off the major roads. Become invisible. With an abrupt jerk, she jerked the steering wheel to the right. The Audi swerved, the tyres briefly lost grip, then she caught it again. Adrenalin shot through her veins. "She's going down!" shouted Lena.

Bodo followed her, controlling the pace. The country road was narrow, lined with tall trees that bent under the storm. No street light, only darkness and the thundering rain.

Then - lights.

**A tractor. Directly in front of her.**

Katrin jerked the steering wheel round. Tyres squealed. The world was spinning. An uncontrollable undertow pulled her along.

The Audi skidded, crashed into the side of a tree, was thrown around and crashed with full force into the ditch.

A dull thud. Then silence. Only the rain filled the night. Bodo slammed on the brakes. The police car came to a halt a few metres away. Lena tore the

Open the door. Her heart pounded as she walked towards the wrecked Audi.

The engine was still running, sputtering.

The passenger door was half open. Katrin was sitting in the car. Her fingers clutched the steering wheel like a drowning man clutching a lifebuoy. Her chest rose and fell violently.Her face was pale, damp with rain and sweat. Slowly she turned her head. Her eyes were empty. Her lips quivered. Then a whisper:

**"I could have made it..."**

Lena held her gaze. "No, Katrin. That was your last mistake."

Katrin's shoulders slumped. The last remnants of resistance evaporated in the cold of the night. Bodo stepped forward and calmly pulled out the handcuffs. A soft click. A final chapter closed.

"Katrin Broder, you are under arrest." In the distance, sirens wailed through the rain. Reinforcements had arrived.

Katrin's escape was over. But Lena knew that this wasn't the end. **Sorokin was still out there.**

And he wouldn't wait.

# *Chapter 44*



*2004 Flashback*

*The ticking of the grandfather clock cut through the silence like a scalpel. Every beat vibrated through the room, precise, inescapable - like the distant rumble of an approaching storm. Heinrich Broder sat motionless at his mahogany desk. His fingertips on the cool surface while dusk fell through the window and cast shadows across his face.*

*But behind the mask of serenity, something was fermenting - a restlessness as thin as tissue paper that could tear. This table had once signified power - here he sealed contracts, moulded careers, destroyed existences. A bastion of wood and steel where he dictated the fate of others. Today it was just a silent witness to dwindling control.*

*Outside, the wind whipped across the dockyard, making rusty containers shake. The rain drummed against the windows, running down the trenches in dirty rivulets as if the ground itself were bleeding. The air was saturated with the smell of oil, metal and damp concrete.*

*There was a single sheet of paper on the desk. One name. Dmitri Sorokin. Heinrich's fingers hovered over the letters. The lump in his throat tightened. He had underestimated him, thinking for too long that he was untouchable. His wealth, his connections, his power - They had always protected him. But protection was an illusion. A soft knock shattered the silence. "Mr Broder?" Marie Hoffmann's voice was calm, but a barely*

*perceptible undertone gave her away. She had been work-
ing for him for years - loyally, discreetly. But today she
hesitated.*

*"Someone is waiting for you outside." Heinrich closed his
eyes for a moment. He knew who it was. His gaze glided
through the office - the tall filing cabinets, the models of
old ships, the large window overlooking the dock. And
the grandfather clock.*

*Unstoppable. Relentless. He rose slowly, as if he could
delay the course of events. The coat over the back of the
chair felt strange.*

*"I'll be right there."*

*He opened the door. The latch closed with a dry click.
Outside, metal walkways gleamed under the floodlights.
The few workers kept their heads down against the rain.
No one looked at him. A black BMW was parked under
one of the lorry cranes. The engine was idling. The tinted
windows concealed what was happening inside - but
Heinrich knew that his fate had long since been decided.*

*A figure stepped out of the shadows. Deliberate steps. In
no hurry. A cigarette glowed between two fingers. Then
it extinguished with a controlled kick.*

*Alexei Sorokin. His gaze was calm. Unyielding. "Hein-
rich." No question, no command. Just a quiet judgement.
"Get in."*

*Slowly, Heinrich started to move. The door of the BMW closed with a muffled click.*

*Nobody spoke during the journey. The rain beat against the roof of the car, a monotonous rhythm that became heavier. They didn't go far. Down. Deep inside the ship-yard. The corridors became narrower, colder. Pipes ran like veins through the ceiling, some dripping rusty water. The concrete beneath Heinrich's feet was cracked and damp. The large steel gate slid silently open. Darkness waited behind it. A single strip of neon flickered, casting a pale blue light onto the floor.*

*Sorokin was standing at a small metal table. Two glasses, an open bottle of cognac.*

*"Come on, Heinrich. One last drink." Broder hesitated. His gaze lingered on the amber-coloured liquid.*

*A gesture of mercy? Or a judgement? Sorokin raised his glass. "To old times." Heinrich took the glass. His fingers trembled. The cognac burned in his throat - with an af-tertaste he couldn't put his finger on. A movement in the shadows. Karin. Her gaze lowered, her shoulders tense.*

*"Karin ...?"*

*Her name barely left his lips. She looked at him. No trem-bling. No tears. Just the cold echo of a decision made long ago.*

*"You deserve it, father."*

*Sorokin nodded. Two men grabbed Heinrich and dragged him through a narrow corridor. He stumbled. The floor tilted under his feet, his body became heavy, his muscles no longer obeyed.*

*His heart was racing. Poisoning. The cognac. "Give him a few more minutes," Sorokin said. "Let him feel every-thing."*

*Karin averted her eyes. Her hands clenched into fists, but she said nothing. Heinrich's breathing became shallow. A tingling sensation ran through his limbs. Shadows danced before his eyes. The last thing he heard was the muffled scraping of stones. Mortar being pressed between joints. The world became narrow. His heart stumbled. His body grew cold.*

*Then it was dark.*

*And Heinrich Broder was gone - forever.*

# *Chapter 45*

2024

The rain fell in thick, cold veils on the Gatjebogen, making the streets gleam and the wind whip against the windows. The darkness of the early morning settled over the city like a heavy blanket, while fine wafts of mist crept over the pavements.

Inside, in the warm silence of her bungalow, Lena sat on the couch, her legs bent, her fingers tightly closed around her coffee cup. The floor lamp bathed the room in subdued light, making shadows dance across the furniture. But despite the cosiness, there was no trace of security. Her gaze was fixed on the rain-soaked windows, while her mind was already in the interrogation room.

Bodo stepped out of the kitchen, another cup of coffee in his hand. He settled silently beside her, the warmth of his body an unobtrusive sign of his    presence. They sat in silence for a moment, the distant drumming of the rain the only sound.

"Are you actually going to sleep any more?" he finally asked, his voice quiet but firm. Lena accepted the cup, a tired smile twitching around her lips. "Not tonight."

He scrutinised her for a moment, then placed a hand on hers - warm, reassuring. For just one breath. Then the touch was gone again. "Not going to be easy today."

"I know." Her eyes followed a single trail of drops running across the window glass. "Karin is not an easy opponent."

"No." Bodo leant back and ran his hand over his face. "But everyone makes a   mistake at some point." Lena nodded slowly. "And we're damn close to it." She took a deep breath, put her cup down and straightened up. Her tiredness disappeared in a determined look. "Let's get going."

Bodo returned her gaze. "Ready?"

She pulled on her jacket. "Always."

The interrogation room was a grey box made of concrete and glass, sober and cold. Here, words sounded sharper than they should. The surveillance camera on the wall flashed red - every detail, every movement was recorded.

Lars Lammers and senior public prosecutor Dr Roland Becker stood behind the tinted glass, silent observers of the impending duel. Lena pressed the button on the recording device and leant forwards. Her voice was calm, but her eyes sparkled with determination:

"Today is 15 October 2024, Chief Inspector Lena Berg and Inspector Bodo Zimmermann are present. The interrogation begins at 8:12 a.m." She let the words hang in the air for a moment,    before turning to her counterpart.

Karin Broder sat stiffly on the chair, her hands clasped together. Her gaze flitted over the empty walls, looking for orientation - or a way out. But there was none here.

"Mrs Broder, you are suspected of being involved in the killing of Heinrich Broder." Lena's voice was razor-sharp.

"You are aware of your rights . You know that this conversation is being recorded. Can you confirm that?"

Karin slowly raised her head. Her face was a mask, but something flickered in her eyes - a trace of fear? For a moment it seemed as if she was going to say something, but instead she moistened her lips while her fingers tensed. Her chest rose and fell faster than before.

"Yes."

Silence. Seconds passed. Lena's gaze remained relentlessly fixed on her.

"Why did you kill Heinrich Broder?"

A barely perceptible twitch at the corners of her mouth. Her fingers clutched at the fabric of her trousers. She opened her mouth - a reflex to deny immediately - but no words came. Her breathing became shallower, more irregular. Her shoulders slumped slightly, as if she was trying to make herself invisible.

Bodo leaned back and relaxed, his tone a hint of mockery. "Karin. Come on." His eyes bored into hers. "We have enough evidence to arrest you. The only question is: will you work with us, or will you allow yourself to be sacrificed for someone who hasn't thought about you for a long time?"

Karin flinched almost imperceptibly. Her eyes flickered as if he had hit a sore spot. Her fingernails pressed so deeply into her palms that it had to hurt.

Lena crossed her arms. "You thought you had everything under control, didn't you? But now there's no plan B. No one to get you out. Just the truth."

Karin took a deep breath, but her breath stopped halfway through. Her hands trembled slightly. She lowered her head as if she was going through all the options again before finally raising her eyes.

Bodo leant forward slightly. His voice was gentle, almost compassionate. "Then explain it to us."

A tremor ran through Karin's shoulders. Then - finally - her tension was released in a resigned sigh. Her lips quivered and her voice was barely more than a whisper as she formed the first words.

And began to speak. The interrogation room was still filled with silence, but it had a different weight.

Words had dug themselves into the walls, inescapably and definitively.

Bodo rubbed his temples. "Damn."

His voice was barely more than a whisper.

"She's in deeper than we thought."

Lena stared at the table, her stomach tightening.

"This isn't just a murder case."

Her voice was toneless.

"It's about power. Influence. And Karin isn't the end - she's just the beginning."

Lars Lammers moved behind the glass pane, his gaze hard, his jaw tense. Dr Becker spoke to him quietly, but every word seemed to put a new piece of the puzzle into the picture.

Bodo stood up slowly, crossing his arms.

"So let's start from the beginning."

Lena looked at him. "We?"

He raised a brow.

"Did you seriously think I was going to leave you alone with this crap?"

It remained silent for a moment. Then Lena took a deep breath - and a hint of a smile flitted across her lips. "Okay."

She straightened up.

"Then let's shed some light on this."

Outside, the rain continued to lash against the windows, but this time it no longer felt oppressive.

This time it signalled a new beginning.

# Chapter 46

The wind had shifted overnight. Now it was whipping in from the sea with irrepressible force, shaking the windows of the Emden police headquarters as if it wanted to shout something to the people inside - a warning, a threatening rumble. Cold rain slapped against the windows, running down in lazy sheets as if the city were weeping.

Silence reigned in the meeting room. Not one that calmed - but one that weighed heavily. The light from the neon tubes was harsh, cutting hard contours into the faces of those present, making tiredness, doubt and tension stand out even more mercilessly. The room was functional, functional - a place for facts, not for feelings. And yet there was an unspoken heaviness in the air.

On the table between them lay the truth - or at least the part of it they had snatched so far. Two black notebooks, their leather covers tanned by the years. Printouts of the latest laboratory analyses that still smelled of printer's ink. Autopsy reports that told a story on cool paper, darker than anything they had expected.

Lena let her eyes wander over the men at the table. Lars Lammers, who was usually always confident, had a deep frown on his face today. Bodo, her closest confidant and partner, sat there with his shoulders slumped, his face was as hard as chiselled. And Dr Roland Becker, the senior public prosecutor, drew two fingers across his forehead as if he could dispel the invisible pressure that was weighing on them all. Lars was the first to break the silence.

"The diaries have been almost completely analysed."

His voice was calm, but what he said caused the tension in the room to rise further.

"Entries up to 2004, the same names over and over again: Sorokin. Fedorov. Lasker. Falk. Some passages blacked out, others difficult to read - but enough to weave a web from which no one can escape."

He turned to Becker. "What does forensic medicine say?"

The senior public prosecutor hesitated. Then, with a heavy look:

"Heinrich Broder was poisoned with arsenic."

Silence.

Becker ran a hand over the back of his neck.

"The diaries confirm it. Broder wrote of a vague uneasiness, of fear. Of the feeling of being watched. He knew that someone wanted to kill him."

Lena felt her stomach tighten.

"This 'someone' often remains vague. But Sorokin's name comes up too often to believe in coincidence."

She stroked her fingers over the leather of the diary. The material felt strangely cold.

"And Karin Broder? She claims to have only been a marginal figure. But the entries show a different picture. She knew it. She knew it for a long time."

The tapping of a pencil broke the silence. Bodo held it between his fingers, letting it tap on the table in a steady rhythm while his thoughts raced. Then he raised his head.

 "The crucial question is: how do we get her to talk?"

His voice was calm, but an inner fire lurked within it.

"If we confront her head-on with the evidence, she'll shut down. We need a lever. One that she can't ignore."

Becker nodded slowly.

"So far, she's suspected of being an accessory to murder. But she's hardly admitting to anything. If we make her realise that Sorokin has long since given up on her, that she no longer means anything to him - then maybe she'll crack."

Lars opened a file, his thumb stroking a note.

"The diaries speak of a second man. Someone who operates in the shadows. If we put too much pressure on Karin, it could be dangerous for her ... and for us."

Lena remembered Karin's face from the last interrogation. The dark circles under her eyes.

The shoulders that hung low. The fear that showed in tiny twitches in the corner of her mouth - and yet there was would have been something else. Defiance. A last spark of hope that Sorokin would not drop her.

"She's clinging to a lie,"

Lena said quietly.

"Maybe he promised to protect her. Maybe she still believes it. But we both know how promises like that end."

Bodo snorted softly.

"Like this: We present her with individual passages from the diaries. Let her think we have less than we do. As long as she thinks there's a loophole, she'll try to wriggle through it - and make a mistake."

Becker leaned back.

"And if that's not enough?"

Lars closed the file in front of him.

"Then I'll issue a search warrant for her private and business documents. If we find anything else there, she'll be trapped for good."

For a moment, nobody said anything. Outside, the rain lashed against the windows. A shadow flitted across the wet street, distorted by the drops running down the window pane.

Lena massaged her temples. Tiredness crept through her thoughts, but there was no time for that now.

"We'll get everything ready. Interrogation room. Recording equipment. Mark the relevant passages. And then ... then we'll see how far Karin Broder's loyalty extends.

Dr Becker stood up. His gaze travelled over the faces in the room.

"Be careful. This case has reached a dimension that we can no longer control. There are people who would do anything to stop us."

Lars, Bodo and Lena exchanged glances. They knew it. They knew that the next step would drag them further into the abyss. But there was no way back.

Lena took a deep breath, forcing herself to make a determination she didn't quite feel.

"Go on then."

Her heart beat faster.

They had a long day ahead of them

# *Chapter 47*

The rain lashed incessantly against the barred windows of the interrogation room while the storm of the night raged outside. The rough sea was not far away, and in the gusts there was a merciless cold that crept through every crack in the old-fashioned walls of the Police Department . The neon light on the ceiling flickered briefly, as if trying to rebel against the darkness, before falling resignedly back into its sterile glow.

Lena sat motionless at the worn wooden table, her gaze as sharp as a razor blade. In front of her lay the diary bound in black leather - a relic of a dark past. The yellowed pages ducked away from the light, as if they had lain in the shadows for too long. The musty odour of old paper mingled with the acrid sterility of the disinfectant. Lena stroked the cover with her fingertips, feeling the fine grooves of the leather. A touch that was more than just a gesture. It was a silent pact with the past.

A soft breath. Then she opened the book.

Heinrich Broder's fine, almost calligraphic handwriting spread out before her like a map to a long-forgotten world.

Karin Broder sat on the other side of the table. Her eyes, framed by dark shadows, flitted unsteadily across the table. She looked like a woman fighting an enemy that only she could see.  A shadow that slowly but inexorably settled over her. Her breathing was shallow, her fingers clasped together.

Lena let the silence take effect. She knew that this was the moment - the narrow gap between lies and truth.

The interrogation room was small. A room of bare walls that became heavy over time. The confinement, the loneliness, the realisation that there was no escape here - all this gnawed at the people sitting on this side of the table. Lena knew that. She had experienced it countless times. Now was the time.

"We have everything, Mrs Broder."

Her voice was calm, razor-sharp. Karin twitched barely noticeably. A blink. A slight tremor at the left corner of her mouth.

Lena saw it.

The curtain of lies began to crumble. Outside, a gust of wind hit the window, causing the pane to shake. Lena flicked slowly through the pages. The scent of old ink and paper rose to her nose, while the

Words looked down at them like relics from another time.

Then she began to read. "29 April 2004, he knows too much. I'm afraid he'll talk. But Sorokin told me there was a solution..." Karin's breath hitched. Her hands clenched tighter. Lena gently put the book down. Her gaze lifted.

"Sorokin told you there was a solution?" A hard shake. "No... no, that... that can't be."

Her voice was tight. Not loud, not upset - too controlled. And that was the problem.

"It's your handwriting, Karin."

Silence.

Then she shook her head again, but it was no longer a firm 'no'. It was a rebellion against her own truth.

"That's not true," she whispered.

Lena took the diary and leafed through it.

"3rd May 2004, I'm scared. He forced me. If I say no, I'll be next..."

The room became narrower.

The draught from the storm beat dully against the window, an ominous pounding from the night. Karin pressed her lips together. Her fingernails scraped the wood on the edge of the table. "He forced me..." Lena repeated. "Who forced you, Karin?" Nothing.

A blink, a quiver of the eyelashes.

"We  know you knew."

Lena's voice was just a breath now, but it struck like a scalpel. Karin sucked in a sharp breath. Her gaze wandered around the room, looking for an escape, a door, a hole in the net that stretched around her.

Then, quietly: "I had no choice." A tremor in his voice.

"Everyone has a choice," Lena replied coldly.

Bodo Zimmermann folded his arms behind her. He was a rock in the surf - tall, massive, unshakeable. He saw it coming. That moment when a truth became too heavy to bear.

"He told me they were going to kill him... and that there was nothing I could do about it." Lena nodded slowly. "Who?" Karin closed her eyes as if she could wipe the answer from the world.

"Sorokin."

A word that glided through the room like a shadow.

Then - a twitch in her shoulders. A quiet sob. "And someone else. Someone I didn't know... but he was always there. In the background. He pulled the strings."

Lena's heartbeat accelerated imperceptibly. Another one. A name that had been missing. The last crack in the façade. Karin slowly raised her head. Her eyes were wide, driven by a fear that went deeper than any lie.

"I didn't kill him."

A soft whisper, bordering on madness.

"But I was watching."

Then it broke.

Lena let the silence cut like a blade. "Then tell me every-thing." A tremor, a deep breath. Then it came. The words that whipped through the room like a hammer blow.

"His son."

The night lay heavy over the city. A leaden sultriness hung in the air as Lena left the police headquarters. The rain had subsided, but the streets were still shiny and damp, as if they were reflecting what had happened. Emden seemed to be holding its breath - as if the city knew that something inevitable was approaching .

Bodo was waiting by the car. A cigarette was stuck be-tween his fingers, but he had barely taken a drag. The smoke rose in thin spirals, merging with the fog over the tarmac. When he looked at Lena, his gaze was calm – too calm. She had known him long enough to recognise that it was the calm before a storm.

"Tough night," he finally said. Lena leaned against the roof of the car, rubbing her temples with two fingers. "Yes. But we've got her. Karin was talking."

Bodo nodded slowly. "It was only a matter of time." He took one last drag and stubbed out the cigarette. "But that doesn't mean it's over."

Lena felt the pressure in her chest. She shook her head. "No. It means we have to turn over the last    stone. And that Sorokin now knows we have him."

Without another word, they got into the car. The engine roared to life with a low hum, a comforting sound in the oppressive silence. Lena let her head sink against the headrest and closed her eyes for a moment. "Drive off. Just somewhere. I need some air."

Bodo scrutinised her out of the corner of his eye, raised a brow, but didn't comment.

He slowly steered the car out of the parking space, letting the city pass them by.

The streets were almost deserted. Only a few figures emerged from under lanterns - shadows that disappeared into doorways as if they didn't want to be seen.

In the reflecting puddles, the city lights flickered like broken stars.

After a few minutes, they stopped at the quayside of the harbour. The water was still, the ships bobbed gently in the current as if they were silently waiting for something. The lights cast long reflections on the dark surface, distorted lines that dissolved with every small wave.

Lena opened the door, got out and stepped closer to the edge. The smell of salt, diesel and wet wood hit her nose - a mixture that brought back memories. It was the smell of homecoming and farewell, of beginnings and endings.

Bodo stepped up next to her and crossed his arms. "You've been thinking." Lena laughed softly. "I always do."

"Too much." She turned towards him. His dark eyes seemed even deeper in the dim lighting, as if they could swallow secrets.

"This goes deeper than we thought, Bodo. Karin has only given us part of the truth. But there's more. And Sorokin won't just disappear."

Bodo let his gaze glide over the black water. "He has nothing left to lose."

"That's what makes him so dangerous." Lena's voice was quieter than she wanted. "And that's what scares me."

He remained silent. Seconds passed, only the distant creaking of a ship could be heard. Then he placed a hand on her shoulder - a simple gesture, but one that grounded her.

"We'll get him,"

he said quietly. He didn't promise anything he couldn't keep. And that was exactly why she believed him.

Lena took a deep breath.

"Then we should prepare for it."

She turned round and walked to the car.

Bodo followed her, but when she opened the door, he stopped short, a wry smile on his lips.

"What, no spontaneous holiday? No romantic trip to Borkum?"

Lena shook her head, a small, exhausted smile playing around her lips.

"Maybe later."

She looked at him.

"We have work now."

They got back into the car. The engine hummed deeply as they drove off into the night.

Behind them, the harbour sank into darkness. Ahead lay the unknown. And the next step would decide every-thing.

# *Chapter 48*

The muffled roar of the engine echoed eerily between the warehouses as Lena Berg steered the car through the narrow alleyways of the harbour area . The smell of salt, diesel and cold metal was heavy in the air. Bodo sat next to her, silent, but his eyes kept darting into the rear-view mirror.

Then they turned up.

Two headlights, far behind. Inconspicuous at first, but Lena's instincts screamed an alarm. Her stomach tightened. As they passed the last quay, she turned abruptly to the right. Seconds later, the other car did the same.

"Bodo?" Her voice was calm, but a hint of tension vibrated in it.

He followed her gaze, his jaw grinding. "Definitely not a coincidence."

Lena forced herself to calm down. The dark-coloured car behind them kept exactly on course, as if it had clung to her. The harbour was deserted at this time of day. Only the rattling of loose metal plates and the tugging of the wind on old cranes broke the silence. A few rubbish bags sailed across the tarmac like lost ghosts.

She pressed the accelerator pedal down. The engine rumbled, vibrated under her fingertips on the steering wheel.

The pursuer stayed on. A shadow, silent, patient.

"Hold on."

Without warning, she stepped on the accelerator. The car shot forwards, the engine roared. The dark-coloured car behind them did the same. They had barely reached the narrow bridge over the city canal when their pursuer appeared beside them.

Tyres screeched.

Suddenly he pushed brutally into her lane.

"Shit!" Bodo tore himself free, clawing at the door handle.

Lena jerked the steering wheel round. The rear end swerved - just for a moment - and then she caught the car. The narrow side street in front of them was barely wider than their vehicle. The walls of the old warehouses flew menacingly close to them.

"He's not just trying to scare us," muttered Bodo.

"He wants us."

Then the next problem. A second car emerged from a side alley.

No coincidence.

Not a mistake. They had been waiting for her.

"Lena!" Bodo's voice was as sharp as a knife. Her chest tightened, her heart raced. A ditch on the left, an endless fence of rusty metal on the right. No chance of turning round.

There was only one way out.

An unsurfaced access road, littered with rubble and mud. A suicide mission.

Lena had a second. Maybe two.

Then she did the only thing she could do.

She stepped on the accelerator.

The car thundered over the gravel track, stones spraying in all directions. The rear broke away again, but she stayed on course. The first pursuer hesitated - the second did not. He stayed on, his driver was good. No amateurs.

"Lena, this is getting damn tight!" Bodo shouted, his hands cramped on the dashboard.

She ignored him. Her eyes scanned the surroundings. On the left, an old ramp that led to nowhere. On the right, a gap between two containers.

A narrow access road."Hold on!" She wrenched the steering wheel round. The car skidded through the narrow alley. Metal flashed as her side mirror grazed a brick wall.

There was a thud behind them - one of the pursuers had misjudged. A jolt went through the car as something hit it from behind, but she ignored it.

The second chaser stayed on.

Then suddenly: darkness.

Lena switched off the light.

The car rolled silently into an old loading bay, hidden between stacked containers. The engine vibrated under her hand - then she switched it off.

Seconds have passed.

Silence.

Then the low hum of the pursuers racing past them, continuing their search. Bodo was breathing heavily. His chest rose and fell rapidly. "That was damn close." Lena released her cramped fingers from the steering wheel, her pulse pounding in her ears. Then she reached for her mobile phone.

"Now we'll call Lars."

Fifteen minutes later, they pulled up in front of the police headquarters. The rain had started to fall, turning the neon light into liquid reflections on the tarmac. The smell of wet concrete and petrol was in the air.

Lars Lammers was already waiting at the entrance, his brow furrowed .

"You look like you've been through hell."

"That's more or less how it feels,"

Lena replied dryly, brushing a damp strand of hair from her face with a trembling hand.

Lars took a look at the damaged side of the vehicle.

"View of the drivers?" Bodo shook his head.

"Tinted windows. They lured us into the trap, but we managed to get away."

Lars nodded.

"I'll have patrols look for the cars. But you should go home and get some rest. We'll sort it out tomorrow."

Lena exchanged a look with Bodo. They both knew they wouldn't get any rest.

But for the moment, the hunt was over.

# Chapter 49

The autumn evening lay over Constantia like a protective blanket. A fine mist hovered over the canals, bathing the modern detached houses in diffuse twilight. Street lamps cast golden flickers on the wet pavement, while the wind blew scattered leaves along the pavements. No rain - as if Emden was holding its breath.

As if the city knew that this was no ordinary evening.

Lena leaned exhausted against the doorframe of her bungalow. The cold had eaten deep into her limbs, the operation on the south quay and the interrogation had drained her. She took a deep breath, feeling the tension slowly easing.

Someone moved silently behind her.

"Heavy thoughts?"

Bodo's voice - deep, familiar, an anchor in her stormy everyday life.

She turned round. His gaze lay calmly on her, warm and firm at the same time.

A moment of silence.

"It's just ... a lot." She sighed, letting her shoulders slump.

The next moment she felt his arms around her.

The embrace was strong, but not oppressive - a hold without holding her tight.

"Then we'll let it go. At least for a few hours." His lips brushed her hair, a fleeting kiss on her forehead.

Lena inhaled the familiar scent of leather and a hint of peppermint. But a dark thought nagged at her.

What if one day she could no longer return to this embrace?

The thought was so real, so tangible, that she tried to push it away with a deep breath.

She released herself a little from his embrace and looked at him. "And what do you suggest? A bottle of red wine and ignore the old files?"

Bodo grinned wryly. "I was thinking of a hot bath. For both of us."

Lena laughed softly. For the first time that day, her chest no longer felt so heavy.

"You're incorrigible."

"No, I'm just a man with a plan."

He took her hand and gently pulled her into the house with him. Past the scattered documents on the kitchen table - to the one place where there were no unsolved cases, no shadows from the past.

Just the two of them.

But the shadows were waiting. And they would soon show themselves.

Steam hung in the air, bathing the bathroom in a warm cocoon. Drops ran down the dark tiles.

Lena leant back, her neck resting on the edge of the bath. The heat slowly released the tension in her shoulders. But it wasn't just the water that helped her to let go.

Bodo sat behind her, his arms wrapped loosely around her. His fingertips drew barely noticeable circles on her skin - so lightly that she almost missed it.

But she felt every touch.

"I know you're brooding again." His voice was close, warm, a gentle counterpoint to the carousel of thoughts in her head.

Lena grinned, stroking her fingers over his forearm. "I'll try not to."

"So?" "I think about the case. Of the evidence that doesn't fit together. And the fact that I sometimes wish we had an evening where nothing else existed but us."

Bodo let his lips slide over her shoulder. "Then let it happen. At least for now."

Lena let her head sink against his chest and closed her eyes. His heartbeat was a calm rhythm, a reliable beat in her chaotic life.

But she couldn't let go of the thought.

How many times had they said that to each other?

That they should enjoy the moment? And yet reality kept catching up with them - a new clue, a lead, a sudden twist.

How long would this peace last this time?

Bodo seemed to read her thoughts. "Do you know what I love about you?"

She opened her eyes and turned her head slightly towards him.

"I'm curious."

He smiled. "That you're so damn stubborn. That you never settle for half truths. And that you're here anyway. With me."

His words struck something in her. A warmth that had nothing to do with the hot water spread.

She turned to face him, her face only centimetres away from his.

"You're a damn good investigator sometimes, you know that?"

Bodo grinned before kissing her - slowly, intensely, as if he wanted to take in every moment.

Then - a noise.

Dull. Removed.

Lena opened her eyes. Was that...?

Bodo had heard it too.

A vibration alarm.

Her eyes met his. No words. Just mutual understanding.

She slowly pushed herself out of the bath and reached for the towel. Dripping wet, she stepped out and wrapped it around her.

The vibrating stopped. But when she entered the living room, the mobile phone on the table was flashing.

A new message.

Reality had caught up with her. Number suppressed.

An uneasy feeling crept into her stomach.

She reached out for the mobile phone. It vibrated again.

"Don't answer it," Bodo said quietly.

Lena ignored him. She took the call.

"Mountain." Silence.

Irregular breathing.

Then a distorted, mechanical voice:

**"You are playing with fire. The shadow will devour you
"** A harsh tone. The call was over. Lena stared at the
display. Her heart was beating faster - not from

Fear, but because of the ice-cold vigilance that spread
through her like a hunting instinct.

"Damn," she muttered.

Bodo took the mobile phone from her and looked at the
call history. "Number suppressed. No tracing possible."

Lena clenched her fist. "I hate it when they start playing
these games." Then - a knock at the door.

Too late for visitors.

Lena instinctively reached for her gun. Bodo peered through the peephole.

"Damn it. It's Lars."

Lena opened the door.

Lars' face looked serious.

 "You have to come with me now."

Lena felt her pulse racing. "What's happened?"

Lars took a step closer.

"There was a second call. This time someone called a name." Bodo straightened up.

"Whose name?"

Lars looked at him. Then Lena.

**"Yours."**

The wind howled outside. It had begun.

# Chapter 50

The city slowly awoke. Fog hung heavy over the streets, stretching like a pale veil through the narrow    alleyways. The first rays of sunlight broke through the grey, casting distorted shadows across the cobbled station forecourt. A distant train thundered over the tracks, its deep roar vibrating through the ground.

In the conference room at Emden police headquarters, Lena stood motionless at the window. Her gaze wandered across the station grounds, lingering on the commuters moving through the cold with their heads bowed.

Everyday life continued. But everything had changed for her.

**"You are next."**

The threat echoed in her head. A cold shiver crawled up her spine, icy all the way to her fingertips.

The door opened behind her. Footsteps. Then the muffled sound of a folder falling onto the table.

"Lars has spoken to the public prosecutor's office."

Bodo's voice sounded rough, tired.

"Katrin Broder remains in custody."

Lena turned round. "Did she ask for a lawyer?"

Bodo shook his head. "No."

"That's worrying."

He leaned against the table and crossed his arms.

"Maybe she knows it's over."

Lena pressed her lips together. "Or she's waiting for Sorokin to get her out."

The air in the room felt heavy. Then Lars entered the room, a tablet in his hand. His look was serious.

"We have a new lead."

Lena felt her stomach tighten.

"Which one?"

"One transaction - 250,000 euros. Offshore account in Liechtenstein."

Lena leafed through the files, her eyes darting over the lines.

"The same pattern as back then with Heinrich Broder."

Lars turned the tablet towards them. The name on the screen caught their attention.

**Andreas Falk.**

Bodo sucked in a sharp breath.

"Damn. We didn't have him on our radar."

"Robin had Lasker in his sights," said Lena. Lars nodded. "He had. But the payment went through Falk.

An old business partner of Lasker's. He laundered Broder's money - and now he's trying to cover his tracks."

A muffled clap. Bodo had hit the table with the flat of his hand.

"We have to find him."

Lars looked over at him. "Then we'll talk to Aniko again. Maybe she can tell us more."

Bodo nodded curtly. "Lena, come with me. We're going to the safe house."

### Safe House

The Safe House was an inconspicuous terraced house in a quiet residential neighbourhood. The façade looked neat but unimportant - the perfect place to avoid attracting attention. Two civilian CID officers stood guard, one inside the house, one outside in a car.

Aniko was sitting in the small kitchen. Her hands clutched a teacup, but she didn't take a sip. Her gaze was blank, her lips barely quivered.

Lena sat down opposite her.

"How are you?"

Aniko slowly raised her head, dark shadows lay under her eyes.

"I want to see Robin."

Her voice was rough, a thin whisper.

Lena took a deep breath. "I can't do that. It's too dangerous."

Aniko clenched her hands into fists.

"He's hurt and there's nothing I can do! I'm scared, Lena. They almost killed him and now he's sitting alone in hospital while I'm supposed to hide here?"

Bodo stepped to the window and peered through a gap in the curtain. The civilian car was still there. No movement. No danger - for the time being.

"We're not doing this to lock you up."

Lena took Aniko's hand, her voice was calm, firm.

"But to protect you. Sorokin is out there. And he warned us."

Aniko blinked, fighting her tears.

"I can't do that. I can't sit here and wait    ."

Bodo turned round. His gaze was implacable, but not without compassion.

"You've already helped. Without you, we wouldn't have discovered the connection to Falk so quickly. But you have to persevere."

It was quiet for a moment.

Then Aniko nodded. Hesitantly. Vulnerable. But it was enough.

The A31 lay ahead of them, a dark ribbon under the grey sky. The rain had stopped, but the   tarmac was still shiny and damp.

Bodo sat at the wheel, his fingers clutching the steering wheel. Lena beside him, her eyes fixed on the sat nav.

Falk's house was on the edge of the forest. The shutters were closed, the property looked deserted. No light. No movement.

Bodo drew his gun. "Ready?"

Lena nodded. They moved silently along the gravel path. He knocked on the door. "Andreas Falk? Emden police."

Silence.

A shadow behind the curtains. Barely visible - but there.

Then - a shot. Not out of the house.

Very close by. Bodo jerked his head round. "That came from there!" They ran off.

A motionless figure lay in the car park. A single bullet hole above the heart, clean and precise.

Next to it - a note. **"You're too slow."**

Lena closed her eyes. Sorokin was one step ahead of them again.

# *Chapter 51*

The rain had cleared, but the air was still saturated with moisture and cold. Dark puddles shone on the cracked tarmac like broken mirrors, reflecting the flickering blue lights of the emergency vehicles. The metallic smell of wet concrete was heavy in the air, mixed with something Lena knew only too well. Blood.

Drops splashed from the edges of the concrete façades, as if the sky wanted to prove that the city was not yet dry.

Lena hunched her shoulders as a sudden gust of wind pressed the wet fabric of her jacket against her skin. The cold crept deeper, biting into her bones. Bodo stood next to her, his hands buried deep in his pockets, motionless as a statue. His gaze was fixed on the body bag, as if he could see through the black, shiny material. Water dripped from his hair, running down his face in cold streaks - as if the rain itself had marked him.

In the centre of the spooky scene, framed by red and white barrier tape and the bright lights of the forensics team, lay another body - this time uncovered. Andreas Falk. His uniform was soaked with rain, the darkness of the fabric blending into the wet concrete.

Lena knelt down next to the dead man, ignoring the cold that made her fingers stiff.

A single bullet hole above the heart - clean, precise. No struggle, no traces of a desperate attempt at defence.

No chaos. Only silence. Precision.

Someone had known what they were doing. Or wanted to leave exactly that impression.

Bodo ran his hand slowly over his three-day beard, his gaze gliding scrutinisingly over the scene. His face remained calm, too calm. But Lena knew him well enough to notice the barely perceptible twitch in his jaw - a sign that he didn't like something.

"Neat work," he muttered. "One shot. No hustle and bustle. No chaos. The perpetrator was a professional - or wants us to think just that."

Lena breathed shallowly through her mouth. The air tasted of concrete, oil and something metallic. Blood.

This wasn't just a murder.

That was a message.

A movement out of the corner of their eye made them look up. Corinna Stein, the team's forensic investigator, approached them with an evidence bag in her hand. A small cartridge case gleamed between the tips of a pair of tweezers.

"**.22 calibre**," she said curtly. "Quiet. Effective. A single, well-aimed shot. No sign of a second. No panic."

Lena nodded slowly. Her gaze wandered over the car park while her mind was already searching for patterns.

For the bigger picture. And then there it was - the name that appeared like a shadow in her mind even before she consciously thought it.

**Sorokin.**

"I want to check the surveillance cameras," she said quietly. "Something must have been recorded some-where."

Corinna shrugged her shoulders. "The cameras here at the car park were switched off. But there's a petrol station directly opposite. Maybe we'll be lucky."

Lena was just about to turn away when she saw it.

Something white flashed out from under Falk's left hand. A tiny piece of paper, soaked, half hidden. By chance? Or deliberately placed?

She bent down and carefully pulled it out. The edges were softened by the rain, the letters hastily thrown down - but still legible.

**"Two trains behind."**

Freezing cold. The shock went right to her fingertips. Her breath caught - just for a moment, but long enough for her to realise that this was an invitation.

Bodo had stood up in the meantime and was also looking at the paper. Nobody said anything for a moment. Then he put a hand on her shoulder.

**"Sorokin?"**

Or someone who knew exactly how to direct her thoughts?

Lena swallowed dryly. She reached for the note with pointed fingers and let it slide into an evidence bag. Her fingers were ice-cold.

Deep, barely audible thunder rumbled in the distance.

The wind had changed.

And the bitter certainty spread through Lena's stomach:

**They didn't play this game.**

**They were the figures on it.**

The wind had died down, but the cold remained. A frosty breeze drifted through the dark streets as Lena walked with Bodo through the corridors of the forensic centre. The sterile neon light burned brightly above them, making the white walls seem even colder, as if they were reflecting the evil that was gathering in these rooms.

Their every step echoed dully on the cold floor.

Lena felt the crunch in her jaw as she pressed her lips together. The note with the message **"You're too slow"** lay sealed in her jacket pocket, but it was as if the writing was burnt directly into her mind.

Bodo walked beside her, his eyes fixed ahead. But she knew him well enough to sense his tension - in the way his hands clenched into fists, the way he ran his tongue over the inside of his cheek.

"It's not just a murder," Lena finally said, her voice quiet, almost choked by the hum of the ventilation shafts.

Bodo nodded barely perceptibly. "It's a demonstration of power."

He stayed in front of the door

**"Forensic medicine - access for authorised persons only**

took a deep breath and then pushed it open.

The acrid odour of disinfectant and cold stainless steel hit them. Dr Julia Müller, the forensic pathologist, was already standing at the dissection table, tweezers in hand. Corinna Stein stood next to her, her arms crossed in front of her chest, her gaze frozen  the pale, motionless figure of Andreas Falk.

Julia gave them a curt nod. "I have an initial overview." She touched the corpse's pale skin with the tweezers. "The angle of the bullet is precise. 22 calibre, as Corinna already suspected at the crime scene. The shot pierced the heart almost in the centre. Perfect execution."

Lena stepped closer. Falk's face looked... calm. Almost too calm.

"Traces of defence?"

Corinna shook her head. "None. He was either surprised - or he knew he was going to die."

A well-aimed shot. No superfluous violence. No fight.

Lena let her gaze glide over the exposed upper body of the dead man. Everything was frighteningly... clean.

"Did he say anything else before he died? Did anyone hear anything?"

Julia stepped up to a stainless steel trolley and pulled aside a sealed evidence tray. A small, silver object lay inside - barely larger than a fingertip.

Lena frowned. "A... USB stick?" Julia nodded. "He must have swallowed it. Either to hide it - or because he had no other choice."

Bodo sucked in a sharp breath. "Damn. If he swallowed it, he knew his time was up."

Lena stared at the stick.

**A digital nail in the coffin.**

Whatever was on this stick - it had cost Falk his life.

Julia crossed her arms. "I'll do a toxicological examination. Anyone who dies like that could have been administered something beforehand."

Lena nodded. "Thank you, Julia. As soon as you have the results, let me know."

Then she turned to Corinna. "What do you think of the stick? Can we get anything out of it?"

Corinna raised a brow. "Depends on whether it's encrypted. But if it was that important, I guarantee you one thing - **someone will protect it.**"

Lena let her gaze glide over the dead Falk once more.

He had known something. And someone had done a hell of a lot to ensure that this knowledge died with him.

### IT laboratory, Emden CID

The doors to the IT lab opened with a soft whirring sound. Bluish light flickered on as the monitors booted up.

Corinna was already sitting at her desk, her fingers flitting across the keyboard. Numbers and lines of code raced across the screen, cryptic strings of characters formed into folders and files.

Next to her, Jan Müller and Lars Lammers bent over the laptop. Their posture revealed that they knew was going on here.

**Damn important things** happened.

Lena entered the room with Bodo at her side.

"Tell me we're lucky," she said.

Corinna shook her head slowly. "The thing is secured to the roof. Strong encryption, fragmented data sets - but I was able to extract a few fragments   ."

Several folders appeared on the screen. One of them immediately caught Lena's eye:

"Payment protocols."

Jan clicked on it. A list of transactions opened. Names, amounts, codes - one line made Lena freeze.

**Sorokin - 250,000 euros.**

There was absolute silence for a moment.

Then her eyes met Bodo's.

That was proof. Real proof.

But before she could say anything, it happened.

The screen twitched. First a brief flicker - then a new message appeared in the centre of the monitor.

**"You're too slow."**

An icy sting ran through Lena's stomach.

"It's not from us, is it?" Jan asked quietly.

Corinna sat as if petrified. Then she moved jerkily, her fingers racing across the keyboard.

"Damn. The stick isn't just a data storage device - it's a trap."

Bodo leant forward. "A trap? In what way?"

Corinna hammered on the keys. Her eyes narrowed.

"As soon as I plugged it in, it established a connection to the outside world. Someone knows for sure that we're investigating him."

Lars rubbed his forehead. "Does that mean someone is watching us live?"

Corinna nodded. "And not only that. I've put up several firewalls, but this thing dodges everything I put in its way. It's a bloody zero-day backdoor - customised."

Lena felt her fingers clench into fists. They had fallen into a trap. "Is there anything we can use?"

Corinna scanned the last fragments. Then she paused. "Here's something else... An abbreviation: **'V.T.'**"

Lars furrowed his brow. "What's that supposed to be?"

Before Lena could ask any more questions, the screen began to flicker again.

A new line appeared. **"You are too slow."** This time it flashed **red**.

Corinna froze. Then she abruptly ripped the stick out of the laptop. The screen went black.

Everything remained silent for a moment.

Then Lena knew: **this storm had only just begun.**

The noise in her head was louder than any thunder coming from outside. Lena let her gaze wander over the darkened monitors - a moment ago they had been twitching, flashing lines of data as if they were breathing. Now everything was dead. Only the reddish emergency light from the servers flickered on the walls, casting eerie shadows on the faces in the room.

She felt Bodo's presence behind her. His breathing was calm, controlled, but Lena knew it was a mask. His pulse was racing just like hers. On the table was the USB stick that Corinna had just torn out of the laptop - small, inconspicuous, and yet a ticking bomb.

"A diabolical gift," Corinna said quietly. Her hands gripped the back of her chair so tightly that her knuckles turned white.

"Has anyone rebooted the IT firewall yet?" Lars' voice was cutting but controlled. His gaze was fixed on the flashing server lights, as if he could read the answer from the chaos.

Corinna took a deep breath. "Yes, but whoever controlled this now knows exactly where we are - and how far we've come."

Lena closed her eyes briefly. Images formed in her head: Andreas Falk, motionless on the cold concrete. The precise bullet hole. The note with the  words *Two moves behind.*

The USB stick, the hard-to-decipher data records. And then this abbreviation that had burnt itself into her memory: **T. F.**

"We have Sorokin - and now T. F.," she murmured. "Two players on a board that we don't have an overview of."

Bodo stepped up next to her. He had taken off his jacket and his shirt was slightly creased. The adrenalin was still coursing through his veins. "Maybe T. F. isn't just any name. What if he or she is behind Sorokin? Or is working with him?"

Nobody disagreed. The silence was heavy - not out of helplessness, but because they all shared the same fear.

Corinna turned back to the monitors. Her fingers flitted across the touchpad, then stopped abruptly. "There's a minimal amount of data left here. No  clear indication - just a cross-link to offshore accounts. Same source for multiple transactions."

"T. F.," said Jan, his voice sounding muffled. He was standing behind Corinna, dark circles under his eyes, as if he had lost a piece of his innocence in the space of an hour. "The abbreviation keeps popping up. Some kind of phantom pulling the strings."

Lena straightened up. "We need to speak to Karin Broder again.

If her name is on the lists - together with   Andreas Falk
- then perhaps a trail leads to this T. F."

Bodo nodded. "I've got her a secure cell. But nothing is
safe here right now."

Lena felt the tension in her shoulders as she packed up
the few printed pages. The USB stick was still lying on the
table, as if it was just waiting to cause mischief again.
Corinna grabbed it, put it in a padded evidence bag and
locked it in a steel cabinet. Double.

"I can't guarantee that we haven't been bugged here for a
long time," she said, "but if someone has managed to do
that with a zero-day breach, we have nothing left but caution."

Jan ran his fingers through his hair. Lars cleared his
throat. "I'll set up a system backup. Maybe we can restore
more if we use the right tools."

Lena nodded. "Do the best you can. Anything we find
could untangle this web."

The hum of the neon lights hung heavy in the air. It was
as if there was no oxygen in the room. Without another
word, they stepped out into the corridor, which was
bathed in gloomy emergency lighting.

The door to the IT lab closed with a soft click.

Outside, they were greeted by the biting night air. Bodo pulled on his jacket and raised his eyes. The sky was overcast with low clouds, the rain had subsided - but the storm was still in the air, lurking like a predator ready to pounce.

"This storm has only just begun," Lena said quietly.

Bodo looked at her for a moment. In his eyes glowed that fighting spark that had carried them both through darker times.

"Then let's get ready."

With one last look at the illuminated police building, they got into the car. The engine hummed quietly as they drove off. In the rear-view mirror, the lights distorted into long streaks, as if they were diving into another world.

And just a few streets away, in a half-lit office, the next revelation was waiting.

# *Chapter 52*

The wind tore at the last leaves, pulling them from the branches like an invisible hunter mercilessly hunting its prey. Golden and deep red flecks swirled through the streets, dancing in the light of the lanterns. Then they died out, sucked in by the darkness. Fog crept over the tarmac, heavy as a veil of oblivion, muffling sounds and distorting contours.

### *IT room, police Department*

The only light in the room flickered from the monitor, on whose surface numbers and characters streamed down in endless streams. Jan sat bent forwards, his forehead bathed in light, his shoulders tense. The quiet hum of the servers was the only rhythm in the silence - the metallic pulse of the digital world.

The room smelled of hot electronics, stale air and cold coffee.

His fingers scurried across the keyboard, traversing a labyrinth of codes, proxy servers, disguised transactions. Offshore accounts, encrypted documents - a web of lies, finely spun like spider silk.

Then - a jolt. Jan's eyes narrowed. A line flashed on the screen.

**T. F.**

He stared at the letters for a few seconds. A familiar abbreviation? No. No entry, no connection. But why did it trigger this tingling in the back of his  neck? As if someone had whispered his name while he was alone.

His fingers lingered over the keyboard. Suddenly the room felt tighter, the air denser, heavier. This abbreviation was not a loose piece of the puzzle.

It was the key.

And perhaps he should never have found him.

### *detention cell*

The neon light flickered and cast harsh shadows on the grey walls of the cell. The room was barren, little more than a hole in which time did not flow but lay trapped within itself.

Karin Broder sat on the narrow cot, her shoulders pulled forwards, her hands folded in her lap. Her fingers kneaded the fabric of her jacket as if she could hold on to it - the last bit of control she had left.

The door opened with a soft click.

Lena and Bodo entered.

No words. Only silence, which settled on the scene like an invisible weight.

The door slammed shut. A muffled sound. A judgement.
"Mrs Broder," Lena finally said. Her voice was calm but razor-sharp.

Karin raised her eyes only briefly, as if she was afraid of losing herself in it.

"I have nothing to do with the death of Andreas Falk."

The words came quickly, almost too quickly. Like a reflex. But her fingers betrayed her. They had stopped kneading the fabric and now lay rigidly in her lap.

Bodo stepped closer. His gaze was calm but firm.

"Karin."

No title. Just her name.

A brief twitch.

"We know that you know more than you're saying."

Her breathing became shallower.

"Sorokin doesn't leave anyone alive who knows too much."

A tremor ran through her shoulders, barely visible, but pure fear flashed in her eyes for a moment. Lena saw it. She knew that this was exactly where she had to start.

Slowly, she pulled the USB stick out of her jacket pocket and turned it between her fingers.

"Jan has decoded a list."

Her voice was soft, almost casual.

"Your name is on it. Andreas Falk's name too."

A short, hard breath.

Then Lena dropped the last words almost like a casual detail:

"And then someone else: T. F."

The world stopped.

Karin's shoulders stiffened. A subtle, uncontrollable jolt went through her body. Her gaze flickered.

"Who's that?" asked Lena quietly.

No threat. No harshness. Only calm.

But the effect was stronger than any interrogation.

Karin's lips opened a crack. No sound came out.

Her chest rose and fell unevenly.

Her hands - still rigid a moment ago - suddenly clenched into the fabric of her jacket.

An escape movement that no longer existed.

An inner struggle.

A glance at the door - as if she could find an answer there that she didn't want to give.

"I..."

The word broke off.

Lena's gaze remained calm, but she gave her time.

Seconds have passed.

Then - a whisper.

Almost too quiet to hear.

"It... it wasn't just Sorokin."

Bodo paused.

His gaze bored into hers, leaving her no chance of escape.

"Then who was it, Karin?"

Seconds have passed. Agonisingly slow.

The fight was over. A deep breath. Her gaze lifted.

"T. F."

A name that was cut into the silence like a wound.

"He... he directed everything."

Lena felt her pulse racing.

That was it. The moment they had been waiting for.

Bodo leaned closer.

"Who's that?"

Karin's lips opened.

A breath of words - then a hesitation.

One last desperate look at the door, as if she could find the answer she didn't want to give there.

"I... I can't say."

Outside, the wind rattled the windows as if it wanted to whip the last lie out of her.

# Chapter 53

The cold light of the neon tubes cut the darkness into sharp edges. The rhythm of the heart monitor counted the seconds - a quiet, relentless ticking. Outside, behind the windows of the Emden hospital, the city lay in muted silence. But in here, time seemed frozen, trapped in sterile motionlessness.

Robin Ahlers sat upright in the narrow hospital bed. The pressure bandage on his shoulder throbbed dully - a constant reminder of his last collision with the truth. A secure laptop lay on his knees.

His colleague had brought it with him - with a terse warning: "For internal investigations only."

Robin took a deep breath. The air smelled of disinfectant and stale fear. He knew he was entering dangerous territory. His fingers glided over the keyboard - precisely, routinely. Firewall after firewall. Security layer after security layer.

But nothing was insurmountable. Not for him.

Then the name came up. **Andreas Falk.** A single message. No explanations, no details.

*"Meeting with T.F. at the old quay. Discreet."*

Robin massaged his temples, his stomach tightened. **T.F.** - a name that was not allowed to exist. But in his head, fragments of an old

File together: **Arms trade. International connections. Disappeared evidence.**

If Falk wanted to meet him ... then perhaps that was the reason why he was dead.

Then - a noise. Quiet. Barely perceptible.

A click.

### *Safe House*

Outside, the city was not asleep. Muffled noises penetrated the walls: the wailing echo of a siren, the distant hum of engines.

Aniko stood motionless at the window. Her shoulders tensed, her hands clenched into fists. But there was more than unease in her eyes.

Determination. "I want to see Robin"

Lena, leaning against the door, folded her arms. Her voice was as calm as steel. **"Forget it."**

An order. Sure, final.

***"The press want someone to blame for Falk's death. They need a face - and you're the perfect target."***

Aniko swallowed, her fingers digging into the fabric of her jacket. "What if they attack Robin again?"

Lena exhaled audibly. Her eyes flickered for a   moment - barely noticeably.

"Don't you think I know that?" She took a step forwards. "But that's exactly why we can't make a mistake now."

Then - a shrill beep. Lena's mobile phone vibrated.

No name. No number. Just a single message:

*"She's next."*

Heavy silence. Freezing cold.

Aniko stared at the screen. Her breathing remained calm, but an inescapable realisation was forming inside her.

There was no hiding. No waiting.

She raised her eyes. "I'm not going to wait for them to find me."

Lena returned the look. She only seemed to think for a moment - then she reached for the radio.

**"Pull up the fuse. Nobody can get in or out any more."**

*Presidium Emden*
A dull thud.

The newspaper landed on the table.

**"Andreas Falk - Murder covered up? Who protects the perpetrators?"** Lars Lammers' gaze travelled across the team. Not a word was spoken. The air in the meeting room was as tense as a tightrope.

He took a deep breath. Then, without taking his eyes off the newspaper: "This is escalating." His voice was calm but firm.

**"We must issue an international alert for Sorokin."**

Corinna Stein nodded. "If he's still in the country, he has to get out. If he's already gone - then we need to know where."

Jan Müller leaned forward. "And T.F.? If Falk wanted to meet him ... could he be Sorokin?"

Lars' jaw ground. "If it's him, it won't be an easy target."

He pushed the newspaper aside and leaned forward. **"Find out about it. And quickly."**

### *Emden Hospital*

Robin rubbed his forehead. His head was throbbing.

Then - a noise. Quiet. Barely audible.

A click at the door.

His body tensed.

The door opened slowly.

A carer entered.

Robin exhaled. Relief - for a fraction of a second

But then ...

- the posture

- the corridor

- the wrong shoes Black leather no hospital Crocs.

His heart hammered against his ribs.

The door fell quietly into the lock.

The dim light from the bedside lamp cast harsh shadows on the man's face - angular, emotionless. Something metallic shone in his hand. Robin swallowed. His fingers twitched towards the emergency button on the bed.

Too late

The man moved with lightning speed. A grip, firm, cold, on Robin's arm. But then - a noise from outside

Heavy steps.

A shadow fell on the frosted glass pane of the door. The man paused, peering to the side. The moment of distraction was all Robin needed

He threw himself to the side with all his strength, pulled the infusion stand with him and hit it against the attacker.

The door flew open.

**"Police!"**

Jan Müller stormed in, gun at the ready. The man whirled around, pulled something out of his jacket - a knife. A shot broke the silence. The attacker gasped, slumped against the bed and slowly slid to the floor

The blade fell onto the tiles with a clink. Jan stepped closer, kicking the knife out of reach

**"Are you okay?"**

Robin nodded, breathing heavily. His gaze fell on the man's breast pocket, where a thin envelope was sticking out. Jan carefully pulled it out and unfolded it.

There was only one word on the note:

**"Done?"**

Lars and Robin exchanged a glance. No signature. No return address. But one thing was clear:

**Someone wanted to make sure Robin didn't survive the night.**

# *Chapter 54*

The wind tugged at the shipyard buildings, sending tendrils of mist dancing through the gloomy harbor district of Emden. Rusty cranes loomed like ghostly skeletons against the night sky, while warehouses projected distorted shadows upon the pavement. Somewhere nearby, a loose chain clanged metallically against a ship's hull, its echo swallowed by the darkness. The salty tang of the sea merged with the musty aroma of oil and rust.

Inside the car, the heating blazed at full capacity, yet an unyielding cold still crept up Bodo and Lena's limbs. Half-hidden between two containers, the vehicle's only beacon in the oppressive dark was the faint glow of the dashboard. Bodo drummed his fingers on the steering wheel, visibly tense, as Lena stole a glance at her watch. The informant's arrival had been long awaited.

Then—a movement within the fog. A silent shadow, patiently waiting.

Rico emerged from the darkness. His scuffed leather jacket and the cigarette hanging from the corner of his mouth marked him as someone accustomed to danger. For a moment he stood motionless, as if the stray beam of light were deliberately highlighting his presence. Slowly, he exhaled a wisp of smoke before advancing.

Lena opened the door; her footsteps crunched on the gravel. Bodo remained inside, scanning the area. Rico rarely came alone.

"You're burning your fingers—and you don't even realize it,"

Rico said, his voice rough and laden with subtext. Smoke curled languidly in the frigid air.

"Sorokin is keeping a low profile, but his connections run deeper than you think."

Lena crossed her arms. "How deep?"

Rico took a deliberate drag on his cigarette and fixed her with narrow, scrutinizing eyes.

"International money laundering. Arms smuggling. Falk was merely a small cog in a vast, bloody machine. But that isn't your biggest problem."

An ominous tension spread through Bodo. "But?"

Stepping closer, Rico lowered his voice.

"Someone else has taken over. Broder was just the beginning."

Lena shot Bodo a quick, questioning glance. "Who?"

Rico hesitated, his fingers drumming on the worn leather of his jacket. Then, quietly, he uttered: "T.F."

Lena frowned. "What does that mean?"

Rico dropped the cigarette, stubbing it out with the toe of his shoe. His gaze darkened.

"If it's who I think it is... soon, you won't be the hunters—you'll be the hunted."

The ride back to the police department passed in a heavy silence. Rain pattered monotonously against the windshield, thick droplets tracing erratic paths on the glass. Lena clutched her notebook and ran her thumb over the rough, textured paper. The first page bore only one line: T.F.

Inside the office, the air reeked of stale tension and old coffee. Neon lights flickered briefly, then bathed the room in a sterile glow. Lena sank into her chair, drew the keyboard closer, and keyed the letters into the police database. No hits.

Biting her lip, she navigated through international wanted lists as the low hum of the computer filled the room. Her eyes darted over the entries—until one name stopped her in mid-scroll. Her fingers froze above the keyboard: Timofej Fedorov.

Bodo, pausing mid-pour as he filled his coffee cup, saw his face darken. "Damn." His voice was rough, now imbued with a firmer edge. "Don't tell me that's the Fedorov."

Lena turned the screen toward him. Though his gaze remained fixed, his grip tightened around the cup until his knuckles went white. "Eastern Europe's most notorious arms dealer," she whispered. "A ghost.

He cooperated with Sorokin but never operated directly in Germany. If his name surfaces in Emden now, we're in deep trouble."

Bodo sipped his coffee slowly before setting the cup down. "We have to bring Becker in on this."

Rubbing her forehead wearily, Lena replied, "He'll be thrilled." She reached for the phone. Dr. Roland Becker, the senior public prosecutor, was a man who brooked no nonsense.

When he answered, his voice cut through the line as sharply as a razor blade.

"You're telling me an internationally wanted arms dealer is involved in our case?"

"Yes," Lena said calmly, though her heart pounded.

"And there are indications that Sorokin may be using him for a new delivery."

A long silence followed, punctuated only by a deep, measured breath on the other end.

"I'll get in touch with the federal police. But until then— no going it alone, do you understand?"

Lena closed her eyes briefly. "Of course not." She hung up, aware that she'd already bent the truth. The silence was broken by the sound of someone clearing their throat.

Corinna Stein, the forensic scientist, stood in the doorway holding a plain brown envelope.

"This came in an hour ago."

Lena took it and tore it open, revealing a single sheet of paper. Handwritten, the message was scrawled in haste:

You ruined Thomas. Who's next?

Her heart began to race. Bodo stepped up beside her, reading over her shoulder. "Shit."

Corinna folded her arms. "Someone's trying to unsettle you."

"Or stop us,"

Bodo replied, his tone grim as he looked toward Lena.

Lena turned the paper over between her fingers, noting that the handwriting was markedly different from previous threats—restless, hasty, and smudged.

"Someone was in a hurry." Corinna nodded.

"I'll run an analysis. We need to know who we're dealing with here."

Lena looked up from the page. They had been battling a dead end for weeks—but now they had a name. Timofej Fedorov.

And if Sorokin truly worked with him, this was no longer just about Emden. This was a deadly hunt.

# *Chapter 55*

The early morning weighed heavily over the police head-quarters. A grey haze crept through the streets as damp mist beaded on the windowpanes. The first rays of sunlight struggled to break through the dense gloom, casting a pale light on the wet asphalt. The city lay in a strange, suspended state – silent, lurking, as if holding its breath.

Inside the police department, the neon light in one of the interrogation rooms flickered, its constant hum the only sound in the otherwise oppressive quiet. Karin Broder sat at the table, her gaze fixed downward. Her face appeared drawn and pale, her fingers interlocked as if clinging to an unseen lifeline. A slight tremor in her right hand betrayed her inner turmoil, and every slam of a door outside made her shoulders tense—as though she expected someone to come and drag her away.

Lena allowed the silence to stretch; she knew that sometimes, quiet could dismantle walls. Leaning back, her eyes remained cool and observant, waiting. The seconds dragged by, punctuated only by the relentless ticking of the wall clock.

"Mrs. Broder,"

Lena finally said, her tone gentle yet sharp as a blade,

"you know you haven't told us everything yet."

A tremor ran through Karin's lips as her eyes darted across the table, desperately seeking an escape.

But there was none. The invisible weight upon her shoulders grew heavier until, almost as a whisper—barely more than a breath—she spoke:

"Timofej Fedorov... he was often in Wolthusen. In an old warehouse building."

Lena let the words sink in, carefully noting every shift in Karin's expression.

"What exactly was going on there?"

Karin pressed her lips together, as if battling the urge to reveal forbidden truths. Her fingers gripped the sleeve of her jumper until, with a short, uncertain breath, she continued:

"I was there."

Her voice came out hoarse, almost broken.

"I saw Fedorov meeting with men... not Germans. They exchanged money, weapons, data." Her voice cracked. "I saw... Sorokin himself."

Lena's stomach tightened—this was a real lead. But it didn't feel like a triumph. Sorokin never made mistakes, and if he did, they were only those he allowed himself.

"When was that?" Lena asked.

"A month ago." Karin exhaled shallowly.

"But Fedorov was afraid. He said that..."

Her hands began to shake noticeably. Closing her eyes as if summoning the strength to continue, she whispered, "He said... there's a list. Names. And anyone not on it is already dead."

Lena held her breath. "A list?"

Karin nodded so imperceptibly that it was almost nothing more than a shadow of approval.

"Fedorov warned that if Sorokin finds out he's no longer needed… then he's next."

Behind the mirrored window, Lars Lammerts, Jan Müller, and Bodo exchanged grave glances. This conversation had changed everything.

*Meeting Room*

A large map of Emden lay spread across the table. Village Wolthusen was delineated with thick lines, and the warehouse building was circled in red. Lars tapped on it with his finger.

"This is our chance. If Sorokin really hired Fedorov, then the trail leads through him."

Bodo folded his arms, his gaze cool and deliberate.

"If Sorokin has made a mistake, then it's one we should capitalize on."

"Then we'll put Fedorov under pressure," Lars declared, his voice calm yet resolute.

"He must believe he's already a dead man to Sorokin. Then he'll talk."

Lena nodded. "Bodo and I will take over surveillance—no rash moves."

"Jan, comb through all digital traces. I want to know if anything points to a planned deal."

"Understood,"

Jan replied, his fingers dancing over the keyboard. Moments later, his breath caught.

Lena straightened up abruptly. "What exactly have you found?"

"The money transfers—they ceased on the very day Falk died. And the account? Completely vanished. The trail leads directly to Sorokin."

Suddenly, a shrill ringing cut through the mounting tension.

The landline telephone—unused, forgotten—rang. Every head snapped toward it as Lars reached for the receiver.

"Lammerts," he said.

Silence.

Then a crackle on the line, followed by a distorted voice amid disturbed signals:

"... not over the threshold... the first who dares dies."

With that, a click. The line went dead.

For a few agonizing seconds, nobody moved. Lena exchanged a look with Bodo, while Jan frantically pounded keys.

"Someone has hacked our line,"

Jan murmured. "No trace left behind."

In the distance, a muffled sound—neither a shot nor a bang, just something heavy, like a fall or an impact—echoed briefly before fading into silence.

Bodo swiveled around sharply. Lars shot Jan a piercing look.

 "Have you found anything else?"

Jan shook his head.

"Just a moment... nothing on the servers yet."

Lena pulled her jacket tighter around her, an unsettling premonition creeping in.

Something was wrong. Sorokin knew it. He had known all along. And now, he also knew that they were drawing ever closer.

# Chapter 56

The night pressed heavily upon Emden. Wolthusen lay shrouded in darkness, the dim flicker of a distant street-lamp casting restless shadows against the weathered warehouse. Hours of rain had slicked the tarmac into a glassy black sheen, reflecting the dull glow of the city's scattered lights. Water trickled in thin streams along the cobbled street, the faint drip of overflowing gutters the only sound in the silence.

The investigative team had spread out, strategically positioning themselves around the building.

Bodo Zimmermann and Lena Berg crouched in the surveillance vehicle, the windows cracked just enough to keep the entrance in sight. Jan controlled the drone, its camera hovering soundlessly above the rooftop. In a separate, inconspicuous car, Jan Müller sat with his hand on the radio, waiting.

Lena lifted the binoculars.

"Nothing for an hour."

Her voice was barely a whisper.

Then—movement.

Two figures slipped from the shadows and approached the entrance. One was tall, broad-shouldered. The other moved with nervous energy, lanky, his motions jittery.

"There they are,"

Bodo murmured, adjusting the camera zoom.

"The tall one is Timofej Fedorov."

Lena sucked in a slow breath. Fedorov—Sorokin's right-hand man. A man deeply entangled in corruption, in unseen power plays. But Sorokin himself was nowhere to be seen. Jan activated the directional microphone. Static crackled in their earpieces before voices broke through—muffled, distorted by the thick warehouse walls.

A sharp hiss. A Russian curse.

"... the card index must never come to light. Do you understand? Not after what happened to Andreas."

Lena's head snapped around.

"Andreas?" Her voice came out hoarse. "The dead man from Broder's shipyard?"

Bodo rubbed his chin. "That's no coincidence. If they're hiding a card index..."

"Then this could be the list." Jan's fingers hovered rigidly over the keyboard. "The list of everyone involved." A dull thud echoed through the earpieces.

Silence.

Lena stiffened. Then—the scrape of shoes on concrete. A metallic clatter. "He's getting suspicious," Lena breathed. Her voice was taut, razor-sharp. "Stand by."

But it was too late.

The rear exit burst open. Fedorov exploded from the doorway like a coiled spring, his coat whipping through the air.

"Damn it! Move!"

Bodo shoved the door open. Jan was already on his feet. Fedorov bolted down the street, his boots slipping on the rain-slick pavement before he caught himself and pushed forward, faster.

Jan took off after him, Bodo right behind. But the Russian was quick—too quick.

A narrow passage loomed between two warehouses. Fedorov lunged toward it. Jan reached the alley barely two seconds later—

But it was empty.

Only the open attic door, swinging lazily in the night wind.

Lena exhaled sharply.

"Damn it. We had him." Bodo clenched his fists. Slowly, his gaze lifted, meeting Lena's. All was not lost. "We know the card index exists," he said, voice measured but firm. "And Fedorov is terrified it will be found."Jan closed his laptop with a snap. "Only one question remains." Lena nodded, her pulse steadying. "Where is she?"

# *Chapter 57*

Karin Broder sat in the stark interrogation room of the Emden police headquarters. The cold neon light showed no mercy, carving deep shadows beneath her eyes. Her hands clutched a coffee cup long gone cold. She didn't drink; she only held on, as if it were the last thing keeping her grounded.

Lena Berg leaned against the wall, arms crossed, her gaze locked onto Karin. "Sorokin sacrificed you. And Timofej Fedorov as well."

A bitter laugh.

"You think that surprises me?"

Karin rubbed her face, as if she could wipe away the years. "I covered for him half my life. But when things got serious, he cut me loose."

She hesitated, her voice lowering.

"If I help you... can I expect a reduced sentence?"

Lars Lammers, seated at the table, exchanged a glance with Lena before giving a barely perceptible nod.

"Cooperation is always taken into account."

Karin took a deep breath, as if standing on the edge of a decision she could never take back. Then, she whispered:

"There's a file—a digital card index. It contains every money laundering deal that passed through the Broder shipyard. Every transaction, every sum, every name involved."

Lena's pulse quickened. "Where is it?"

"On an encrypted server at the shipyard. Access is restricted to a single terminal—biometrically secured. Sorokin designed it so no one could breach it remotely."

Lars continued noting details. "Do you think he's still in Emden?"

Karin shook her head.

"He's too smart to stay. But before he disappears, he'll erase his tracks. If you want to catch him, you'll have to move fast."

Lena leaned in. "How fast?"

Karin's voice barely rose above a whisper. "Faster than you think."

While Lena and Lars processed the information, Jan Müller sat at his workstation, scanning surveillance footage. He rewound a clip, then froze the frame. "Here." He pointed at the timestamp. "Last night. 03:47. A freighter was loaded at the outer harbor. And guess who showed up?"

On the grainy screen, Timofej Fedorov moved through the frame, flanked by two men in dark jackets. They vanished behind a row of containers.

Lena's jaw tightened. "Sorokin is moving the last of his money." Lars rubbed his chin. "He never acts impulsively. Which means this is our best shot at catching him." Jan zoomed in, focusing on another detail. "There."

A silver van sat parked near the container stacks. The logo of a shipping company was emblazoned on the side. Only the company didn't exist. Lena narrowed her eyes. "What if it's not just about the money?"

Lars studied her. "What are you thinking?" Lena gestured at the screen. "Sorokin was never just about cash flow. If this is his last deal, he'll have something bigger in play."

She turned to Jan. "I need a full manifest of those containers. Now." Jan's fingers flew over the keyboard. A minute later, he looked up.

"You're not going to like this." The pressure was mounting. Robin remained in the    hospital. Aniko was secured in a safe house. And Lena herself had been receiving threats.

Lars' tone was grave. "We have to protect our people. I don't want another attack." Jan nodded, but doubt flickered in his eyes. "What if we're too late? If Sorokin vanishes again, we'll be left with nothing."

Lena placed a steadying hand on his shoulder. "Then we turn him into the hunted. He can't hide forever." Jan exhaled, staring out the window as if the answer might be waiting beyond the glass.

"Let's hope you're right. Because if we're wrong—" Then Lena's phone rang. She answered. "Berg."

Silence.

Then a voice, low and cold, that made her blood freeze.

**"You're playing a dangerous game, Inspector. One you cannot win."** Lena's grip tightened on the phone.

"Hang up now, and your team might still have a chance." A click. The line went dead. Lars' eyes drilled into her. "Who was that?"

Lena slowly exhaled. "Sorokin."

The room fell silent, heavy as lead. Jan looked at her. "So he's closer than we thought." Lena grabbed her jacket. Her hand trembled slightly, but her voice was steady. "We have to get to the shipyard. Now."

Jan reached out, stopping her. "Lena—what if it's a trap?"

She met his gaze, unwavering. "Then we make sure we're the ones waiting for him."

# *Chapter 58*

Lena stepped out of the heavy glass doors of the police headquarters. The cool night air struck her like a blade. Normally, she relished this moment—the brief relief when the weight of the day lifted, even if just for a second. But tonight was different. There was something in the air, an invisible heaviness, as if the darkness itself carried more than just shadows.

She needed a break. Just a few minutes to gather her thoughts, maybe grab a bite to eat. Across the station square, a small snack bar stood in the dim glow of a streetlamp, little more than a serving window and a fryer hissing with oil. The thought of something so mundane, so normal, felt like the last thread tethering her to reality.

Then—a bang.

Not the murmur of the city, not the hiss of a bus, not the dull thud of a suitcase on cobblestones.

One shot.

Lena reacted on instinct. Before her mind had even processed the sound, she was in cover, her body pressed hard against a concrete pillar. Her breath hitched, her pulse pounded in her ears. Eyes scanning the square. Searching.

There—a dark car, windshield cracked open just slightly. A shadow shifted behind the glass. Then the engine roared to life, tires screeched, and the car was gone.

Shit.

A warning—or a real attempt to take them out. Either way, the message was clear. They had dug too deep.

Her fingers trembled slightly as she pulled out her phone. Before she could dial, it buzzed in her hand.

Lars.

"Are you hurt?"

"No. I'm... okay."

"That was Sorokin. They're moving against us. I've already had Aniko transferred to another safe house. Robin is under full surveillance."

Lena's jaw tightened. No more grey areas. No more maneuvering. They were on a death list.

A shadow in the corner of her vision. Rico.

He stepped out of the darkness as if he had been there all along. His worn leather jacket hung loose on his shoulders, hands buried in his pockets. But his eyes gleamed—not with excitement, but with a restless energy, the kind that came from knowing something dangerous.

"Lena," he whispered, barely audible over the hum of the streetlights. "Timofej Fedorov is planning something.

Something big. He's stashing cash in the old warehouses at Outer Harbor. I can take you there."

Her mind worked at lightning speed. Information like this never came for free.

"What do you want?"

Rico shrugged. "Immunity. Protection."

Lena studied him. Words weren't enough. The question was—could he be trusted?

Her gaze drifted to the darkness. The flickering lights. The whisper in her head that said: Do it. What choice do you have?

She exhaled slowly, her decision already made.

"We're going."

Rico nodded. "But if you fuck me over, you'll regret it."

"That goes both ways."

The night closed in around them—cool, oppressive, swallowing up any way out.

The harbor district loomed ahead. Lena sat beside Rico in the car, the engine humming like a mechanical heartbeat against the silence. The streetlights flickered across the dashboard, casting distorted shadows across their faces before disappearing into the blackness.

There was no turning back.

A single shot. The blink of an eye. And suddenly, nothing was the same.

The night felt heavier now, thick with the weight of unseen threats. Lena stared out at the passing facades, cold concrete walls that seemed both defenseless and menacing. Every alleyway a potential ambush. Every shadow a trap waiting to be sprung.

"Do you think he knows what he's doing?" Her voice was quiet, barely more than a breath against the hum of the car. Maybe the question was meant for Rico. Or maybe for herself.

Rico met her gaze briefly in the rearview mirror, his dark eyes unreadable. "If you hesitate, you lose. And we can't afford that."

The city thinned out as they neared the harbor's edge. The orderly chaos of urban life gave way to rusting container stacks, abandoned shipyards, and empty parking lots. The wind carried the sharp tang of salt and oil, colder here, harsher.

Lena felt it pressing against her chest. Not just fear. Not just the adrenaline of the last few hours. It was something deeper. A shadow she had carried for years.

The voice that always crept in when the path forward held no return. A whisper of past choices, of mistakes that refused to fade.

"We still have half an hour to Outer Harbor," Rico said, his tone as sharp as a scalpel. "It's not just Fedorov waiting there. This is where all the threads come together. You need to decide how far you're willing to go."

Lena leaned her head against the window. The cold glass stung against her skin, a brief, grounding contrast to the heat coiling in her gut. "I already know," she said, her voice steadier than she felt. "If we stop now, it's over—for all of us."

The car turned down a side street. The glow of the streetlights stretched long, reaching across the pavement, casting the skeletal remains of old warehouses into looming sentinels. The city felt distant now. Only the murmur of the engine and the restless wind remained.

Then her phone vibrated.

A single pulse. A signal traveling up through her fingers, a warning before she even saw the name.

Lars.

She lifted the phone, her heartbeat quickening.

Short words. No more than a message.

**Situation has worsened.**

Lena swallowed hard, bracing against the surge of dread. She glanced at Rico, saw his face reflected in the glass—calm, unreadable.

"Ready?" he asked, voice quiet, as the headlights cut through the mist ahead, illuminating the wet cobblestones of the harbor entrance.

Lena nodded.

No more hesitation.

No more doubts.

The city faded behind them. Before them, the vast, silent expanse of the harbor stretched out, dark and endless, waiting to consume them whole.

A place of no return.

# *Chapter 59*

The wind drove the damp autumn air across the outer harbour, causing the harbour lanterns to flicker in the puddles and throwing empty plastic containers across the asphalt. The smell of diesel, salty water and rust hung heavy in the air. The night was moonless, the water pitch black. Shadows moved between the warehouses - silent, determined.

Lars Lammerts had planned everything precisely. Weeks of investigation led to this night. The Emden CID, supported by the Swart Team, had strategically positioned themselves around the warehouses. Covered by containers and empty lorries, the officers lay in position. No whispering, no radio. Just tense silence, electrified by the approaching raid.

Bodo and Lena pressed themselves against a concrete wall, their breath steaming in the cold. In front of them were the harbour workers - seemingly routine, but in between them were men who didn't belong there. The men they were looking for.

A dark-coloured van rolled to the end of the pier. The sliding door slid open silently. Timofej Fedorov got out, flanked by two broad-shouldered men. His gait was calm, almost casual - but Lena knew better. Behind this  façade lurked a predator.

Fedorov stepped up to one of the containers. He opened it and ran his eyes over the contents - bundles of money, carefully packed. A smaller box, sealed. Lena's pulse quickened. Was this the proof they needed?

Then - a sudden disruption.

A black SUV rolled up. Silent, sleek as a predator. The light from the harbour lanterns was reflected in the tinted windows. The way the car moved left no room for doubt.

Sorokin.

Fedorov froze. Sorokin had given him clear instructions: No fuss. No risk. And yet here he was.

The door opened slowly. Sorokin got out. His coat collar turned up, his eyes as cold as North Sea waves. He stood motionless, scrutinising Fedorov from a distance - a brief, deathly silence. Then he spoke. A single word in Russian.

Bodo felt his fingers tighten around the grip of his weapon. An uneasy feeling crept into his stomach, cold and heavy.

"This is going wrong..."

Fedorov hesitated. Just a second. Then - a movement.

A gun flashed.

Lena's heart stopped.

**"Access!"**

The night exploded.

Shots whipped through the darkness. The sound echoed from the warehouses. Swart officers fired from cover, their orders drowned out by the chaos. Screams. Shattering glass. The metallic smell of gunpowder lingered in the air.

Sorokin backed away, sliding behind his car. Fedorov's men raised their weapons, seeking cover . A thud - one of them collapsed  hit.

Fedorov saw his plan collapse. His gaze flitted frantically across the battlefield. Then he whirled around - his weapon aimed at Sorokin.

Sorokin did not move. No twitching, no emotion. Icy. Calculating.

One second. Two.

Then - without any hurry - he turned round. And ran off.

**"Damn!"**

Lena jumped forwards, sprinting after him. Her heart was racing, adrenalin burning in her muscles.

An engine howled. Screeching tyres ate into the asphalt. The car sped onto the pier, trailing a cloud of dust and smoke behind it.

Fedorov took advantage of the chaos. He ran.

**"He's getting away!"**

Bodo whirled around. Nothing. Just shadows. The distant roar of engines. And the gnawing feeling that they had lost him.

But her real opponent was not Fedorov.

It was Sorokin.

And he was already on his way into the unknown.

# Chapter 60

The harbour was in flames. Black smoke rolled across the water, drifting lazily like a living creature trying to suffocate everything. The fire was reflected on the smooth surface, cut by the flashing blue of the sirens. Screams, radio transmissions, the thud of boots on metal - an inferno of light, noise and chaos.

The attack was successful. But the battle was not over.

Two shadows emerged from the tangle of people and machines.

Sorokin and Timofej Fedorov.

Predators on the run. Sorokin was the mastermind, but Fedorov had the evidence.

Lena felt the decision like an electric twitch in her muscles. "Fedorov! He's got the data!"

She raised her weapon and started moving.

Behind her, the Swart Team responded. Bodo chased Sorokin through a labyrinth of containers, stairs and warehouses. The Russian knew the terrain and moved with unsettling precision. A shot whipped through the night. Then silence.

Lena forced herself not to look. Fedorov was her target.

He sprinted over rusty tracks, dodging wrecked machinery. His breathing was intermittent. But she was faster. Unstoppable.

Then - a mistake. A stumble.

He caught himself and started again. But it was too late.

He tore open a door and disappeared into a dilapidated factory building. Metal slammed shut with a crash.

Lena threw herself against it. The rusty steel frame crunched and gave way. The cold struck her. The smell of oil, rust and old metal was heavy in the air. Shadows crept across the walls, distorted by the flickering fire outside.

He was here. Hidden. Lurking.

Her radio crackled. "Lena? Nobody can get out of here. We've sealed everything off."

Then - a noise. A dull thud. A suppressed curse.

Lena turned round. Too late.

Fedorov had Jan

He pressed him against a workbench, the gun to his temple. In his other hand he held a thick briefcase. His face remained motionless, only his eyes sparkled.

"That's your problem, Commissioner." His voice was gentle, almost regretful. **"You hunt men like me. But you don't understand who's really pulling the strings."**

Lena held the gun out to him. Her hands remained steady. But her heart hammered against her ribs.

"Drop the folder, Fedorov. Now."

A smile flitted across his face. No twitch of fear, no trembling. Just cold amusement.

"Sorokin is long gone. You'll never get him."

A twitch.

A muscle, barely visible.

Lena reacted instinctively.

Her shot shattered the silence.

Fedorov cried out. The gun clattered to the floor. The folder slipped from his fingers.

He staggered back. Blood seeped from his wrist, dripping in thick drops onto the dusty concrete.

Lena grabbed him, twisting his arm into a secure grip.

Jan gasped, rubbing his temple. "Bloody hell... that was close."

Lena ignored him. The folder.

Her fingers trembled slightly as she picked up the papers. Her gaze flew over the pages.

Names. Account details. Transactions.

The whole damn swamp.

Her radio crackled. A second of silence.

Then - Lars' voice. "Lena?"

His voice sounded rough, tense. "Where are you?"

Lena took a deep breath. "We have Fedorov. And we have the evidence."

Silence.

Then - a breath of relief.

"Damn good. But Sorokin..."

Silence.

Lena stepped out of the hall. Cold night air hit her sweat-covered skin. Blue lights danced across the harbour area. Police officers ran, securing the last suspects.

*The harbour belonged to them.*

*But the ocean?*

*It belonged to Sorokin.*

*And he was gone.*

# Chapter 61

Lena stood at the window of the Police Department and looked out at the grey sky over Emden. The rain had subsided, but a heavy blanket of cloud still hung over the city. A fitting conclusion - the case had been solved, but the shadows of the past lingered as if they would never go away.

The breakthrough came with Timofej Fedorov's map file. It contained everything: names, places, bank details - neatly documented. Within hours of the discovery, raids were carried out in several cities. High-ranking members of the network were led away in handcuffs, warehouses were stormed and secret accounts were frozen.

The news showed heavily armed police units searching luxurious villas and sealing up office complexes. A criminal empire that had operated in the shadows for years was collapsing.

Lars Lammerts came into the room with a thick stack of files and placed them on the table with an audible plop. "We now have 37 arrests nationwide, six in East Frisia alone. The BKA has taken care of Sorokin's main contacts in Berlin. His network has practically been smashed."

Lena turned round. **"And Sorokin himself?"**

Lars shook his head. "Disappeared. The traces lead to South America, but nothing concrete."

**"So he remains a ghost."**

Lars nodded. "A very rich and dangerous mind. But it will be difficult for him without his network. He's on the run - and at some point, everyone makes a mistake."

Bodo, who was leaning against the wall with his arms folded, sighed. "That means we can't close this thing here for good. I don't like that at all."

Lena smiled wryly. "Welcome to reality,  Zimmermann."

While Sorokin's empire was crumbling, another web was tightening around the Broder family.

"How do you think it's going to end?" asked Jan as he entered Lena's office.

Lena leant back. "It depends on how good her lawyer is. But with the evidence we have, she'll disappear behind bars for a long time."

Jan nodded slowly. "And Alexei? What about him?"

Lena sighed. "He'll go into hiding. But men like him don't just disappear. They wait."

Lena stepped out of the Police Department . The rain had finally stopped, but the air was heavy from the humidity of the day. She pulled her jacket tighter around her and took a deep breath. The case was solved - officially at least. But the nagging feeling that they had overlooked something would not leave her.

She walked slowly to the car park. A tingling sensation ran up the back of her neck - that instinctive feeling that had never deceived her over the years.

She stopped. Looked round.

The street lay there quietly. A few lanterns flickered in the wind, their light reflected on the wet tarmac.

Nothing suspicious.

Then - a movement.

On the opposite side of the street, half-hidden in the shadow of a house wall, stood a figure. Too far away to recognise any details, but long enough to make it clear that she was being watched.

The person made no effort to hide. But neither did he make any effort to approach her.

A silent observer.

Lena held her gaze. Seconds passed.

Then a taxi drove between them. When it rolled on   the figure had disappeared.

Her stomach tightened.

She unconsciously clenched her hands into fists. Who- ever it was knew exactly how to move unseen.

Perhaps the case was officially closed. But her gut told her otherwise.

With one last look into the darkness, she got into her car. She pulled the door shut, started the engine - and stopped.

Something was different.

Her fingers trembled slightly as they stroked the steering wheel.

Then she spotted it. A damp imprint on the windscreen. No trace of rain - just a single, blurred imprint, as if someone had wiped their hand across it.

She inhaled sharply.

**It was over.**

**Or not?**

Chapter 62

In the evening, the entire team gathered at the Grandcafé in the city center. Nobody had actually planned on going out today, but after the last few weeks of fear, investigations, and danger, this was exactly what they needed—a moment to catch their breath. Someone had suggested the idea, and no one had disagreed. Now they sat there, tired, yet with a quiet contentment slowly spreading through their bodies.

Bodo leaned back, swirled his beer glass, and shot Lena a sideways glance.

"You look like you could use a week of sleep." Lena snorted and took a sip of red wine.

 "Thanks for the charming analysis, Zimmermann."

He grinned. "Anytime. But seriously—what now?" Lena let her gaze wander around the group; her colleagues looked just as exhausted as she felt. But besides sheer fatigue, something else was evident on their faces—relief, and perhaps even a hint of pride.

"First, let's enjoy the fact that we've won. After that?" She shrugged. "We'll see what the future holds."

Aniko sat next to Robin, her fingers curled around a steaming mug of tea. Her eyes kept drifting toward him, as if she needed to confirm he was really there—alive and on the mend.

Robin ran his thumb over the label of his beer bottle. "I've been thinking…"Aniko looked at him, one eyebrow slightly raised. "Yes?""Well…"

He cleared his throat. "I'm wondering if you'd like to have coffee somewhere other than the office. You know, without corpses and case files."

A faint smile crossed Aniko's lips. "Is that an invitation to a date, Robin Ahlers?"He turned bright red. "Uh…maybe?" Aniko gave a soft laugh. "I think I can consider that."

Jan, watching the scene with a grin, nudged Bodo. "And you? What are your plans?" Bodo took a long swig from his glass. "I'm thinking of starting a quiet life by the water somewhere."
Lars, who had been listening in an easygoing manner, leaned forward. "You? A quiet life? You'd last about two weeks before finding some new mystery to solve." Bodo grinned. "You're probably right."

Corinna, swirling her second wine spritzer, gave a sigh.

"I think I'm the only one who's looking forward to a normal workday. Finally, predictable chemistry instead of unpredictable criminals."

Jan laughed. "Sure, tell yourself that. Give it two weeks, and you'll be bored without all the chaos."

Lars grinned. "Any idea when Julia will get here? She's never late when there's something to drink."

Almost as though she heard him, the glass door slid open at that very moment, and Julia entered the café, slightly out of breath. "Sorry, guys. Had to close out another case, but now I really need a glass of wine!"

A chair was freed up, and she settled into it with a relieved sigh. "What did I miss?"Lena grinned.

"Robin just asked Aniko out on a date."

Julia arched an eyebrow at Robin, who was now sinking deeper into his chair. "Finally! About time!"

Laughter rippled through the group, conversations flowing in waves—sometimes boisterous, sometimes thoughtful. Eventually, they pushed their chairs closer together and clinked their glasses in a toast. For a moment, everyone forgot just how close they had come to the edge.

Outside, a fine drizzle hung in the air like a soft veil over the city. The warm glow of the streetlamps reflected off the cobblestones, making the night appear calm and peaceful, as if it had decided not to be threatening for just this moment.

Gradually, the group went their separate ways, each saying goodbye—not forever, but to take a break from everything. Robin and Aniko were the last to leave the café. Robin shrugged on his jacket and hesitated, as though he wanted to say something. Then he turned around. His eyes found Lena's—grateful, but also resolute.

"Thank you…for everything."

Lena regarded him for a moment, a barely noticeable smile on her lips. "Take care of yourselves. Both of you."

They disappeared into the night, hand in hand, their silhouettes fading in the soft glow of the streetlamps.

**A Few Days Later**

Lena and Bodo stood on the pier. The wind carried the salty scent of the North Sea, tugging at their jackets and tousling their hair. Seagulls circled above, their shrill cries blending with the low rumble of the ferry that lay moored at the quay. The setting sun painted the sky with a golden and blood-red glow, while the water reflected the vibrant colors.

The ferry was ready to depart, ready to carry Robin and Aniko away for a while. Bodo stuffed his hands into his pockets, his gaze fixed on the ship. "Are you going to miss him?"

Lena let her eyes wander over the gently rolling waves. A faint smile flickered across her lips—somewhere between wistfulness and acceptance. "Yes. But this is his path. And he'll be back. Eventually."

The gangway was retracted, and the ferry's muffled horn shattered the silence. Slowly, it began to pull away from the quay.

Robin and Aniko stood at the railing side by side, the wind ruffling their hair. Robin raised his hand to wave goodbye. Lena returned the gesture and felt a pinch in her chest. Longing mixed with relief—a strange balance between letting go and staying hopeful.

Bodo said nothing; instead, he placed a hand on her shoulder—a quiet, wordless gesture that spoke volumes.

The ferry grew smaller on the horizon until it became just a dot in the vastness of the sea. Lena drew in a deep breath. Tomorrow would be a new day.

## Later in the Evening

The rain had passed, and the city lay still under a clear sky. The damp streets reflected the glow of the street-lamps, bathing Emden in a silvery sheen.

Lena and Bodo returned home. In the living room, a fire crackled in the fireplace, wrapping them in its warmth like a comforting blanket. Bodo sprawled out on the sofa, a glass of red wine in hand. "This is what a peaceful life

might look like." Lena leaned back and let her gaze roam around the room. "Yes, maybe." But was that really true?

The memories of the past days still clung to her like shadows she couldn't quite shake. She remembered the moment Robin went missing. The suffocating fear that she might never see him again. The trembling of her hands when news came he had been found—alive but marked.

She suddenly realized how tired she was, weary to her core.

Bodo put an arm around her, and she nestled against him, seeking comfort in his presence, in the fire's warmth, in the soft crackle of the wood. One breath. Two. For a moment, she allowed herself to sink into that deceptive sense of security. For just the briefest instant, all felt right in the world.

Eventually, she set her glass aside and sank deeper into the cushions. Her eyelids grew heavy, her breathing steadied, and she drifted off in his arms.

## Elsewhere, Something Was Stirring

Night had fallen at Police Headquarters. The open-plan office lay in darkness. Only the quiet hum of a computer broke the silence. A screen flickered. A system came online. A message appeared, large and impossible to miss:

**"You thought it was over. But we've only just started, Lena."**

**The Trial Against Karin Broder**

While Lena tried to return to everyday life, the trial against Karin Broder drew ever closer. The courtroom was packed when the presiding judge declared the proceedings open. The charges ranged from money laundering to aiding and abetting arms trafficking and involvement in a criminal organization.

As the prosecutor presented the overwhelming evidence—including the diaries of her father, Heinrich Broder—the defendant remained emotionless. Witnesses from her criminal circle testified against her, and attempts to shift blame onto Sorokin failed in the face of irrefutable proof.

After weeks of intense hearings, the verdict was delivered: a long prison sentence.

The guilty verdict triggered mixed reactions in the courtroom, while Karin herself sat motionless. A reporter asked for her reaction. Slowly, she raised her head, her lips forming an almost mocking smile.

"Sorokin isn't so easy to pin down."

**December 10, 2025 – Emder Newpaper**

*"CID Takes Down International Money Laundering and Arms Trafficking Network"*

Emden—The East Frisian port city was the scene of a spectacular criminal case that caused a stir not only in the region but throughout Germany. It has now come to light that the Emden Criminal Investigation Department, in cooperation with international authorities, has broken up a ring spanning several European countries.

At the heart of the investigation was Karin Broder, daughter of former shipyard manager Heinrich Broder, who has now been convicted of involvement in money laundering and illegal arms trading.

The case began with the discovery of a body in the cellar of an old shipyard. The investigation quickly led to the Broder family. The victim's diaries revealed not only dark secrets from the past but also entanglements in a criminal network.

Through painstaking efforts, the Emden CID gathered enough evidence to make several arrests. Particularly explosive: the investigation uncovered international connections.
"This case shows how globally organized crime can leave its mark even on small cities," said lead investigator Lars Lammerts.

Not only did the Emden press cover the events extensively, but national media outlets such as Newspaper

Der Spiegel,

Die Welt,

and TV Daily News also gave prominent coverage to the spectacular trial. Experts consider the blow against this network an important success in the fight against organized crime. "The Emden case will go down in police history as a prime example of effective investigative work," commented a crime expert to Daily News.

However, the verdict against Karin Broder did not mark the end of the proceedings. Her suspected accomplice, the Russian businessman Sorokin, remains a fugitive, and an international manhunt is in full swing.

## A Damp Morning in Emden

The cold morning air clung to Lena's coat as she got out of her car and looked toward the old harbor area. The wind blew in strong gusts from the sea, carrying the salty tang of the North Sea and churning up foam on the waves in the muted light beneath the gray clouds. In the distance, the rusted cranes of the disused docks loomed against the faint glow of dawn like skeletal silhouettes.

Emden lay under a haze, but Lena's thoughts were razor-sharp: she felt the aftermath of the previous autumn in every fiber of her being. They had only just officially closed the last chapter. Sorokin, still on the run, lingered in Lena's mind like a phantom. His incomplete trail worried her more than she cared to admit. Even now, she sensed his shadow hovering over Emden—like a time bomb that could detonate at any moment.

Bodo Zimmermann had reported for duty early, alerted by a call about a body found down by the harbor. Troubled by the vague report and his own dark suspicions, he waited within sight of the taped-off area. As soon as he spotted Lena, he gave her a grim nod. "I'd have liked to let you sleep a bit longer," he said quietly, and the look on his face showed that this was no routine call. "Sleep is overrated anyway," Lena replied, pulling her hood tighter. "What do we know?" Bodo jerked his chin toward a row of shipping containers, where the eerie glow of blue lights danced across the steel walls. "Not much yet. But there's plenty of reason to believe it wasn't an accident. And when I think of Sorokin…"

The hairs on the back of Lena's neck stood on end. She couldn't shake off the weight of her memories: their last encounter, the menacing hints that had burned themselves into her mind. Now, however, there was no time to hesitate. Taking a short, steadying breath, she followed Bodo toward the crime scene—determined to chase down this new lead and solve the case before the shadows of the past could close in on them again.

## Acknowledgement

Dear readers,

I would like to thank you from the bottom of my heart for your interest in my second volume of the crime series,

**Resonance of the Hidden** It is a great pleasure for me to share my stories with you. I hope that this thriller has also given you some exciting hours.
Please bear in mind that all the plots and characters in this book are fictitious. Any similarities with real persons or events are purely coincidental.

Your support is essential for me as an author. Tell others about this book and, if you enjoyed reading it, leave a review on the relevant portals. Your feedback is not only a motivation for me, but also helps others to discover my work.

For more information about my books or myself, please visit my website:

www.bodo-lehwald.de.

There you will also find the latest news and perhaps soon information on upcoming events. Thank you for your loyalty and interest. I look forward to taking you on another captivating journey through the secrets of East Frisia in the next volume.

With best regards,

Yours, Bodo Lehwald

*"The truth does not remain hidden forever. It just waits for the right moment to come to light."*